THE SURROGATE THIEF

Other books by Archer Mayor

GATEKEEPER
THE SNIPER'S WIFE
TUCKER PEAK
THE MARBLE MASK
OCCAM'S RAZOR
THE DISPOSABLE MAN
BELLOWS FALLS
THE RAGMAN'S MEMORY
THE DARK ROOT
FRUITS OF THE POISONOUS TREE
THE SKELETON'S KNEE
SCENT OF EVIL
BORDERLINES
OPEN SEASON

THE SURROGATE THIEF

ARCHER MAYOR

NEW YORK   BOSTON

May

Mysterious Press
Warner Books

Time Warner Book Group
1271 Avenue of the Americas, New York, NY 10020
Visit our Web site at www.twbookmark.com.

Printed in the United States of America

First Printing: October 2004

10 9 8 7 6 5 4 3 2 1

Library of Congress Cataloging-in-Publication Data
Mayor, Archer.
    The surrogate thief / Archer Mayor. — 1st Mysterious Press ed.
      p. cm.
   ISBN 0-89296-815-X
   1. Gunther, Joe (Fictitious character)—Fiction. 2. Police—Vermont—Fiction.
3. Vermont—Fiction. I. Title.
   PS3563.A965S87 2004
   813'.54—dc22   2004014369

To Jean-François and Geneviève DuLac
for the examples you set and the inspirations
you helped ignite

Acknowledgments

As with all my previous books, this one would never have left shore without the help of a great many people and organizations. They gave freely of their time, knowledge, and expertise and supplied me with the informational gold mine I rummaged through as I wrote. If there are errors as a result of this process, however, go no further than the messenger. The fault will be mine, and not the fault of those listed below. To them go only gratitude and best wishes.

John Applegate
David Ainsworth
John Martin
Von Labare
Herb Maurer
Dana Bonar
Eric Buel
Karen Carroll
Robert McCarthy
Kali Erskine
Yvonne Shukovsky
Karen Carroll
Mike Crippen
Castle Freeman, Jr.

Carol Boone
Euclid Farnham
Paco Aumand
Letha Mills
Evan Hodge
Garry Lawrence
Kathryn Tolbert
Richard Guthrie
Bob Kirkpatrick
Bill O'Leary
Paula Yandow
Dan Davis
Peter Shumlin
Julie Lavorgna

Wyn Glover
Darlene Littlefield

Peter Langrock
Tammy Martell

The Brattleboro Police Dept.
The Vermont Forensic Lab
The Vermont Dept. of Public
  Safety
The Gloucester Police Dept.

The Vermont State Police
Court Reporters Assoc. Inc.
The Tunbridge World's Fair
Windham Co. SA's Office

Chapter 1

Dispatch to 0-30."

Officer Paul Kinney unhooked his radio mike and answered, "0-30."

"Domestic disturbance, 63 Vista Estates. Neighbor called it in. Address listed to a Linda Purvis."

"Ten-four."

Kinney replaced the mike and pulled into a smattering of traffic. It was almost midnight, and, even in a town of thirteen thousand like Brattleboro, it was still Vermont, where phoning people after nine and staying up past eleven remained unusual, even slightly inappropriate, behavior.

Kinney was feeling good. It was summer, two days ago he'd been released by his training officer to patrol on his own, and he was flush with self-confidence. To his thinking, all that remained was to learn the ropes thoroughly with the Bratt PD, establish a reputation, put out some feelers, and pick from a variety of plum federal jobs, from the FBI to Homeland Security to God knows what. He felt poised before a veritable trough of opportunities.

He headed west on Route 9 into West Brattleboro, the main town's smaller offshoot. Given its less urban makeup, West B played host to a choice of trailer parks, from the seriously upscale—expansive, complete with paved roads, car parks, and garages—to the barely solvent, where the odds favored Mother Nature repossessing her own.

Not surprisingly to Kinney, the loftily named Vista Estates fit the latter category.

He wasn't concerned. He didn't know this address specifically, but he judged himself pretty adept at handling domestics. He'd studied his FTO's style—an old-timer who'd been a field training officer for too many years—and, as a result, had mostly learned how not to behave. And even though he'd handled only a couple of domestics on his own, Kinney was convinced of the merits of his technique. People under stress didn't need a friendly ear. They were secretly yearning for the comfort of a little imposed discipline.

Vista Estates was to hell and gone, almost out of town, and proffering neither vistas nor estates. A trailer park whose assets were better known to the tax courts than to any Realtor, it was a threadbare clearing among some roughly opened woods, crisscrossed with narrow, root-tangled dirt lanes and populated with as many empty lots as decaying trailers.

The one thing the park owners had bothered with, Kinney noted gratefully, was numbering the addresses. He found 62/63/64 without much trouble, clustered together, although only after he'd used his flashlight to see better out his side window. Vista Estates had clearly deemed streetlamps a luxury.

Kinney drew abreast of the rough scratch in the dirt serving as a trifurcated driveway, told dispatch of his arrival, and pulled himself free of the car. Before him were two distant trailers and an empty space for a third. The home on the left was blazing with light, its neighbor all but dark, save for a single curtained window.

He drew in a deep breath, both enjoying the cool summer air and preparing himself for the show of command he saw coming, and set off down the driveway.

He considered stopping by the neighbor's first. That was certainly protocol. But instinct and vanity pushed him toward the direct approach. Slipping between the pickup and the small sedan parked out front, without checking their registrations, he climbed the worn wooden steps up to the narrow homemade porch and paused at the thin metal front door.

He certainly sympathized with the neighbor's complaint. There was a knock-down, drag-out screaming match taking place inside, accompanied by the thumping of inner doors and the smashing of crockery.

Kinney passed on simply ringing the bell and removed his flashlight from the slim pocket sewn into his uniform pants.

He used it to smack the door three times.

"Brattleboro police."

The immediate silence was like pulling the plug on an overly loud TV set—utter and complete. In its sudden embrace, he felt abruptly and paradoxically defenseless.

The door flew open without warning, revealing a large man with a beard, a T-shirt, and an oversize revolver in his hand pointed at the floor. "You get the hell away from here or she's dead. Got that?"

Kinney felt his stomach give way, along with his bravado. Transfixed by the gun, he imagined himself as the human-size target he so frequently perforated at the range, and could visualize the barrel rising to the level of his eye, an enormous flash of light, and then nothing.

Instead, the door was merely slammed in his face.

" 'You get away from here or she's a dead person.' That's all he said. He had a gun."

Ron Klesczewski closed his car door and leaned back against the fender. He rubbed his face with both hands, still chasing the remnants of a deep sleep from his brain, before peering into the wary, almost belligerent expression of the patrolman before him.

"You got the call? I mean, you were the one this guy talked to?" Ron spoke deliberately, hoping to project a calming influence. In fact, being the senior officer here, he felt his own anxieties beginning to roil inside him, a nagging insecurity he'd wrestled with all his life.

"Yeah. It didn't sound like a big deal from dispatch—a routine domestic. I knocked on the door, he opened up, delivered the one-liner, and slammed the door. There was a woman behind him, crying."

Klesczewski took in the tight shooting gloves, custom gun grips, and strained nonchalance and identified a neophyte's attempt to camouflage insecurity with accessories. "She look all right otherwise?"

To his credit, the patrolman became clearly embarrassed. "I guess. I was sort of looking at the gun. That's when I figured I better call for backup."

Klesczewski studied him for a beat before asking, "You okay? Did he point it at you?"

There was a moment's hesitation, as if Ron had asked a trick question. All traces of initial swagger vanished at last in the response. "No. I mean, yeah, I'm all right, but no, he didn't point it at me. It was a little scary, is all. Not what I was expecting. But I'm fine . . . And she's fine . . . I'm pretty sure . . . The woman, I mean."

Brattleboro's police department was known either as a lifer colony, where laid-back older veterans spun out entire careers, or as a turnstile agency, where baby cops hung around just long enough to decide between a flashier law enforcement job elsewhere and getting out.

Ron wondered if the latter option wasn't circling this one's head right now. As it was, he was so new that Ron couldn't remember if his name was Paul or Phil. His name tag just read "P. Kinney."

"How long ago did this start?" he asked him, deciding he looked like a Phil.

Kinney checked his watch. "Maybe half an hour ago." He keyed the mike clipped to the epaulet of his uniform shirt and muttered into his radio, "Jerry? It's Paul. You remember when I called for backup?"

"Twenty-three fifty-three," came the brisk reply.

Okay, Ron thought, so it's Paul. Things better improve from here. "The scene secure?"

Kinney nodded. "Only three sides to worry about. Jerry's covering the west and north. We're on the east, and Henry's got the south. Good thing the trailer park's half empty. Makes life a lot easier."

That last line was delivered with pale, leftover flair. Ron shivered slightly. Even summers in Vermont could get chilly, especially if you were fresh from a warm bed. "You've got more coming, though, right?"

"Oh, sure. The state police are sending a couple. The sheriff, too. I asked Dispatch to get hold of the chief and Billy Manierre, but no luck so far."

"They're both out of town," Ron said with some regret. He was head of a four-man detective squad and the department's only hostage negotiator, both positions that put him closer to the upper brass than to the uniforms chasing tail-lights—the latter of whom he envied right now.

"You better show me around."

Paul Kinney stumbled over an exposed root as he turned, increasing his awkwardness. "Watch your step," he said needlessly. "It's just around the corner, past that fir tree."

They weren't using flashlights. The moon supplied enough light to see by, and they didn't want to stir up the man in the trailer in case he was looking out.

Kinney lowered his voice as he drew abreast of the tree. "There it is."

Klesczewski peered into the gloom. Looking slightly de-flated, like a small grounded blimp needing air, the trailer sat alone in the middle of a narrow hardscrabble yard. To one side of it was a blank rectangle showing where a simi-lar home had once stood. To the other was a second trailer, some twenty feet away, lights blazing from every window. In the distance, a row of trees and a hill blocked off the scene like a set piece on a stage. A swaybacked pickup and a rusty compact were parked next to the home they were interested in.

"Jerry's out behind?" Ron asked, pointing at the trailer.

"Right, and Henry's alongside the other one."

"Why're all the lights on in there? Are the neighbors still inside?"

Kinney answered more emphatically than the question deserved, making Ron think he might have addressed this problem later than he should have. "No, no. We got them out. And I talked to them, too. Got some good information. I guess we forgot about the lights."

"We can turn them off after the tac team gets here," Ron placated him, noticing that the primary trailer had only one lighted window, its curtains drawn. "How did this go down?"

"Neighbors complained," Kinney explained. "Said they were screaming at each other next door and breaking things. That's sure what they were doing when I arrived."

"We know who 'they' are yet?"

"Linda Purvis is the owner of record, and according to the neighbors, the man sounds like her ex, Matthew. That matches the two vehicle registrations and the physical descriptions I got."

"Any kids?"

Kinney's face turned toward him in the half light, looking blank. "I don't know," he stammered. "I didn't ask."

"So, there may be others in there." It wasn't a question.

"Yeah," the younger man admitted. "I guess so. If it helps," he added, "Dispatch said this wasn't the first time. Purvis is in the computer for prior domestics here, complete with a restraining order issued yesterday."

Which was probably what triggered this, Ron thought. One of the hallmarks of these kinds of situations, taught during his negotiator's training, was the so-called precipitating event. Almost without fail, it was lurking somewhere, usually acting as the proverbial one straw too many. In the worst cases, you got what they called the triple— three cataclysms striking virtually at once, like a freakish planetary alignment.

"You smell liquor on his breath?" he asked.

Kinney nodded. "Big-time."

Such as a drinking binge, Ron thought. He turned away and looked down the rutted road leaving the park. He saw the twinkle of blue strobes approaching in the distance.

"Get on the radio and tell everyone to respond Code Two. I don't want to crank this guy any tighter than he is."

Kinney did as asked, and they both watched the strobes wink out moments later, while the headlights kept bouncing toward them over the uneven ground.

Klesczewski didn't look at Kinney as he continued, "As soon as everyone gets here, I want those smaller tire spike kits quietly placed under both Purvis cars, all other trailers within easy shooting range evacuated, and a perimeter established and sealed."

"Who's the shift commander tonight?" he finally asked.

"Captain Washburn. It was supposed to be Lieutenant Capullo but he's out sick."

Ron looked up at the night sky, dread settling in. That made Washburn top dog for the duration, since the chief and his second in command, Manierre, were out of town. Negotiation by its nature was tough enough, especially when you had as little experience as Ron had. Adding Washburn's built-in animosity for him wasn't going to make it easier.

The only missing stressor now was a gung ho tac team, champing at the bit to turn that trailer into the Alamo. And that much was a given with the team's new leadership—a transplanted Boston cop named Wayne Kazak. Ron smiled at the irony. Now he had his own triple to deal with.

He sighed softly and said, "Okay, let's get the van down here and set up a command post. Better count on this taking a while."

Chapter 2

Two hours later, Ron Klesczewski was sitting in an airless van, headphones binding his ears, his eyes half closed in concentration, listening to Matthew Purvis ranting on the other end of a dedicated line. This last detail was actually the PD's "throw phone," which Ron had managed to get him to accept after forty-five minutes of persuasion, using the ruse that Ron's cell, which he wasn't actually using, was running low on power.

The advantage of the throw phone over a standard line was being revealed right now, since Purvis wasn't actually talking to Ron, but yelling yet again at his estranged wife. Since the unit was unfamiliar to him, he'd merely put it down instead of hanging it up as he might have normally.

Which in turn was helping to enhance one of the pillars of good negotiation: information gathering. Anything the negotiator could learn about the subject, using all available methods, gave him something extra with which to defuse the situation.

"It's sounding like Linda thought Matt was cheating on

her with her own sister," Ron murmured, still eavesdropping. "Either that or she's deliberately heating him up." Directly across from him, a whiteboard was mounted on the van wall, attended by a patrolman who now carefully wrote down, "Matt slept with Linda's sis?" and added the exact time.

Already there was quite a lot on the board, acquired from Ron's observations; computer searches; interviews with neighbors, friends, and family; and anecdotal tidbits from any officers who'd dealt with either Linda or Matthew Purvis in the past. Despite the hour, all across town, Ron had people digging for more. Even the town clerk was awakened for access to any records she might have.

Ron waited for a pause in the argument before punching the button on his console that made the throw phone ring whether it was off or not, noting in the back of his mind that Linda was standing her ground, giving as good as she got.

The phone rang twice before Matt picked it up.

"What?"

"It's Ron, Matt. I was a little confused when you put me down just then. I thought we were working a few things out."

"Like what? Like how you're going to blow me away as soon as I shoot this bitch?"

"That's not what I was hearing," Ron said quietly, knowing that the man's emotions needed to resettle after his last screaming match. "Before we were interrupted, we were talking about what you've just been through—how we might be able to put your life back together."

There was a third man in the van with Ron: an official liaison with the incident command post outside, equipped with a pair of headphones connected to the ICP, and assigned the task of passing notes to and from the negotiator as directed. The notes were color coded according to their urgency. The one he placed before Ron now was purely informational. Klesczewski glanced at it and passed it along to the officer at the board, who wrote, "Fired from job two days ago." With this morning's restraining order and his by now admitted alcohol dependence, that earned Matt Purvis the "triple" designation Ron had mused about earlier.

"There's nothing left *to* put together," Purvis was yelling. "Don't you get it? I'm not fucking around here. I will kill this bitch because she's world-class evil, and then I'll kill myself to save you the trouble."

"Jeez, Matt. I'm hearing a lot of frustration."

"No shit, Sherlock. You'd be frustrated, too, all the crap I have on my plate."

"Maybe you'd like to get some of that out of your system."

There was a pause, then a tentative, "What're you saying? More talk? I'm sick of talking."

The liaison handed Ron another, higher-priority note. Ron silently read "Let's get moving"—clearly Washburn's words—crumpled it up, and dropped it on the floor. There were others like it already scattered about, making him ever more grateful for the protocol prohibiting all but a select few from entering the van. The incident command post was only fifteen yards away, near the trailer park's entrance.

"I'm talking about blowing off a little steam. You ever scream at the night sky? Just let her rip?"

"Everybody's done that."

"That's all I'm saying. Maybe it'll help a little—clear your head some."

Matt Purvis was incredulous. "What? Step outside and start yelling? That's crazy. You'll shoot me."

"Why would we do that, Matt? You haven't done any-thing to us."

"I'm in here with a gun, for Christ's sake."

"Every Vermonter I know has a gun," Ron countered.

"I'm threatening to shoot my wife."

"Matt," Ron persisted, "I hear you telling me you want us to kill you, but we're not going to do it. We're here to see you and Linda both end up safe. So you can step outside and scream your lungs out. We'll just watch."

Purvis was clearly baffled by this turn of events. "You're crazy."

Ron laughed. "You're not the first to say that. Go on—give it a try."

"Just step out and yell?"

Ron could hear the fascination growing in the other man's voice. He glanced up at the whiteboard as if for con-firmation and read what they'd learned earlier from one of Matt's drinking buddies: "Acts out in public."

"Sure," he suggested.

The regular phone rang inside Matt's trailer.

"Hang on," Purvis said, and put Ron down with a bang, again not actually severing the connection.

Ron killed his mike switch, swore softly, and said to the note taker, "He just got a phone call."

He hunched over, listening carefully.

"Who?" he heard Purvis say. "A reporter? I don't . . . What?" His voice grew. "A nut with a gun? Who the fuck told you that? . . . Yeah, the cops're here . . . It's none of your business . . . I got fired, all right? I got fired and my bitch wife slapped a restraining order on me and I'm about to be thrown out of my house for back rent and life is shit. Is that what you want to hear?"

Klesczewski punched a transmit button on his console,

switching his line over to the incident command post. He slipped one of his earphones off so he could listen to Purvis and the ICP at the same time.

"Washburn."

"He just got a phone call from a reporter."

"What?"

"I think we should cut the trailer's phone line. It might be somebody from the *Reformer*, but whoever it is, is working him up all over again."

"Goddamn it, Ron, let's give Kazak and his guys a shot."

Ron grimaced at the last word. Wayne Kazak was Washburn's kind of action-oriented guy. "It's your call, but I'd like to hold off on that for a bit. Before the phone rang, I almost had him out the door."

He refrained from detailing that overly rosy bit of fiction.

As intended, his phrasing put Washburn on the spot. Were the incident commander to choose a possibly bloody assault over a negotiator making progress, heads would roll, especially in a town as prone to argument—and suspicious of its police department—as Brattleboro, a famous bastion of liberal debate.

"All right. We'll cut the line. How fast do you think you can get him out?"

"You know I can't answer that, Ward. But I'm making progress."

"Right." Washburn hung up.

Ron readjusted his headphones. Purvis was still talking on the other phone, but now Linda was throwing her oar in, yelling at him to stop jerking himself off and make up his mind, calling him a loser and a dickhead who couldn't even make a standoff with the cops work. Ron could almost feel the tension building in Matt's head as the latter's responses, to both reporter and estranged wife, became increasingly terse.

Come on, Ron began repeating to himself, *cut the goddamn wire.* He hesitated pushing the button triggering the throw phone's ringer, unsure whether he'd be giving Matt a calmer harbor that way or merely adding to the pressure.

Just before he was about to go ahead, a shot went off, sharp as a whip's crack, audible even through the van's wall.

All hell broke loose. The note taker whirled around at the whiteboard, dropping his marker, Linda let out a scream over the headphones, and Washburn's voice yelled through the van's override speaker, "What the Christ happened, Ron?"

Ron could hear Kazak outside, shouting orders over his radio to his team, preparing for an assault.

He first spoke on the intercom, "Hold everyone off. Let me find out," and then rang through on the throw phone.

From habit alone, Matthew Purvis picked up. "What?"

Ron struggled to control his voice, happy to hear Linda still complaining in a grating voice in the background. "I thought I heard a noise, Matt. Just wondered if you were all okay in there."

"Fuck no, we're not okay. What the hell do you think?"

"Is anyone hurt?"

Purvis was borderline hysterical. "I didn't shoot her, if that's what you mean. Wouldn't make any difference anyhow. I'd need fucking silver bullets to do any good."

Ron hesitated a split second and then laughed outright, in the meantime scribbling a note, "All's okay. Hold," and handing it to the liaison for transmission.

"What're you laughing at?"

"Did you hear what you just said, Matt? Jesus, man. That's one sense of humor."

Thankfully, Purvis laughed, too, dropping the tension a notch. "Yeah, well. What've you got left, right?"

"Right," Ron agreed. "I mean, things could be worse."

He grabbed his forehead at his own choice of words. What the hell was he thinking?

But again Purvis surprised him. After an excruciating pause, he commented, "You're pretty funny yourself. How worse could they get?"

"Okay, I know you've had a pisser of a day, Matt. You're in a world of hurt." Relieved to be back on track, Ron studied the board across from him. "Your job, your apartment, the restraining order, falling off the wagon . . . Pretty understandable that you feel shoved in a corner."

"You have no idea," Purvis muttered.

"You're right. I don't. But I've helped a lot of people who have. That's why I'm here now. I hear you have a son."

A silence followed this abrupt change of subject. "Yeah."

"What's he up to?" A note on the board read "Army."

"He's in the service."

"Sounds like you're real proud of him."

"Yeah. He's a good kid."

In the background, Linda called out, "You talkin' about Chris? A loser and a faggot, just like his old man."

Ron winced, wishing to hell she were in another room or unconscious. She sounded drunk. With any luck, eventually she'd pass out.

The phone rattled as Purvis dropped it again to scream at her, "You goddamn bitch. Don't you say that about Chris. You say one more thing about him and I'll blow your fucking brains out, you hear me?"

"Hear you? The whole town can hear you, Matthew." She drew out his name tauntingly.

The liaison presented a note reading "Tac team has a clear shot through curtain gap."

Ron winced and wrote "NO SHOOTING" in block letters before handing it back.

He called out over the phone, desperate to head off another blowup. "Matt. You there? Hey, Matt?"

"What?" he said finally.

Reacting to his own pressures, Ron decided to become more direct. "How does it make you feel, being in there with her?"

"Pissed off."

"You think there may be a solution to that?"

"Yeah. I could walk into a hail of bullets."

"From us?" Ron made his voice sound surprised, heartened that Purvis hadn't mentioned killing his wife first. "We're not going to shoot you. I want you out safe and sound, Matt. Nobody shoots somebody because they're having a shitty day."

"The place is surrounded by guys with guns. I'm not that stupid."

Ron tried steering him away from a conversation they'd had several times already. "What do you think of me? Personally?"

"I don't know you."

"Don't you?"

Ron let the silence drag on.

Finally, Purvis admitted, "I guess you're okay."

"Would you be willing to come outside if I was there to greet you? We could keep talking later, face-to-face, away from the guns."

"I've seen how that works on TV. You guys beat the shit out of me."

"You really think I'd do that?"

Purvis hesitated before admitting, "Maybe not you. I was thinking about those ninja bastards in black. I saw them out there."

"Well, I'm the one we're talking about. Let's get this done, Matt. You and me, at the front door. I'll walk up and call out, so you recognize my voice; you open the door and come out with your hands up. Then we can talk more in private over some coffee, without interruptions. You can tell me about Chris, and I can brag about my kid."

The silence was punctuated only by Linda's growled aspersions in the distance, sounding like a crow on amphetamines.

Matthew Purvis got the message. "Okay."

"All right," Ron said with relief. He reached out and pushed a button activating a parallel line to the command post, allowing Washburn and Kazak to listen in and understand what was about to happen. "I have to tell you how this works, so pay attention. I'm not the head guy here, so I have to coordinate with the ninjas you just mentioned. I'll be there, like I said, front and center at the door, but they'll be there, too, armed and scary-looking. That's their job and there's nothing I can do about that, okay?"

"I don't trust them."

"They're there to protect me, Matt. They don't know you like I do. To them you're just somebody who might try to hurt me. And my boss, who is probably just like yours was, he'll fire my ass if I don't follow procedure. But you'll be fine, okay? I promise you that. I'll be the first one you see when you open that door. I'll be wearing a bulletproof vest over a white shirt and brown slacks. You listen to my voice only, okay? Ignore everything else."

"They'll see the gun and shoot."

"Then slide it out first or leave it behind. Put it down on

a table somewhere. Just make sure when you come out that your hands are up and that we can see they're empty. You got that? Are we squared away on this?"

"Yeah. I guess." Purvis was sounding suddenly exhausted.

"Hang in there, buddy. I'll be there in three minutes. Put the gun down, go to the door, and wait for my voice."

"Okay."

Klesczewski made sure Matt had left the phone before leaping to his feet and throwing open the van's door.

Across the way, he saw both Washburn and Kazak emerging from the command post, actually an old converted ambulance. They'd heard everything he'd said.

"I don't like it," Kazak said predictably. "As soon as he turns that doorknob, we should go in hard and take him down."

Ron merely looked at Washburn as he slipped a black vest over his head and strapped it in place.

Thankfully, Ward Washburn understood. "We'll do it his way, Wayne."

Ron nodded. "Thanks." He began trotting toward the trailer around the corner as Kazak coordinated the surrender with his team over the radio.

Halfway up the driveway, a shot exploded from inside the trailer.

Moments later, the door opened, spilling light across the patchy grass, and a woman appeared, swaying on her feet, a gun in one hand and a bottle in the other. She was laughing.

"*Come on in, you assholes,*" she shouted into the night. "I did your job for you. I shot the son of a bitch."

Chapter 3

Joe Gunther cupped his cheek in his hand and looked at his old friend. "Ron, you can't beat yourself up over this. You did it by the book—better, even. Who knew the wife would kill him? And don't say, 'I should have,'" he quickly added as Klesczewski opened his mouth to speak.

Ron spoke anyway. "I didn't do it by the book, Joe. I should never have told him to put the gun down. I knew that—especially the way she was acting. I might as well have told him to hand it to her direct. That exact scenario was in my training. I was just so relieved I was about to get him out safely, I forgot. And I got him killed."

Gunther shook his head sadly. He'd known Ron for years—had once been his boss as head of Brattleboro's detective squad—and had seen his younger colleague agonize over issues large and small. It was simply the nature of the man—what helped make him a decent human being, if maybe not the most forceful of leaders.

"Honestly?" Joe told him now. "I doubt it. I think in their own weird way, Mr. and Mrs. Purvis had it worked out long before you showed up. Some people are just built that way—the definition of a love-hate relationship. There's no getting between them. If you had saved him this time, like you say, they would've hooked up later to play it out for keeps."

Ron was still looking glum.

A knock on his office door caused them both to look up. Sheila Kelly, who'd been promoted to detective after Joe's departure, was standing there with a sheet of paper in her hand.

"Hi, Joe," she said with a wide smile, leaning forward to kiss him on the cheek—a rarity among cops. "I haven't seen you in ages. You'd never know you worked upstairs. How are you?"

Joe acknowledged the gentle rebuke. He was employed by the new Vermont Bureau of Investigation nowadays, was in fact their field force commander, which meant he spent most of his time on the road. Logically, he should have moved to Waterbury, near the center of the state, but he'd worked in Brattleboro his whole career and was loath to leave. So far, his bosses had allowed the eccentricity.

"I'm fine, Sheila," he said. "Busy, but doing okay."

"And Gail?"

That called for a more measured response. Gail Zigman and he had been romantically linked for more years than most married couples, although they'd never tied the knot. So the question was reasonable enough. But there was also Gail's latest ambition to consider—a small hot potato, at least in the traditionally conservative environs of a police station.

"Now, *there's* busy," he answered. "I suppose you heard, she's going to run for state senate. Every night her place looks like headquarters for the Normandy invasion."

Sheila laughed. "Nope. I didn't have a clue. Guess that shows how politically involved I am. Well, if anyone can do it, she can. Tell her I wish her well, even if I won't vote for her."

Gail's liberal views were legendary in this corner of the state, where she'd already been a selectperson, a local prosecutor, and forever a standard-bearer of almost every left-leaning cause available, of which there were many. In short, not the typical cop's sort of politician, which often made Joe's colleagues wonder how he could keep her company. Actually, although he did agree with Gail on many points, politics was a topic they tended to avoid, if not always successfully. This made him less than thrilled with the hotter-than-ever partisan debate now surrounding her.

"I'll do that," he said simply.

Sheila Kelly handed the sheet of paper to Ron. "Fax just came in from the crime lab on that gun. Kind of interesting."

Ron took it from her, explaining as he did, "Purvis's gun was an old Ruger Blackhawk. The serial numbers had been ground off, so I thought the lab might like a look at it."

Sheila wandered back into the squad room just outside Ron's office. Joe watched her settling down at her desk as Ron read the contents of the fax, thinking back to when he used to head the unit. By now, Ron and their forensics expert, J. P. Tyler, were the only original members left. The other two, Sammie Martens and the infamously difficult Willy Kunkle, had moved with Joe to the VBI. Nobody here had ever admitted missing having Kunkle around.

His expression guarded, Ron handed his old boss the fax. "You might want to read this, Joe. The bullet they test-fired from Purvis's Ruger matches one you gave them thirty-two years ago."

*   *   *

Vermont is shaped like a broken wedge pointed south. It's barely over 40 miles across at the bottom, 90 across the top, and 160 in length. It has two interstates: I-91 running north-south, and I-89, which it inherits from New Hampshire in a diagonal jaunt from Boston to Montreal. The Green Mountains sew the state together like a protuberant spinal column, the vertebrae a series of picturesque, tree-topped peaks that slope down to the Connecticut River on the east, and Lake Champlain to the west.

It is tiny, rural, landlocked, unindustrialized, politically quirky, among the whitest states in the union, and the forty-ninth in population. Its capital, Montpelier, is the smallest of its ilk in the nation, and the only one not to have a McDonald's restaurant.

Ask anyone in the country about Vermont, and you are almost sure to be given some impression, however inaccurate. From the Green Mountain Boys to maple syrup, skiing, fall foliage, and cows—not to mention civil unions and some surprisingly high-profile, plain-speaking politicians—Vermont tends to stick in people's minds, if not always benignly.

It is a place with resonance beyond its modest statistics, and, for Joe, a world in itself.

He knew it better than most, too. Even when he worked at the Brattleboro PD, he made it a point to get out and visit other departments. There are only about a thousand full-time police officers in Vermont, and no jurisdictional boundaries— a cop is a cop anywhere in the state, fully certified and responsible to act as such if necessary. Gunther was keenly aware of that fact and saw the whole as a single tribe, if made up of different factions. His joining the VBI, in truth, had less to do with personal advancement, and more with easing the turf struggles he saw only slowly fading among many of the almost seventy law enforcement agencies across the state.

It was a great source of satisfaction to him, seeing how the growth in information sharing had resulted in a commensurate decline in unsolved crimes.

Which only added to the irony that he'd been the one involved in—and possibly responsible for—one of the more notorious of the state's still open cases.

Thirty-two years ago.

He watched the familiar countryside roll by as he drove toward Waterbury and the forensics lab along one of the most beautiful traffic corridors in the Northeast. It was a trip he never tired of, and one he'd come to use, in good weather and poor, as an opportunity for reflection. If meditation was best pursued in peaceful, supportive, nurturing environments, Joe could think of none better than this smoothly curving road through the mountainous heart of his home state.

And, in this instance, such solace was a blessing, for the long-dormant thoughts created by the discovery of Purvis's gun were a muddle of loss and mourning and lasting disappointment.

Thirty-two years ago, Gunther had been a fresh-faced detective on the Brattleboro force. A bright, hardworking patrolman, he'd made the transition to plainclothes quickly and had been in the unit about a year. He was good at what he did, made his bosses happy, and had a reputation around town for fairness and discretion.

The latter was crucial back then. The department had had no more than fourteen officers total, versus twice that today; the town was the same size then as now, and the crime rate had seemed rampant. Many a time Joe had to choose between arresting and processing someone and thereby leaving the street, and letting him go and hoping a lecture would suffice. Sometimes a phone call to an overworked but decent parent was enough; sometimes a little old-fashioned intimidation was called for. Miranda rights had just barely been introduced and were undergoing judicial adjustment. They certainly weren't yet routine. A police officer's discretion—and his knowledge of whom he was dealing with—was often the better guide than the rule book. Shoving a nightstick down someone's pants and frog-walking him across the bridge to Hinsdale, New Hampshire, to get rid of him for the evening had worked more than once.

But discretion could be pushed too far. On the night that Klaus Oberfeldt was found battered and unconscious on the floor of their store by his wife, the ambulance was called and the bare facts recorded. But it wasn't until the next day, when Joe came back on duty, that he first heard of it. No neighborhood canvass had been conducted, no evidence collected, no statements or photographs taken. The beat cops at the time had written it off as a mugging and had filed it for a detective follow-up.

Nobody had liked old man Oberfeldt, as the lack of initiative made clear.

Joe dropped by the store the next morning to see Maria Oberfeldt, Klaus's wife. He was embarrassed by her incredulity at the official poor showing, which helped him bear her tongue-lashing. She, like her husband, was short-tempered, judgmental, imperious, and distrustful. Together they'd turned the area around their small grocery store into a social fire zone. Kids, animals, vagrants, and often customers knew to expect a hostile and suspicious reception. The police were called regularly to investigate thefts and vandalisms and even loitering that often wasn't so. Not that some abuse didn't exist. The town in those days was a magnet for teenagers on the loose, who often threw eggs or paint at store windows for the hell of it. To many, as a result of this chemistry, the Oberfeldts only got what they deserved.

Nobody argued that Klaus's beating was wrong, but few were surprised, and no one besides Maria grieved for him.

She greeted Joe at the store's locked door—she hadn't opened that morning—and gave him an earful for thirty minutes straight. Then she stopped, fell apart, and collapsed crying into his arms.

It turned out that not only was Klaus comatose, but they'd been robbed of $12,000—a small fortune in earned savings that they'd kept under a floorboard in the back room.

Joe finally led her back upstairs to where she and Klaus shared an apartment, and convinced her to take a small drink and lie down for a rest. He then returned to the store, grateful that it hadn't been overly contaminated since the attack, and began treating it as it should have been from the start: as a major crime scene.

Joe left the interstate at Exit 10 and entered the town of Waterbury, best known for its proximity to Ben and Jerry's ice cream plant and as the home of the Vermont State Police.

The latter's headquarters were located in the vaguely named State Office Complex, a large gathering of redbrick buildings that had slowly grown around the original state mental hospital, built in the 1890s and now almost empty. All of it looked to Joe like some manic-depressive architect's vision of a college campus for the imaginatively impaired.

The Department of Public Safety building was located off

to one side of the campus, as institutionally bland as the rest although bristling with antennas and microwave dishes.

Joe abandoned his car on the grass bordering the chronically full parking lot. He entered the building's lobby, was buzzed through by the dispatcher behind her bulletproof glass, and began climbing the staircase to the top floor.

The building's top, or third, floor hosted the crime lab, Criminal Justice Services, a couple of meeting rooms, and the office of VBI's director, Bill Allard. As a result, while the lab was Joe's destination, he knew it would be impolitic not to drop by Bill's office first.

This wasn't a chore by any means. They were good friends, a couple of warhorses who'd come up through the ranks riding the learning curve that transformed so many law enforcement leaders from hot dogs into problem solvers—an evolution that had made both of them attractive to the creators of VBI. The Bureau was a bit of a thorn to the law enforcement community. A statewide major-crimes investigative unit culled from the best of each agency across Vermont, it had seriously rocked the boat when the governor and a compliant legislature had given it birth. The state police, which still had its own plainclothes unit, saw it as an unnecessary rival, while every municipal department complained it would lure away their most talented personnel.

Being accurate made both views hard to dismiss, although the politicians kept trying. Gunther and Allard, the latter of whom had spent his whole career in the state police, didn't bother. They just kept proving, in case after case, that the VBI was there for the overall good as a highly qualified, well-funded support unit that only came into a case by invitation, did its job discreetly and competently, and then disappeared, making sure the credit always went to the host agency. It had been a successful tactic so far, and a small but growing number of former critics had been heard to admit—if only off the record—that maybe VBI wasn't as bad as had been feared. So far.

Allard was sitting at his desk in an office so small it barely allowed for two folding guest chairs. He was gazing with apparent wonderment at some cluttered document on the computer screen, his large, stubby fingers poised over the keyboard as if frozen.

His face lit up as Gunther crossed the threshold.

"Joe. I didn't know you were coming up. Have a seat. You're not hand-delivering bad news, are you?"

Joe sat down, shaking his head. "Nope, no fouls, no errors, and no need to ask forgiveness as far as I know. I'm just up here checking on something at the lab."

Allard raised his eyebrows. There were five VBI outposts across the state, including a unit downstairs, and Bill Allard made it his business to be at least aware of every case they were working on. "From your neck of the woods?"

Gunther waved his concern aside. "No, the Bratt PD had a domestic a couple of days ago—ex-wife shot her husband. But the gun was missing its serial number, so they had the lab run a check. Turns out the same gun was used in an old case of mine."

"No kidding?"

"Yeah. I never solved it. It's bugged me ever since."

"A killing?"

"Didn't start out that way. It was a robbery-assault at a mom-and-pop grocery store. Nobody liked the victim, an old grouch named Oberfeldt, and at first we didn't even bother finding out their life savings had been stolen. The bad old days with a vengeance. The guy wasn't dead; he was just in the hospital—although the word 'just' doesn't do it justice. He was in a coma. But the selectmen were on the rampage for us to clean up the bars and get the kids off the street to make the town more appealing. The case pretty much fell to me on my own."

"What happened?" Allard asked.

A lot, Gunther thought to himself—almost more than he thought he could bear at the time, or bear to remember now.

"Not much," he said instead. "Six months later, old man Oberfeldt died without regaining consciousness. His wife sold the store and left town. I never found out who did it."

"And now the gun's resurfaced," Bill Allard suggested.

"Yup. Three decades later."

Allard let out a low whistle. "Jesus," he said, and then pointed toward the door. "Okay, you've officially proved you have good manners, Joe. Go to the lab and nab yourself some bad guy who's probably using a walker by now. Thanks for stopping in."

The Vermont Forensic Lab took up the entire top floor of the building's longest wing. It was a narrow, cluttered, bizarrely designed layout, clearly never intended for its present use. Old equipment lined the walls of the dark, close central hallway; doors to either side revealed impossibly jam-packed labs or eccentric secondary parallel halls. Half the time Joe couldn't discern if what he was looking at was a storage room or a workplace that only resembled a mad scientist's attic.

Ballistics was housed at the far end, across the corridor from latent prints. None of this was labeled or looked the role, any more than the whole remotely resembled any popular perception of a crime lab. Joe simply knew where to go from past experience. In a state so thinly populated, it was understood that you could figure out how to get some-where by merely wandering about for a while.

In the old days, when the state police ran things, techni-cians were officers on rotation. Times had changed. Now the place was a part of Public Safety's Criminal Justice Ser-vices—as was VBI, for that matter—and staffed by people qualified enough in their specialties to have earned the lab national accreditation. An honor indeed, given that it ap-peared to be housed in a condemned high school building.

Malcolm Nash had been in ballistics for over fifteen years, first as an assistant but recently as the man in charge. He was tall, stooped, and energetic, and Gunther thought he'd probably always looked as he did now, and forever would: a somewhat geeky mid-forties. Pure hell in high school, no doubt, but not too bad as time passed.

"Joe Gunther," he said, clearly pleased, as Joe entered the cluttered office. He crossed the room and extended his hand for a shake. "I thought you might show up. Too in-teresting to resist, right?"

He motioned to a shabby wheeled chair as he perched on the edge of a desk. The room was one of two, this one filled with filing cabinets, a couple of desks, some scientific equipment, and a huge IBIS computer used for bullet and cartridge identification. On semipermanent loan from ATF, it filled a quarter of the floor space like a robot on steroids. The back room, reserved for test firings, contained a cotton box for high velocity rounds, and a water well running down the inside corner of the building, for slower bullets. The latter was a bane to downstairs residents, since any testing resulted in a thunderous explosion reverberating all the way to the basement.

"I read up on that old case of yours," Nash was saying.

"Really fascinating. And relevant, too, since I was able to run some newer tests based on your report at the time."

He reached over to a corner of the desk and retrieved a slim file folder. "Klaus Oberfeldt," he read, "aged sixty-seven at time of death. The ME said that he'd been beaten, in part or in whole, with a gun gone missing, which gun had discharged accidentally as a result." He paused and read on. "At least that was the assumption, since the wife heard the shot, the victim had no hole in him, and you found a bullet buried high in the front door casing. Ballistics here took a guess from all that, combined it with the distinctive signature of eight lands and grooves from the re-covered bullet, and came up with a .357 Blackhawk re-volver, since it had a crucial flaw at the time, where the firing pin rested directly against the cartridge's primer. The hypothesis was that if the gun was used in a fashion where the hammer came in contact with the victim's skull, as in a back-handed return motion, the bullet would go off."

Malcolm Nash looked up suddenly and smiled broadly. "Making my predecessors pretty smart or pretty lucky, since that's exactly how it turned out. I would love to write this up for one of the journals, by the way. Would that be a problem?"

Gunther paused. His own reminiscences of this case were so personal, he had a hard time seeing it in purely ob-jective terms. "No," he allowed. "Assuming we come up with a final chapter."

Nash's eyes widened. "Oh, sure. I wouldn't write about an open case. I was just planning ahead."

"You are sure about the match?" Gunther asked. "I've been told that over time old guns leave different impres-sions on their bullets."

Nash was dismissive. "That's mostly NRA babble. They

don't like the gun control lobby's idea of a bullet and casing record being kept on every factory-fresh gun. In fact, it would take more shooting than you can imagine to alter a gun's impressions. Talk about carpal tunnel—you'd be blazing away every day for years."

He pointed to the IBIS machine. "It's in there if you want proof. Since the beginning of time, this lab used to keep an 'unidentified ammunition file'—literally a chest of tiny drawers with stray bullets in it. That's where yours used to live. Didn't matter where they came from—deer jackings, suicides, murders. If we didn't have a gun to match them to, we kept them just in case."

He got up, crossed over to the machine, and turned it on. "When we got this from ATF, one of the conditions was that we use it as much as possible. It costs a quarter of a million dollars, after all. So, along with encouraging everyone across the state to send us anything ballistic, we also made a file of all those old bullets."

He took the cramped office in with a general sweep of the hand. "It didn't hurt, either, that we could then throw out the chest of drawers." He paused. "Although part of me is a little nostalgic about that. It used to be fun poking through that collection, wondering about all the stories it contained."

He began typing commands, still talking. "Anyhow, as a result of all the data entry, we got a hit right off when we entered the test-fired bullet from the Blackhawk. The computer does that automatically—scans every new item with what it already has in memory."

He abruptly sat back and pointed to the screen. "And voilà, see for yourself."

Joe looked over the scientist's shoulder at the split

screen. There was no denying the similarities between the two color pictures of two matching bullets.

"I see what you mean," he said softly. "Were you able to raise the gun's serial number, too?"

Nash made a face and switched off the IBIS. "No, sorry. Whoever ground it down really went for it. Usually, they stop when they can't see the numbers anymore, not knowing about the visual echo underneath. But either this guy knew his metallurgy or he was just luckily heavy-handed. Anyhow, we couldn't get a thing. The FBI might give it a try, if you'd like. They have fancier methods than we do."

"You think it would be worth it?" Gunther asked.

Nash was appropriately equivocal. "I wouldn't dream of answering that, Joe. Could come home to roost. It ain't cheap, if money's a concern. Whose case is this, by the way? Bratt PD's or yours?"

Gunther looked at him in surprise. "Good point," he admitted. "I better clear that up. I'll let you know later if we should send the gun to the FBI."

Nash gave him a conspiratorial smile and asked, "You're not leaving right off, are you?"

"Why? You have something else?"

"Nothing earthshaking, but it's a nifty confirmation. Something they love in courtrooms, assuming this gets that far."

He returned to one of the desks, from which he extracted a white paper bag. What he laid out on the table was the Ruger Blackhawk, now disassembled.

He picked up the gun's frame and pointed to the slot where the hammer fit when the gun wasn't cocked. "We figured the misfire occurred because the hammer spur came in contact with Mr. Oberfeldt's head, thereby depressing the pin. That would've caused a vicious wound, resulting in a lot of blood coating the gun. At least that was the reasonable assumption." He held up the frame so Joe could see right into the empty hammer slot. "You can't see anything with the naked eye, but I thought that even if the gun had been wiped off later, some blood probably worked its way into the inner workings here." He straightened and smiled again. "And that's just where the folks up the hall found a sample. Its DNA matches the old samples on file from Mr. Oberfeldt."

Joe nodded appreciatively. "Nice work, Malcolm."

Nash poured the gun back into the envelope. "There's more, although now we're wandering into the land of speculation. I don't know if you fully appreciate what I just told you. Blood samples dating back thirty years are pretty rare; getting them in good enough shape to retrieve DNA is telling."

Gunther appreciated the other man's sense of drama. He'd clearly hit a home run and was hoping to stretch out the applause. "Telling in what way?" he prompted.

"Guns see a lot of action, no pun intended," Nash explained. "They get carted around, often get shot and cleaned on a regular basis. They get wet; they're exposed to heat; they're left out in the cold. Especially over a course of decades."

"All of which raises hell with any blood sample," Joe suggested.

"Correct." Malcolm Nash looked at him meditatively. "Which leads me to say that if I were a betting man, which I emphatically am not, I'd venture that up until the time Mrs. Purvis ended her marriage with that gun, it had been leading a peaceful, protected, sheltered life."

He stood up and shook Joe's hand, adding, "I give you that for what little it may be worth."

Chapter 4

It felt as if Tony Brandt had been Brattleboro's police chief since Christ wore shorts, although he'd actually joined the department a few years after Joe. So long a tenure was rarely healthy. Even chiefs once considered innovative and far-thinking seldom managed to maintain that reputation as the years took their toll.

Brandt was the exception. A tall man who wore glasses and tweed jackets and had once smoked a pipe continuously until workplace rules prohibited it, he'd always seemed more like Mr. Chips than a lifelong cop. But a cop is all he'd ever been, and a cop who'd managed to avoid the trends in favor of changes that truly worked, from community policing to use of nonlethal weapons, to streamlining paperwork. It was he who'd made sure the department had a trained hostage negotiator, and despite the outcome of the Purvis shooting, no one was arguing that such programs hadn't improved law enforcement in Brattleboro.

He now sat in his corner office, his feet up on the cubbyhole-equipped desk he'd built himself in his garage, watching Gunther quietly as he had through the years, listening to what his old friend had on his mind.

For his part, Joe always felt comfortable in this role, knowing Brandt to be a thoughtful sounding board, although the absence of the fog of pipe smoke still threw him, apparently more than it did the ex-smoker in question.

"So," Joe concluded, having detailed his recent activities, "it looks like the Klaus Oberfeldt case is open again, or at least deserving of more digging."

"And you want to know if you can have at it or if I want to keep hold of it?"

"Something like that."

Brandt stretched his arms high above his head and let his hands come to rest behind his neck. "There's a no-brainer. It was your case to begin with, felony crimes is what VBI is supposed to do, and I don't have the time, money, or manpower to spend on it. I give it to you with my best wishes, and with full access to all our records."

"I was hoping you'd say that."

"I do have a question, though," Tony said, "which has nothing to do with the actual investigation, then or now."

Joe felt a stirring in his chest, knowing where this was headed. He'd been there a dozen times himself ever since Oberfeldt's name had first resurfaced.

"Case or no case, that was a bad time for you, Joe, at least according to what little you've told me. You sure you're comfortable revisiting that ground? Someone else could check it out without a worry—leave you to get on with your life. You told me yourself you worried that the case went cold because you were sidetracked by what was happening at home. That somehow you felt you dropped the ball."

Leave it to Tony to put his finger right on it, Joe thought.

He got to his feet and moved to the door, pausing there to answer. "That's one reason I want it."

"You didn't, for what it's worth," Tony added. "I wasn't around then, but I know that much."

"Drop the ball?" Joe asked.

"Yeah."

Joe smiled wistfully, all the memories so fresh. "With any luck, maybe I'll get to find that out for myself."

Back when Joe was playing catch-up on an assault that became a robbery and finally a murder six months later, he was married to someone he deemed the love of his life: a kind, gentle, funny, passionate woman named Ellen.

This wasn't exactly objective. She had been all those things, but she'd had her flaws, too. He just couldn't recall them. The adage has it that you can't compete with the dead. Over time, they just keep growing in stature.

And Ellen was definitely dead, killed by cancer over the same six months that Klaus Oberfeldt lingered in a coma.

Joe and she were married for several years and couldn't have children. She worked at the local bank, and whenever possible, they had lunch together. It wasn't a complicated life. They lived in a rented apartment, didn't have pets, thought a drive to Keene was a trip to the big city. There was an ease to their existence that in hindsight seemed like tempting fate, although even now he didn't see enjoying a little peace as anything deserving of punishment. He sure as hell hadn't back then, when, after a tour of duty in combat and a few years lost in confusion and soul-searching, he'd viewed Ellen's arrival in his life as a gift.

What killed her was inflammatory breast cancer. Very rare, very lethal, and very fast.

*　　*　　*

Joe's next stop after leaving Brandt should have been his own office, above the PD in Brattleboro's municipal building. It was late in the day. He doubted that the other three special agents on his squad would be in, which was part of the appeal. Peace and quiet beckoned, especially valuable in the planning stages of a new or, in this situation, revived case.

But he walked out into the parking lot instead and drove west toward Gail's house, as if drawn by the need to compare a love he'd come to idealize with the one he enjoyed now.

He didn't think how doing this instead of going to work highlighted precisely the emotional ambiguity that Tony Brandt had just questioned.

Gail and Joe were an odd pairing, at least to most of their friends: he, the son of a farmer, a native Vermonter, and a lifelong cop; she, an urban child of privilege, an ex-hippie, a successful businesswoman. Theirs was a union in which the emotional integrity, though tested, had never faltered. Through the turmoils they'd shared, the one constant had been that love—placed on a different plane by the hard work and faith supporting it.

Which had created a curious paradox: As a result of that trust, their love had been unhitched from the standard vehicles most couples used for its care and feeding. Joe and Gail were not married, had no children, shared few common interests, did not live in the same house, and didn't even work in the same part of the state for over half of each year. Gail was a lawyer/lobbyist for Vermont's most powerful nonprofit environmental organization and spent months on end in Montpelier representing her cause.

Although, as Sheila Kelly had touched on earlier, this last detail was facing a challenge. On the heels of the retirement of one of the county's white-haired political icons, Gail had announced her intention to occupy his newly opened state senate seat.

This had hit Joe like the news that an old and crumbling dam had finally yielded to the pressures behind it. So many of her intimates had been urging Gail for years to run for statewide office—believing, quite rightly, that she'd take to it as a bird does to flight—that its occurrence had the feel of inevitability about it.

Joe's problem was that while he honored this conceptually, as he had her previous career choices, it was taking place on a whole different level. Unlike any of its forerunners, this campaign was demanding her undivided attention—forcing her to be surrounded virtually around the clock by a flock of supporters, strategists, staffers, and fund-raisers who had helped transform her from an interesting human being into someone who now ate, drank, and lived the pursuit of a single goal.

To Joe, who so cherished their few shared times alone, this sudden and complete myopia had been unsettling. From once having felt that together he and Gail could batten down the hatches during hard times, he was now feeling a bit like a partisan spectator on the fringes of a crowd.

This had been the status quo ever since she'd announced her intention to enter the primary weeks earlier. And up to now Joe had been philosophical about putting his personal needs aside. After all, this was merely a process, and not without some interesting and possibly exciting ramifications.

But that was before Matt Purvis had appeared in his life, carrying a gun from a past so laden with baggage.

For the first time in quite a while, Joe was sufficiently

thrown off balance that his usual stoicism was in real need of Gail's company.

A few hundred yards beyond the I-91 overpass, he turned right onto Orchard Street and began driving uphill, his eyes to the left, hoping her broad driveway would be empty.

It wasn't, and as soon as he saw the half-dozen cars tightly packed as if awaiting a ferryboat, he wondered why he'd hoped otherwise. Had he set himself up for this disappointment on purpose, to reward his perfect memories of Ellen by contrast? He pulled over to the roadside opposite the driveway and killed the engine, silently shaking his head. These were just the kind of emotional gymnastics he usually tried to avoid.

As if to render it all moot, he swung out of the car and wended his way toward the house, looking forward to—if nothing else—being temporarily absorbed into Gail's current maelstrom of a life.

Certainly, that was alive and well, as he discovered hitting a wall of voices upon opening the back door into the kitchen.

There were three women before him, moving between restaurant-size salad fixings and a cauldron of soup and using the phone on the wall—Gail had installed four additional lines since announcing her intentions

One of them stopped talking and smiled at him as he entered. "Hi, Joe. You joining the dinner powwow?"

He raised his eyebrows. "Knew nothing about it, Brenda. Not sure I'd be of much use, anyhow. Is Gail around?"

Brenda gestured vaguely at the door leading into the rest of the large house. "We wouldn't be here without her." She paused suddenly and stared at him. "Actually, the way things are heating up, we might be. You hear about Ed Parker?"

"What about him?" he asked. Parker was a Republican drum banger and local businessman—disarmingly charming, charismatic, and popular at places like the Elks Club, Rotary, and others—who was always writing letters to the editor and talking on the radio about how the state was going to socialist hell in a handbasket. A man who'd married a seductive and appealing style to a rock-ribbed conservative message.

"The Republicans have finally sorted out their differences and made him their choice for the senate. Pretty extreme, if you ask me."

"No primary?" Joe asked.

Brenda looked amused and explained with that odd pride the Democrats have in their particular political dysfunction, "Oh, you know them: one man, one race. God forbid they give the people a choice. Anyhow, Gail is here someplace—check the living room."

He followed the growing noise—still more voices, but supplemented by the plastic tapping of keyboards and the ringing of phones.

He paused at the living room entrance, watching the activities of at least five more people. The comfortable furniture he associated with his moments with Gail—including the couch they sometimes made love on—had been replaced with desks, work tables, and a scattering of office chairs.

A young man frantically clacking on the computer stopped long enough to stare at him inquiringly. "May I help you?"

Another woman, drawn by the comment, looked up and smiled. "Joe," she said as she crossed over and gave him a hug. "I haven't seen you in ages." She nodded toward the young man. "This is my son, Aaron."

Joe shook hands, still looking around, which Aaron's mother correctly interpreted. She touched his shoulder and glanced overhead, murmuring, "She's upstairs. Go on up."

He left the living room and the noise, walked down the long hallway to the foot of the stairs, and began climbing, thinking that against all odds he might get some time with Gail after all.

But again he was disappointed. Halfway up, he saw her appear on the landing above, clipboard in hand, accompanied by her oldest friend and now campaign manager, Susan Raffner. They were deep in conversation and didn't even see him until after they'd started down.

Gail's face broke into a wide smile. "Joe. What a sweet surprise. I didn't know you were coming by." She stooped forward and kissed him awkwardly as Susan looked on. Returning Gail's embrace, he noticed Susan check her watch.

"You know what they say," he answered, trying to sound upbeat, "I happened to be in the neighborhood—not hard in this town."

Gail rolled her eyes. "A town with a lot of people, though. I'm starting to feel like I'll meet every one of them before this is over."

"It's going okay, though, right?" Joe asked. In an attempt to sound both savvy and supportive, he added, "I heard about Parker."

She made a face. "He's such a screwball. Problem is, nobody knows it, despite what he says. Anyhow, he's not my problem. I have to beat all the Democrats in the race first, and nicely enough that they don't take it personally. Such a weird process. Makes running for selectman a total breeze." She paused and touched his cheek. "God, I haven't seen you in days. Feels like forever." She furrowed her brow. "Are you all right? You look tired."

"Just a case I'm on," he said vaguely.

"Gail," Susan's voice dropped between them.

Gail stepped back against the railing and glanced up at her friend. "I know, I know." She looked at Joe again and shrugged helplessly. "I gotta go."

He smiled halfheartedly. "Brenda told me—big powwow."

Her expression was torn. "Right. You want to listen in? God knows I could use the input."

But he begged off. "Too much homework at the office."

Susan took two steps down, pressuring them to take the hint. They did, Gail leading and talking over her shoulder. "God, don't talk about homework. That's all I do anymore— that and eat vegetarian rubber chicken."

She paused again at the foot of the stairs. "Come back later?" she asked, placing her hand on his chest as he drew near.

He took her hand and kissed it as Susan took her other elbow and began steering her along the hallway. "If I can. Good luck."

Joe watched them go and then left by the front door, not wanting to walk through the house again.

Chapter 5

Joe Gunther unlocked the door with the borrowed key and paused before switching on the light, reflecting on the dark stillness before him. He was in the basement of the municipal building, on the threshold of the police department's storeroom. A windowless, airless black cave, it was the endpoint for everything from old parade uniforms to forgotten files, to pieces of hardware that hadn't quite made it to the dump. It also housed hundreds of past case files, labeled by date and name, each box containing records, reports, photographs, and even items of evidence, often as casually tossed together as the contents of a dorm room just before vacation.

The smell of the place was dry and dusty, slightly enhanced by something so subtle, he could only ascribe it to ancient memories. His mind drifted to how many investigations he'd reduced to such a container now tucked away in the gloom before him. It seemed he and his colleagues had unconsciously created a museum of humanity's clumsy chaos in the process, replicating Pandora's box with dozens of tiny, less dramatic facsimiles, rendered all the more poignant for their mundane contents. Drunken brawls, jealous rages, venal dreams—and all the mess they implied—now silenced, defeated, and forgotten, row on row.

He turned on the lights and began walking by the chronologically arranged metal shelf units, counting off the years and heading toward the dawn of his own career. He eventually paused, turned into an aisle, and came to two dust-coated boxes at eye level marked "Oberfeldt."

He piled one atop the other, finding them disappointingly light, and headed upstairs to his office.

Klaus Oberfeldt never returned home after that night, and he never awoke to say who had assaulted him. He made one trip in his remaining half year of life up to Hanover, New Hampshire, to Mary Hitchcock Hospital, for some tests and an evaluation, but it was done out of courtesy or curiosity, or more likely because of Maria Oberfeldt's endless haranguing. Everyone treating him knew what the outcome would be, and when his last breath was expelled, it was accompanied by a collective sigh of relief.

Young Joe Gunther witnessed that with a conflicting mixture of understanding and outrage. Typical of his nature, while he hadn't been spared Maria's generalized contempt, Joe had sympathized with both her sorrow and her fury. She and her husband might have been short on social graces, but neither had deserved what they'd been delivered. Joe happened to be at the hospital when Maria was told of Klaus's death, and he'd seen the last remnant of hope drift from her eyes. The fact that he was at the same place and time because his own mate was dying a couple of doors down both exacerbated his desire to bring closure to Maria's grief and confronted him with his own impotence.

The fusion of their separate sorrows seemed merely to create a void, leaving the case that had united them listless and without chance of resolution.

Joe sat at his desk in the otherwise deserted VBI office, the overhead lights extinguished in favor of a more intimate desk lamp, and spread out the contents of the two Oberfeldt case boxes.

The old photographs told the story best, not surprisingly, if for reasons beyond the mere images they conveyed. They were in black-and-white, for one thing, and large—eight-by-tens. Nowadays crime scene photos were often color Polaroids, or quasi-amateur snaps taken by whatever detective was nearest a digital camera. But, as was common back then, these had been shot by the owner of the local camera store, and they reflected his intuitive feel for lighting, angle, and depth of field. They were creepily cinematographic in their perfection, as if snipped from a moody film noir of the fifties, and they produced a certain artificial immediacy, being at once too good to be true and so real as to be palpable. Looking at them brought Joe fully back to when he'd been standing just to one side of the frame.

The fact that they were monochromatic reminded him of the passage of time, and of the distance he'd traveled in the intervening decades. "Feeling old" was too maudlin to capture the emotion. Joe took the aging process as simply one of life's by-products—something to be undertaken with few complaints and as much decorum as possible. But he didn't dismiss his experience as lightly, and his experience had been to witness such scenes as now littered his desk more times than he could count. That these were old enough to be in black-and-white was a sad and telling reminder of his journey's length.

The Oberfeldts' store had been long and narrow, with the

counter and two freestanding shelf units running perpendicular to the back storage room and the staircase beyond. In a fanciful way, it was reminiscent of a bowling alley, if smaller, a bit wider, and far more cluttered—a truly tiny, old-fashioned mom-and-pop market. In truth, the photographs made it look like a frontier store out of the Wild West, the black pool of blood on the floor only heightening the impression.

The body didn't feature in any of the photographs—it had yet to become a body. For that matter, given that this was initially a robbery-assault, photographs of this quality shouldn't even have been taken. It wasn't standard protocol. Gunther had requested the camera store owner to drop by, and his chief at the time gave him hell for it later. Such a waste of money during tight fiscal times was not looked upon kindly.

Joe had acted on instinct and didn't mind the reprimand. He'd seen Klaus at the hospital, after all, and had been told by the man's physician that he probably wouldn't last long. As things turned out, the pictures had been an extravagance. Although they were requested on the assumption that Klaus would die, his killer would be caught, and such evidence would be needed at trial, only the first had come to pass—and way too late for these images to be of much use, regardless of any clues they contained.

And they did contain clues: a bullet hole near the front door, the violent pattern of Oberfeldt's blood spatter, the open hiding place in the back room's floor where the couple's life savings had been, and—most interesting of all—a trail of smaller blood drops leading away from the scene, along with an open switchblade found lying in Klaus's gore, both presumed to be the assailant's.

Joe selected a picture showing the knife in close-up, the

lighting arranged to best reveal the ridges of a single thumb-print on the blade, peering out from under a thin smear of blood.

There certainly was a nagging anomaly. Why the knife? It was found open, had clearly been taken out for some use, while all of Klaus's injuries had been due to the pistol-whipping.

And yet the knife proved useful. The thumbprint was carefully lifted and compared to the thousands on file at the police department. The officer who fancied himself a foren-sics man spent weeks poring over endless cards with a mag-nifying glass, as intent as a spider weaving a web against all odds, until he finally hit pay dirt in the name of a local thief named Peter Shea. Pete was a relatively low-profile bad boy, had a problem with alcohol, and was generally considered one of the usual suspects when that phrase was still com-mon currency.

Unfortunately, he was not to be found. Nor had he been found to this day.

In a truly ironic paradox, that disappearance hadn't turned out to be all bad news. Clearly, it wasn't good that Pete had vanished, but at least they now had a name to pursue. Until that thumbprint had yielded an identity—and the person owning it had fled—Joe had been getting nowhere.

And he had worked the problem hard—persistent even in his youth. At least, for the first couple of months. He'd conducted several canvasses, chased down every complaint the Oberfeldts had ever filed, checked out all the local crooks with even vaguely similar MOs. He'd interviewed Maria three times, hoping to extract a memory of someone who might have wished them far more than simple ill will.

And he'd pushed her aggressively on who could have known about the nest egg's hiding place.

But it hadn't led to anything concrete—besides the unsettling suggestion that the hiding place had been known to several past employees, all of whom subsequently swore they'd kept mum. By the time Peter Shea was identified, Joe's devotion to the cause had flagged. After all, Oberfeldt was still alive, the case was still a robbery, and Ellen was still dying.

Near the end, Joe had to admit that he really didn't give a damn about the Oberfeldts or their presumed assailant. It was his chief who recognized this first and forced his young detective to take some leave. Joe put up a halfhearted protest. The chief back then was a laid-back, unruffled sort, more mindful of his "boys" than of the public they served, and Joe knew that no one would be asked to put much effort into the case, Shea or no Shea, until Joe himself returned to duty. But honestly, he was grateful to be taken off the hook. Toward the end, every conversation he had, every place he went, all he could see in his mind's eye was Ellen, pale and emaciated, slowly blending into the white sheets encasing her.

Inflammatory breast cancer is a fast-acting killer. Chances of recovery have improved over the years as both treatment methods and drugs have modernized, but it's a toxic disease and, when Ellen had it, a guaranteed death sentence. Chemotherapy, now such a mainstay, was generally considered a last-ditch tactic and most often wasn't even employed.

She'd laughed at the cancer's discovery, when Joe had noticed it during an intimate nuzzle. He'd felt its heat against his lips and pulled back to question her, noticing at the same moment its flushed color. There'd been jokes about how poison ivy could get in a place like that, before they resumed making love.

The image of their naked bodies entwined, moving as one, lost in pleasure and ignorant passion for the last time—the presence of the cancer already hot but unknown between them—plagued him like a nightmare for years afterward.

The following day, she went to the doctor to begin the countdown on their lives together.

It wasn't bad to begin with. Ellen drove daily up the new interstate to Mary Hitchcock Hospital for five-minute radiation treatments. She played it as a lark, ribbing Joe that she'd take advantage of being in what she called "precious Hanover" to do some upscale shopping and destroy their budget. But it became a thin con quickly made tinny by her growing exhaustion.

There wasn't any pain, thankfully—not at first—and her appetite remained normal. For what now seemed an impossibly brief twilight, both of them began thinking there'd been a misdiagnosis, or that she'd be the one that made this disease only 99 percent fatal.

But that didn't last. Joe became so tired of grim-faced people dressed in white lab coats, their eyes at once clinical and sympathetic, telling them nothing but bad news. Ellen and he became experts in the language of disease, speaking in Latin-based polysyllables with an ease they'd once reserved for happier conversations. Ellen and he turned to each other for small moments of pleasure and intimacy in the midst of it all, while feeling like two pieces of flotsam refusing to sink into the sea.

When they made love now, their previous joyful abandon was stained by too much knowledge, as if neither of them wanted to risk rupturing the virulent capsule cradled between them.

Surgery was next—radical, dehumanizing, utterly trans-
forming. Not only was Ellen's breast removed, but, in an
effort at what they blandly called hormonal therapy, her
ovaries as well. The doctors recommended this in hopes of
"an objective response."

She did not respond objectively, perhaps because, Joe
once suggested, no one had bothered to tell her what the
hell that meant.

Not that it mattered, finally. As momentous as had been
their concerns about the surgery, they withered to nothing
after the pain kicked in.

It first appeared in the right upper quadrant of her ab-
domen, and in what both she and Joe had come to expect
as the norm, its cause was optimistically misdiagnosed as
being related to the surgery.

It wasn't. The disease had spread to the liver. The pain
came from the tumor growing faster than the liver could
stretch to accommodate it. With Ellen's now rapidly shrink-
ing frame, Joe began to fantasize at night about the cancer
becoming larger than the two of them put together.

Of all the horrors he'd seen in combat, the self-doubt and
confusion he'd suffered growing up, nothing he'd experienced had prepared him for this metamorphosis of the
woman he'd planned to grow old with, into a pain-racked,
sutured, wan-eyed vessel of an army of pestilent cells.
Every visit to Ellen's bedside reinforced the sensation that a
yawning distance was growing between them, as if she were
slipping below the surface, and all he could reach—plung-
ing as deeply as he could—were the tips of her fingers.

When she died, just two days after Klaus Oberfeldt, she
weighed barely seventy-five pounds—a parody of Joe's
nightmares about the creature growing within her. In the

end, all that was left—all that escaped—was the smile she gave him just before she fell asleep for the last time.

Joe put aside the crime scene photographs and swiveled his desk chair around to face the darkness of the night outside. It was starting to turn cool, creeping toward September, and people had already begun commenting on how summer's grip on the region was beginning to slip.

"Working late, boss?"

He looked over his shoulder at the office entrance. He saw the small, slim profile of his one female squad member, Sammie Martens, barely visible in the gloom, "Hey, Sam. You, too? Feel free to hit the lights."

She approached his desk and settled into his guest chair instead. Of his three younger colleagues, Sam held a special place in his heart. She'd worked so hard to get here, essentially from childhood, that the concept of struggle had become not only second nature but a self-fulfilling prophecy. This wasn't just ambition, although she had that, too. It was more reminiscent of the punch-drunk boxer who can't see the other guy has thrown in the towel. Sam's fate, it appeared, was to keep on swinging without clearly knowing why.

"Not me," she said now. "I was working out at home and saw your light on. Made me curious. We have something going?"

Joe smiled in the semi-darkness. Sam's huge single-room loft apartment, once a post–Civil War dance hall in one of Brattleboro's ancient building blocks, was directly across the street, the better—so claimed her friends—for her to respond to any call. They were only half kidding, and she only half took it in jest.

"Indirectly. It's an old case from the PD days," Joe explained. "Something I worked on when I was starting out.

The gun just surfaced in the hostage negotiation Ron had a few nights ago."

Sam nodded. "That was a bummer. I called him right after at home. Wendy said he'd already gone to bed. I can never figure out how he stays in this business."

Joe considered that for a moment. "Maybe it's lucky for all of us he does."

She understood his meaning but couldn't resist putting her own self-deprecating spin on it, adding, "Yeah. We can't all be hard-asses, right? Did the gun supply a breakthrough?"

He made a face. "Not in so many words. Basically, it's just a new string to run down. There was one thing, though—the crime lab made a wild guess that, until it popped up last week, it's been safely tucked away."

He leaned forward and pushed the crime scene pictures toward Sam for her perusal. "I would love to find out where that little resting place is."

Chapter 6

According to Ron Klesczewski, Linda Purvis denied knowing where her estranged husband had gotten the Blackhawk. In fact, since she'd hired a lawyer, she'd buttoned up entirely. That left Gunther to interview the rest of Matt's friends, family, and acquaintances, starting with his son, an army private in town for the week on bereavement leave.

He caught up to Christopher Purvis at a local funeral home, where he found him being sale-pitched by a dark-suited attendant. A small, slight man, Purvis was saddled with bad skin, poor eyesight, and an oddly shaped skull that only looked worse for its high-and-tight haircut. For those societal misfits that a uniform improved, visually if nothing else, this one was the exception. He stood in the home's viewing room, surrounded by coffins, his hat in his hand and his expression downcast, looking to Joe like a child freshly caught wearing his father's stolen clothes.

Joe started by saving him from what he could. He

stepped before the attendant, whom he knew, and requested a moment's privacy.

They both watched the man glide off with professional smoothness.

"Thought you might need a break," Gunther said quietly as the door closed without a sound.

"What I want is a pine box," the young man said tiredly, removing his thick glasses and rubbing the bridge of his nose.

"You'll get it. These are good folks. They'll listen eventually."

"He was saying he didn't want me to think back a year from now and regret that maybe I didn't pay proper respect by getting a fancier casket."

"Are you paying for it?"

"Some of his buddies have chipped in for most of it." Up to now, Chris Purvis had been staring either at the floor or at the samples along the wall. Now he looked at Gunther for the first time, his eyes magnified behind their lenses. "I know what everyone's saying, but he was a good guy. He just never got a break. Pretty typical that people are there for him after it's too late."

"Still, if it's mostly their money, maybe they should have a say," Joe suggested. "It would help get you off the hook, too."

Purvis mulled that over, finally nodding. "Yeah. Maybe." He scowled slightly, as if embarrassed, and then said, "I'm sorry. Am I supposed to know you?"

Joe stuck out his hand. "No. Sorry. My name's Gunther. I work with the Vermont Bureau of Investigation."

Purvis stared at him. "And you came to see me here? Jesus." He didn't sound angry. It was more like amazement.

But Joe waved that off. "No, no. Don't misunderstand.

This has nothing to do with what happened to your father. I was just told where to find you. But I can leave. I'm not here to add to your troubles."

Purvis barely shook his head, clearly nonplussed. "No. I mean, you're not bothering me. I just . . . Well, thanks for dealing with that guy, anyhow. Did you even know my dad?"

"No, but what I've heard matches what you said: a good guy always at the short end of the stick. I never can figure how that happens to some people." Gunther gestured to the waiting room outside. "Would you like to sit down for a bit?"

The young soldier moved with him to a row of chairs set up near a picture window overlooking the parking lot.

"Had you seen your dad much recently?" Gunther asked as they sat down next to each other, the only occupants in a skeletal array of empty wooden chairs. They were speaking softly, influenced by the somber tones of their environment.

"No, sir," Purvis answered. "This pretty much came out of the blue."

Gunther didn't suggest he not call him "sir." The perception of authority might be handy as the conversation progressed. "You mean the confrontation between him and Linda?"

"That bitch," Chris Purvis murmured, back to staring at the rug.

"They'd been at each other for a while?"

"Forever, seems like. I never understood what he saw in her. She treated him like shit from the day they met."

"Did it ever turn violent?"

He looked up. "From her it did. You bet. She was always

slapping him and yelling at him. He never laid a hand on her."

"But he didn't like it."

Purvis flared with anger. "Well, no shit, he didn't like it. What the fuck do you think?"

Gunther narrowed his eyes. "Watch it."

The other man's face paled, and his chin trembled briefly. "Sorry, sir," he whispered, glancing away.

Gunther let a moment pass before easing him off the hook. "You have a right to be upset. You know anything about your dad's gun? The Ruger? That's what I'm trying to trace."

Chris Purvis was at a loss. "The only gun I ever saw was an old .30-06 he used to hunt with. I didn't even know he owned a pistol."

"Would you have known?"

"Probably. We got along, and I went through his stuff all the time for one reason or another. He didn't care. He didn't hide things." He snorted and added, "Didn't have much to hide and no place to hide it anyhow. You seen where he lived?"

Gunther couldn't say he had.

"A one-room rat hole. That bitch took him for all he owned. He couldn't afford anything else."

"So, he got the gun recently," Joe mused out loud. "Any ideas there?"

Purvis shrugged. "I don't know."

"Any friends who were into guns?"

He was incredulous. "This is Vermont. Everybody's into guns." He scratched his cheek reflectively. "He had a friend named Dick who talked a lot about them. I think he belonged to a gun club. Kept inviting my dad to the range so they could shoot together. He might know."

"Dick who?"

Chris looked up at the ceiling in concentration, sighing. "Oh, boy. I met him a few times. Italian name. 'Ch-' something. I'm sorry. I don't remember. But he worked with my dad at the lumber mill, doing the same thing—stacker, or some such shit. The bottom of the bottom of the heap, was what he used to call it. They were the guys who basically handle the stuff the loaders and forklifts and the rest don't mess with."

A small silence elapsed. Joe stood up. "You miss your dad." He said it as a statement.

Purvis leaned forward, his elbows on his knees. "Yeah. He had a lousy life and made all the wrong moves, but he was okay. He never hurt anybody."

Gunther patted him gently on the shoulder. "Talk to your dad's friends, Chris. They might be more help than you think. It's pretty clear you weren't the only one to think he was a decent man."

Purvis looked up at him, squinting slightly through his thick glasses. "Okay. I'm sorry I got mad earlier."

Joe smiled. "Don't worry about it. Take care of yourself."

This time they shook hands.

Three days after Ellen's funeral, Joe returned to work. No one thought he should. His brother, Leo, and his mother, who both lived in Thetford, Vermont, where Joe had been born and brought up, lobbied him to spend some time back home. The chief, whose name was Canaday but who was never called anything but "Chief," told him to take as many days as he wanted. But Joe didn't think he could stand much more time on his own. For weeks already he'd been traveling between the hospital and their small apartment, seeing day after day how his living alone was slowly eroding all traces of Ellen's presence. His shaving equipment laid permanent claim to the rim of the bathroom sink, where in the past, it used to retreat behind the mirror until needed. Similarly, the kitchen cabinets yielded to cans and boxes of his choosing; the fridge emptied of perishable items and restocked with a few things to drink and little else. Joe's clothes, draped here and there, became almost all there was to be seen outside the closet.

As Ellen was vanishing inside her own body, so was she disappearing at home.

The morning of the service, freshly dressed in black, Joe rented a fully furnished apartment on the corner of High and Oak, just a stroll from the center of downtown, so that after the funeral he'd have a new place to spend the night. He paid the rent on the old place for a couple of months, but he didn't return there for six weeks.

He needed to work, and with Klaus Oberfeldt's death, he hoped he had something that might keep him on track.

But that wasn't all.

He also needed to work because he'd let Maria Oberfeldt down. She'd been the only one railing for someone to address her husband's beating, and no one, Joe especially, had given it proper attention.

Now, in a world without Ellen, Joe could only think of who had killed Klaus Oberfeldt.

Instinctively knowing that it was too late, he started with Shea's inner circle, not including family. As far as could be determined, there was none of the latter. Given up for foster care as an infant, Pete had moved from home to home, establishing no lasting connections, deemed time and again incorrigible. He'd ended up in Brattleboro only because that's where he'd turned eighteen, and had thus been flushed out of the system. As a result, like a parody of a

homing pigeon, Pete Shea had returned to Brattleboro forever after, usually following one of his brief sojourns in the
penal system.

After rummaging through Shea's apartment and meager
possessions, Joe spent days chasing down old cell mates
and drinking buddies and poring over the young man's arrest records, scouring for a name that he hoped might hold
some promise. He finally found it in Ted Moore, who was
listed as having been busted with Shea twice, once for supplying minors with alcohol, again for being drunk and dis-
orderly, and who was suspected of being a fence for some of
Pete's ill-gotten goods.

Given the recent timing of their last known association,
and the fact that Moore had been reported living it up just
two days after the Oberfeldt assault, Joe thought Ted might
well be worth a visit.

At the time Joe set out to locate Ted Moore, Brattleboro
wasn't the gentrified, politically active, socially diverse
place of today. It was something else altogether. Vietnam
was still in full swing; the seeds of the sixties had blos-
somed into protest, violence, and a universal social uneasi-
ness; and all of it was palpable even in this remote pocket
of Vermont. Kids made oinking sounds as police cars drove
by, the sweet aroma of marijuana was in the air and clung
to people's tie-dyed clothing and long hair, jobs were scarce
and the local economy terrible, and thirty-eight licensed
outlets served liquor throughout town. The bars were full
to capacity every Friday and Saturday night, dumping hundreds of quarrelsome patrons into the streets come closing
time.

Things finally got wild enough, regularly enough, that
an edict was issued to all arresting officers: Start cuffing
people flat on the ground—the hoods of the patrol cars are

taking a beating from all the heads being thumped against them.

There was an almost Wild West energy in the air separating the rebellious have-nots from the sheltered gentility. The police force and its famous "thin blue line" fit smoothly into this context, however inaccurately, between those paying them respect and those giving them trouble.

As a result, the cops were in an element perversely to their liking. Underpaid, poorly staffed, overworked, and only marginally supported by the town fathers, they labored more for the mystique than for any job security. This wasn't something you did for income. You did it for the same reason you thought people had once joined the Texas Rangers.

And, to a great extent, you did it alone. When Joe became one of the few in this beleaguered department, it had two cars, one huge portable radio that barely reached base, and a flashing red light system located at the three major crossroads downtown, used to let the beat guys know they were being summoned. Cops learned to keep an eye peeled, depend on their wits, and interpret the law as it suited their needs. Countless disputes every weekend never even appeared in the paperwork, much less made it to court on Monday morning.

It was against this backdrop, driven by guilt and coping with sorrow, that Joe set out to find Ted Moore.

According to his police record, Moore was an itinerant carpenter, and according to the people Joe found loitering outside Moore's run-down apartment building on Canal, he was helping build an extension onto the town garage on Putney Road.

The present Putney Road is a traditional "miracle mile," cluttered with chain stores, gas stations, and motels—as unique to Vermont as to suburban Iowa. When Joe Gunther went to meet Ted Moore, virtually the entire western side of the road was farmland. Not so the eastern, however, which is why Joe was never surprised by how the strip finally ended up. Directly across from the farm, like an urban metaphor for a slow-moving prairie blaze, stood restaurants, a drive-in, a dairy, and a couple of hamburger stands, all poised by the curb like a row of flames straining to jump a firebreak. Once that tourist-laden interstate appeared in the late sixties, just beyond the fields, Joe knew that the farmers' days were all but done.

The town garage occupied the southern edge of those fields. It was a large wooden structure, with a shed big enough for a winter's supply of salted dirt, next to a few stalls housing the salt and the plow trucks. The "few" part was why Moore and others had been contracted to expand the garage.

Joe pulled off next to several pickups and took his bearings. Adjacent to the salt shed was the equivalent of a wing, and at its far end were several men wearing tool belts, working on the roof. Below them, the walls of the extension shimmered in clean, new pine siding.

Gunther walked the length of the building and nonchalantly addressed the first workman he came across. "Is Ted Moore around?"

The man's reaction came as a surprise. Instead of answering directly, he turned and bellowed toward the roof crew, "Hey, Ted, you've got a visitor."

It was neither what Joe had wanted nor expected, and standing flat-footed in the parking lot while his hoped-for interviewee straightened up like a startled gazelle put him at precisely the disadvantage he'd been hoping to avoid.

Sure enough, Ted Moore unbuckled his tool belt,

dropped it with a crash, and vanished over the far side of the roof.

"Thanks a lot," Joe muttered as he set off in a sprint around the corner, hoping to cut the other man off.

But there was no chance of that. By the time Joe caught sight of him, Moore had already leaped from his perch and was hotfooting it south down the length of the garage. Cursing his own stupidity for having parked where his quarry was now headed instead of driving straight to the site, Joe picked up his pace, praying that he was faster and in better shape than the carpenter.

But running wasn't Ted Moore's only tactic. About halfway along, and urged on by the incongruous cheers of his distant coworkers, he paused, doubled over from the exertion, and picked up a three-foot length of rebar from the littered ground.

Joe didn't hesitate. Still coming on at full tilt, he pulled his snub-nosed revolver from his holster and took aim.

Moore dropped the metal rod and resumed running.

This time, however, knowing he was athletically outclassed, he veered toward the towering salt shed beside him, and a small exterior staircase angling toward a narrow access door at its apex—used during the winter to reach the top of the salt pile inside. Joe could see Moore's plan: If he got through that door and blocked it from the inside, Gunther would have to go around, allowing Moore ample time to reach his pickup and escape. Even if Joe didn't try following, he'd probably still be too late to make up for the shortcut.

Joe took the stairs two at a time, the ringing of his shoes against the metal steps matching Moore's high above him.

But not that much higher. Already flagging, Moore was clearly finding his uphill option a real challenge. Gasping for air, helping himself along with both hands on the railing, he was stumbling every few feet, reducing the gap between them.

By the time he reached the door, he didn't bother trying to block it behind him. He merely threw it open and disappeared from sight, Gunther barely ten feet below.

Inside, there was a small platform leading to a ladder that dropped into the salt pile like a straw into a milkshake. The drop would have been thirty feet had the shed been empty. Right now, in preparation for the coming winter, it was over half full.

Ted Moore staggered toward the ladder's top, swung around to face it, and tried to descend. Gunther took a more practical approach. He ran to the platform's edge and kicked Moore in the head, sending him sailing backward through the air to land with a thud ten feet below.

Gunther then climbed down the ladder at a leisurely pace to crouch by the other man's side.

Moore's arms and legs were moving slightly, as if he were keeping afloat in the water. His eyes were wide and fixed on Joe's.

"You almost killed me," he said in a whisper, the air knocked out of him.

Joe rolled him over, handcuffed him, and rolled him back. Moore's sweaty face was now caked with salty sand.

"And what were you going to do with that rebar, asshole?" he asked.

"I didn't know who you were."

"Bullshit. Why'd you run?"

"I thought you were the brother of some girl I knocked up."

Joe picked up a fistful of sand and dumped it onto Ted's face, blinding him and making him choke.

His hands bound, Moore thrashed around for half a minute, spitting and catching his breath. "What the fuck're you doing?" he complained.

Joe picked up another fistful and held it where Moore could see it. "Trying to have a conversation. Why'd you run?"

Moore was blinking furiously against the sting in his eyes. "You can't do this."

Gunther moved to open his hand.

"No, no. Okay. I'll tell you. I ripped off a store last night. I thought you were after me for that." He paused for a moment, his brains almost making noises as he realized his admission. "Weren't you?" he added plaintively.

Gunther smiled and sat back more comfortably, noticing that a couple of workmen had appeared far below, looking up the hill at them from around the edge of the open bay doors. He waved cheerfully and gestured to them to leave.

"I am now," he answered.

Moore closed his eyes tiredly. "Shit."

"Actually," Joe admitted, "I just wanted to ask you about Pete Shea."

The other man grimaced. "What the fuck do I know about Pete?"

"I don't know. Educate me."

Moore tried to look surprised, but the gesture let more dirt into his eyes. "Ah, shit. Come on. Let me sit up."

Gunther pulled him to a sitting position.

Ted hung his head and shook it violently a couple of times. "Jesus, that smarts."

"Talk to me about Pete," Joe said again.

Moore's voice was angry. "Pete, Pete . . . The son of a bitch isn't even around anymore. Hasn't been for months. What's the big deal?"

"Where'd he go?"

Ted looked up at him and slowly enunciated, "I do not know."

Joe pushed him flat onto his back again, swiveled around, and placed his forearm against the man's throat, making him gag.

This time, Joe was the one speaking slowly and clearly. "Cut the crap, Teddy, or you'll be grateful for a mouthful of salt."

"I don't know. Honest," Moore half croaked.

Joe pulled him up again roughly. "Why did he leave town?"

"He was spooked. Said you guys were after him. He said you were going to pin the storekeeper beating on him."

"Did he do it?"

"Like he'd tell me. Of course he said he didn't do it."

"What do you think?" Joe asked him.

"Me? I don't know. It wasn't Pete's style, but what's that worth? A guy gets juiced, somebody pisses him off, then suddenly it's not his style, but he does it anyhow. He was pretty cranked last I saw him."

"What're they saying on the street?"

Ted Moore shrugged. "They're saying he did it. But no-body knows squat. They say Paul McCartney's dead, too."

"Was Pete flashing around any cash before he took off?"

"Nah. He was just acting paranoid. I didn't know any money was involved. That wasn't in the papers."

Joe ignored him. "You were seen spending a lot right after the old man went down."

Moore looked innocent. "Me?"

Joe only had to reach for Moore's throat to make the man concede, "All right, all right. Jesus H. Christ. I had some money. Fine. It had nothing to do with that shit."

Joe looked into his face and believed what he heard. He reached around and opened the handcuffs. Moore massaged his wrists and then rubbed his face with both hands, brushing the sand away.

"You're not bustin' me?" he asked cautiously.

"You still have what you stole last night?"

"Yeah. It's at home."

Joe tilted his head slightly. "Then, no—not if you hand it over. We'll do it now." He stood up and yanked Moore to his feet, not admitting that since he'd cuffed him and had him confess without Mirandizing him, there wasn't a bust to speak of.

"Is there anyone else in town Pete might've confided in?" Joe asked as they sidestepped down the slope.

"Not Pete. Kept to himself, pretty much."

"No girlfriend?"

The other man looked surprised. "Hey, there's always a girlfriend—Katie Clark, if you're interested. They even lived together, but that'll be a dead end, too."

"Why do you say that?"

"Chemistry. Pete's been gone for months, and Katie started hanging with somebody else a week later—no love lost, if you ask me. If he'd contacted her or anyone else, I would've heard. This crowd isn't big on keeping secrets."

He paused and eyed Gunther as if struck by something wholly original. "That's a first, you know? I mean, sooner or later, you always hear about where a guy ends up, even if it's dead. But not Pete. Not so far."

Chapter 7

Joe Gunther was thinking back to that unorthodox salt pile interview when he entered the VBI office, his brain still working on how to link two events separated by three decades.

"Deep in thought?" came a voice. "Better not strain your-self."

Joe glanced over to the one desk in the room that was wedged into a corner. That quasi-defensive positioning combined with the mess spilling over the desk's surface made its occupant look as if he were hunkered behind sandbags. Psychologically speaking, the image fit perfectly.

"Hey, Willy," Joe said distractedly, walking over to his own desk.

Willy Kunkle was the squad's odd man. Though he had been crippled by a sniper bullet years ago and saddled with a dangling left arm, Willy's sour and biting personality pre-dated any such cause-and-effect explanation. Despite the injury, the post-traumatic stress disorder following his stint in Vietnam, his tortuous recovery from alcoholism, and one wildly failed marriage, Willy—as he was the first to admit—was a self-made man.

A boss's nightmare, he was still loyal, intelligent, and tenacious enough to have not only earned Joe's respect but his protection as well. Several times, when Willy had been threatened with termination, Joe had found ways to keep him on board. When asked why, especially by Gail, who openly loathed the man, and even once or twice by Sam, who was currently Willy's girlfriend, Joe usually ducked the issue. Left to their own conclusions, therefore, people considered all possibilities, from Willy's being a substitute son to Joe's becoming senile. There were other, less well known interpretations, however, the most telling of which was that once upon a time, as Ted Moore could have attested, Joe's methods hadn't differed all that much from Willy's own. Both battle-scarred vets, they'd had difficulty reining in the style of retribution they'd witnessed all too often in combat.

Joe had eventually found a steadying mentor in his old, now late squad commander, Frank Murphy. In his heart, he was hoping that he might still serve the same role for Willy, if only partially.

"Sam tell you what I was working on?" Joe asked, pretending to be scrounging through some files.

"Something about you being so bored, you had to go back thirty years for a case?"

That was one way of looking at it. "Yeah, in a nutshell. Who would you go to if you wanted a gun?"

"Around here, anyone who wasn't driving a Volvo or didn't shop at the Co-op."

Joe sighed. "Yeah—pretty much what I was thinking."

"But you're not talking just any piece. You're talking about an ancient hog leg. That smacks of amateur hour to me."

Gunther looked up at him, brightening slightly. "I have the name of one of the dead guy's pals. Worked with him at the lumber mill as a yard gofer."

Willy hitched his right shoulder noncommitally. "That's where I'd start. What's his name?"

"Dick somebody. You want to keep me company?"

Willy snorted and began extricating himself from behind the desk. "Well, shit, since you got it narrowed down to a single Dick, how can I say no?"

The mill in question was south of the Brattleboro town line—an open complex of sheds, stacks of lumber, and a railroad spur. Again recalling his failed approach with Ted Moore, a wiser Joe Gunther went straight to the office, showed his credentials, and inquired about an employee named Dick who was a friend of Matt Purvis and had a last name starting with "Ch." The response from the secretary greeting them was happily instantaneous.

"That would be Dick Celentano. They were quite the duo. I was so sorry to hear about what happened to Matt. That's what you're here about, right?"

Willy had already opened his mouth to ruin this friendly, casual moment when Joe cut him off. "You're right. Very good. And don't worry about Dick. We just want to chat with him about Matt. I hate to wander all over the yard looking for him, though, and I sure don't want to embarrass him any. Is there a way you can page him? Tell him he has a phone call, maybe?"

Joe gave her a conspiratorial smile, causing her to giggle. "Ooh, that's clever," she said. "Okay."

She hit a button on the console before her and announced, "Dick Celentano to the office for a phone call. Dick Celentano to the office for a phone call."

Gunther thanked her and pulled Kunkle over near the front door, murmuring, "I'll wait for him here. Go loiter in the parking lot and discreetly shepherd him in. I don't want him making a run for it once he finds out who we are."

"Ooh," Willy mimicked before heading outside. "That's clever."

They needn't have worried. Dick Celentano was cooperation personified, and easily impressed. "Can I hold it?" he asked after Joe had shown him his badge. The man was completely unfazed by having been lured into the office by a ruse.

Willy rolled his eyes as Joe handed it over.

"Wow," Celentano said, cradling it as if it were a religious icon. "I've read about you guys, but this is a first. You're like the best of the best, right? Like, way better than the state troopers."

"Yeah," Willy said quickly, before Joe could interrupt. "Way better. Be sure to tell them that."

His eyes gleaming, Celentano returned the badge. "Cool. You got it. So, what can I do you for?"

"We're here about Matt," Gunther told him.

Celentano's face fell. "Can you believe that? Unbelievable. I heard about it on the news. I was, like, stunned. I mean, I cried, right then and there."

"I bet," Willy muttered.

"That must've been tough," Joe added, patting the man's arm. "You didn't see it coming?"

"Well, I knew he was bummed out, losing his job here and all. It's not like any of us has money to spare, you know what I mean? And he had less than most."

"Did you know Linda?"

The man's expression soured as he joined the general consensus. "That bitch. Yeah, we met once. She must've been something in the sack, is all I can say, 'cause she wasn't much anywhere else. I never could figure that one out—what he saw in her. She treated me like shit right from the get-go."

"No kidding?" said Willy.

Celentano glanced at him, all happy innocence. "Yeah. I mean, what did I ever do to her, right?"

"So," Joe asked, steering him back on course, "Matt going to confront her came totally out of the blue, as far as you know?"

"Oh, yeah. Totally."

"He had a handgun. What can you tell us about that?" Willy asked.

Dick Celentano furrowed his brow. "I only know about a rifle," he said slowly.

Both detectives stayed silent. Their guest's former enthusiasm had abruptly faded. He, too, remained quiet, leading Gunther to suggest, "But he was looking for a handgun."

"Yeah," Celentano mournfully conceded.

"And you supplied him with one," Willy added, his voice threatening.

This time the other man correctly interpreted Willy's meaning. "No, I didn't. I swear. I didn't want any part of that. I told him so, too."

"So, you knew what he wanted it for?"

Celentano squirmed. "Linda was driving him crazy. He said he just wanted to show her who was boss. I said I wouldn't help—turned him down flat. Just like that. He was drinking again. I wasn't sure what he'd do."

Willy had straightened by now and was looking out the window, his impatience showing. Joe, for his part, leaned in close, still suspicious. "You were best friends, Dick. He was in need. Even if you didn't want any part of it doesn't mean you couldn't help him indirectly. What was he threatening to do? Rob a store and steal a gun? That would've gotten him in really hot water."

Dick cast his eyes down. Clearly one of the world's worst poker players. "It wasn't a store," he said softly. "It was a friend's house he was thinking to rob."

"So, what did you suggest?" Joe coaxed.

"I gave him a name."

Willy took Joe's cue and said with unsettling gentleness, "Dick, we didn't jam you up here. We won't with the next guy, either. We just have to close all the circles with this. Lay it to rest so life can go on."

"His name's John Moser," Celentano confessed, looking deflated. He looked up at Joe pleadingly. "I didn't know what else to do."

Willy abruptly dropped to one knee to better make eye contact, his demeanor hardening yet again. Celentano involuntarily flinched. But Willy didn't raise his hand or his voice, although the impact of what he said had much the same effect: "You call a priest or a counselor, you moron. You hurt your friend's feelings so you can keep him alive. That's what you owe him—not access to a gun."

Gunther never did get any closer to finding Peter Shea, although it wasn't for lack of trying. After collecting what Ted Moore had stolen the night before in exchange for not arresting him, Joe tracked down Katie Clark—Pete's girlfriend at the time he disappeared—waiting tables at one of the town's ubiquitous pizza joints.

He was standing by the back door when she ended her shift.

"You Katie Clark?" he asked, showing her his badge. "I'm Joe Gunther."

"Good for you, pig."

Joe raised his eyebrows. She fit the profile for that kind of response: skinny; long, straight, greasy hair; dirty hip-hugger jeans and sandals; the obligatory tie-dye T-shirt with a peace symbol emblazoning one breast—every effort made to diminish a natural attractiveness. But he knew from asking around which social stratum she inhabited, and it wasn't the protester/college dropout crowd. She was pure working class, a poseur who couldn't care less about what was happening in Vietnam.

"I'd like to ask you about Pete Shea."

"He's gone." She made to brush by him.

"You know where to?"

"Wouldn't tell you if I did."

He addressed the back of her head. "If we establish he killed that man, you'll be in shit up to your ears unless you help me now."

She turned around to face him. "Pete didn't kill anyone. You're the one who's full of shit."

"How can you be so sure?"

She hesitated a split second. "I just know."

"You were with him all that night?"

"Yeah."

"From eleven o'clock on?"

"Right."

Joe made up the next line. "After the two of you got together at the Village Barn just before? We have witnesses to that."

"Sure," she said, but her eyes betrayed her confusion at this total fiction, and her doubts about playing into it.

"Katie," he said, his voice softening, "Klaus Oberfeldt was assaulted just after nine, and I have no idea if you were at the Village Barn that night. If you think Pete's innocent, help me prove it."

She continued staring at him for a long moment, and then finally let her gaze drop. "I can't."

"You don't know where he was at that time?"

"No." She looked up again, reinvigorated. "But I know he didn't do it."

"He carried a switchblade, right? Used to show off how well he could throw it across a room and make it stick to a wall?"

She thought that over carefully. The police had withheld mention of the knife from the papers, as they had the missing money.

"Yeah," she admitted slowly. "But he lost it."

"We found it at the crime scene."

Her lips pressed together and she stared at him angrily.

"Where did he go, Katie?"

"I don't know," she repeated, her fists clenched. "He just left. You want to tap my phone and follow me around, be my guest. I liked Pete—he was gentle and sweet and not an asshole. I don't think he did it, no matter what tricks you want to pull, but I still don't know where he is. He dumped me like a hot rock and I haven't heard from him since. I think it was just more than he could handle. He's had a shitty life and I don't guess it's getting better." She quickly wiped an eye with the back of her hand, adding, "I gotta go."

She turned on her heel and walked off into the night. For months thereafter, Joe did keep tabs on her as best he could. But there was never anything to indicate that she ever reconnected with Pete Shea.

*   *   *

"You know John Moser?" Joe asked Willy as they left the lumber yard. Whereas other people had hobbies like fishing or watching car races, Willy had two: One was pencil sketching, something Joe had discovered by accident and had been sworn never to divulge; the other, known to all, was keeping tabs on the town's underworld. As other men tracked baseball stats, Willy collected intelligence on the activities, alliances, and interactions among likely law enforcement customers. Every other cop Joe knew was content to deal with the bad guys as they appeared on the radar scope. Willy's interest was like a connoisseur's; he liked to be familiar with all aspects of his subjects' progression, from start to finish.

"I know he's not somebody I'd send a friend to see."

Joe scratched his head. "It's not that big a town. You'd think I'd've heard of him."

"You don't keep up," Willy said flatly. "He's from Mass. Springfield. Got too hot for him down there, so he brought his business to the land of the yahoos."

"What business is that?"

"He's a middleman. Drugs, girls, guns, stolen goods— you name it. Cagey, though. Rarely touches the stuff himself."

"Meaning he'll be all cooperation when we ask him about Matt Purvis's gun?"

Willy laughed. "Fer sher—you can count on it."

Gunther took his eyes off the street long enough to cast him a sideward glance. "I'm not sure I like that laugh."

Willy stayed smiling. "Then don't worry your pretty little head about it. I'll find him for you."

It was late by the time Joe finished at the office, having spent several hours catching up on paperwork. Being VBI's number two man meant that he had not only his own case-load and unit to watch over, but the activities and reports of the other four statewide unit chiefs as well, all faxed or e-mailed to him daily.

It wasn't as onerous as it could have been. Since the VBI had been created essentially as a legislative experiment, and run by Gunther and Allard from the start, the two of them had quietly reinvented the standard paper stream common to most police agencies. Each VBI unit was given unusual autonomy, resulting in the correspondence between them being more practical in nature than the Big Brother, from-the-top-down norm. As a result, Joe spent less time check-ing timesheets, doing cost accounting, and going over case management minutiae, and more time staying up-to-date on investigative progress and results. It allowed him to feel more like a doting nurse checking on vitals than a bureau-crat reducing his colleagues to "little people."

Still, it took time, and it didn't compare to being on the street chasing leads, so by the time he called it quits, he was in the mood for some R & R.

In the past, that had usually involved Gail in some way, either by phone or through a visit if she was in town.

He sat in his car, wondering what to do. Dropping by the last time hadn't been particularly successful. It was later now, of course, after the average dinner circuit or run-of-the-mill Kiwanis or Elks meeting.

He started up the car and drove over to her house.

Again, unsurprisingly, it was a mistake. The lights were all blazing and the driveway as jammed as before. He'd set himself up for an avoidable disappointment. Turning around in the middle of the street to head home, he was angry at his own stupidity. Running for high office had been in Gail's blood for years, essentially since he'd known her. Events, traumatic and otherwise, had delayed the inevitable, but her time had finally come. And he knew this was only the beginning. An ambitious, hardworking, intelligent woman, Gail was a late starter, which further fueled her need to excel.

Her goals were thus reasonable, expected, even inevitable. But he still found himself resentful. In the midst of revisiting a past he'd assumed was long buried, he was finding the rekindled grief oddly amorphous, as if no longer applicable to just his loss of Ellen.

He was pretty sure this was a result of frustration and exhaustion. But he also knew that sometime soon the doubts it was raising would have to be addressed.

Chapter 8

"Hello?"

"Hi. It's your firstborn child."

There was an infectious chuckle at the other end of the line—old, thin, and inordinately welcome. "Joseph. My goodness, it's been forever."

"It's been two weeks, Mom. No guilt trips, please. I hope I'm not calling too late."

"Guilt's a mother's best currency, Joe. You should know that. You're the detective. And you know the habits around here. Always up until midnight. Hang on. Let me get your brother."

Joe visualized her backing her electric wheelchair out of the living room docking station she'd created of card tables, shelving, and benches, all laden with books, magazines, and newspapers, and purring toward the back of the house. The need for a chair stretched back years; the need for it to be electric reflected her increasing frailty. It was a sad reality, with an inevitable outcome that Joe did his best not to think about much.

"Leo," he heard her call out, summoning his younger brother. "Pick up. Joe's on the phone."

He also heard the television in the background. The reading material had once been all there was—her window on the world and a symbol of her devotion to the written word. Over the past few years, though, he'd noted sadly that the TV had been growing in dominance. Her eyes weren't what they had been; her attention span was shortening. She still did read and write, but in shorter spurts and with decreasing retention, more out of hard-won habit than with true enthusiasm.

"Joey," came the perpetually upbeat voice of his brother. "How's it hanging? Sorry, Mom."

"That's disgusting, Leo," she countered. "And I didn't hear it."

Both of them allowed for that particular leap of logic.

"Okay," said Joe. "I just figured I hadn't called in a while. A very *short* while. I was wondering how you were both keeping. Why aren't you out on a date, Leo?"

Leo was a lifelong bachelor, a popular and skilled deli butcher in Thetford who wooed the local housewives with charisma, humor, and good cuts of meat. He had a passion for less-than-mint cars of the sixties and for women who saw him as having no promise whatsoever, and a habit of shaking your hand and kneading your arm simultaneously, as if judging both your character and your fat content.

"Woulda been, shoulda been, but her husband got home early."

"Leo," their mother said sharply. "Enough of that. It's not even true. He's not the Casanova he pretends to be, Joe. He spends most of his time with those broken-down cars, making a mess in the barn. If the EPA ever came by for a visit, this place would be on the Superfund list."

Leo still lived in the home they'd known all their lives, the farm Joe's father had worked until his death decades earlier. He'd left behind his two boys, his much younger widow, a few buildings, and little else beyond some free-and-clear acreage, which she'd slowly sold off to pay bills and simplify her life. For some reason, whether habit or a comfortable lethargy, Leo had simply stayed on. His mother had made it easy by leaving him to his own devices, a show of respect that was paying off now that she had a built-in and devoted caregiver.

"You working on any big cases, Joe?" Leo asked, clearly hoping to deflect their mother's attention.

"Not really," Joe admitted. "Just reopened one that goes back a bit. It's interesting but probably academic by now." He generally downplayed his job—a veteran cop's inbred discretion.

"We heard about the shooting down there," Leo continued. "The hostage thing that turned inside out? The TV loved that one. You have anything to do with it?"

"Leave him be, Leo."

"No, that's okay, Mom," Joe answered. "The PD handled it, Leo. Remember Ron Klesczewski?"

"God," Leo said. "He caught that? Poor guy. Sounded like a mess."

Joe couldn't argue. "Just another offering from our so-called dominant species."

"Ouch. That doesn't sound good."

"How's Gail?" Joe's Mom asked, revealing her intuition.

Leo wasn't as sensitive. "Yeah. Boy, she's really making headlines. You think she'll pull it off? That Parker guy could smile the chrome off a fender, and he's well funded, too. I heard what's-his-name—Tom Bander—has thrown in with him. Isn't he, like, the richest guy in the state?"

"I don't think he's that big, Leo," Joe answered. His heart wasn't into talking politics, although he would have had to admit he knew little about the man, aside from his wealth. "It's a famously liberal county. She might have a shot."

"Not much of one, from what the pundits're saying. But hey. I'd vote for her. Guess that's not kosher, though, right?"

"No. Probably not. I'll tell her you offered, though."

"Say good night, Leo," his mother said quietly. "I need to speak with Joe alone."

Leo took no offense. "You got it, Ma. I'm in midautopsy with a carburetor anyhow. Come up and visit, Joe."

"Will do, Leo. Keep out of trouble."

"Ha. That'll be the day."

There was a click on the phone, a momentary pause that often followed Leo's departures, before his mother said, "You don't sound well, Joe."

"I really am. Promise. Maybe a little tired."

"Then what is it?"

Joe's mother had been a parent and a half to him and Leo, since their taciturn and older father had spent most of his days working the fields in stolid silence. He'd been a generous and gentle man, not at all cold, but he waited for people to come to him, and then responded only to direct questions he felt he could answer. It fell to his wife to fill in the blanks, something she did with animated conversation, an avalanche of good books, and an honesty that combined respect with openness.

Joe conceded defeat, which he now realized was why he'd called in the first place. "The old case I mentioned was the one I was running when Ellen died. It's brought a lot of stuff back."

Her voice softened. "Oh, Joe. I'm so sorry. That's got to be very tough, especially with Gail being so busy."

She'd put her finger on it, as she so often did. Years before, after Gail had been raped and her life turned upside down, Joe had almost died trying to bring the perpetrator in. Then, as now, Joe's mother had helped him see clearly through the tricky emotional maze.

"Does Gail even know what you're working on?" she asked.

"No," he confessed. "I haven't had a chance to tell her."

"Because of her schedule or because it involves Ellen?"

He hesitated. "Both, maybe. Mostly the schedule, but I do feel a little weird about this. I haven't thought about Ellen so much in a long time."

"Her death changed your life, Joe. It took years before you allowed someone like Gail to get close, and even then it only worked because she didn't replace what Ellen was for you."

"A wife?"

"More than that," his mother pursued. "Ellen would have been the mother of your children, if you two had chosen to adopt. You've been mourning that all this time, too, whether you admit it or not."

Joe remained silent, pondering the truth of her argument, looking for flaws he realized might not be there.

"Are you feeling a little widowed all over again?" she asked after a few moments.

Joe was caught off guard. "I'm not sure I'd put it that way."

"Maybe you should. It might help you see things more clearly."

"That's a little dramatic."

"Is it? You're not married. You live apart. Your quiet moments together are shoehorned in. What's left if you lose those? I wouldn't downplay the importance of this."

Joe hesitated again, somewhat at a loss. "I can't tell her to stop running. She wouldn't do it, anyway."

"That's not the debate to have. There may not even be a debate. But this has got to be put on the table between you, Joe. You're not going to be able to settle this in your own head. People don't have good conversations in the mirror, not ones that count, anyway."

This time the ensuing silence was respected by both of them, allowing her words to find their proper nesting place.

Finally, Joe sighed. "Thanks, Mom."

"I love you, sweetheart."

Willy Kunkle pointed through the windshield. "That's your man."

Sitting behind the wheel, Joe watched as a thin young hustler with a struggling beard swung off the porch of one of Brattleboro's ubiquitous decrepit wooden apartment houses on Canal Street and began walking west, his body language at odds with itself, hovering between watchfulness and cool indifference.

"John Moser?" Joe asked.

"The one and only."

"You have anything we can use to squeeze him?"

"Not much. Like I told you before, he's cagey that way. I do have a bluff that might work, though. Remember Jaime Wagner?"

Gunther thought back, his brain, like those of most in his profession, filled with a gallery of people no one else would choose to know. "Pimply guy who ripped off the Army Navy store a few years back?"

Kunkle nodded. "I've got him parked at the PD right now on something unrelated. But he works for Moser off and on, and I hear he helped Moser on a job just a few days ago. I'm thinking we can use him for that bogus lineup thing old Frank used to pull."

Gunther laughed. "Father Murphy's rolling, walk-by beauty show? Jesus. God knows what the legalities are of that nowadays."

"Who cares?" Willy answered, opening the door. "It's not like we're busting either one of them."

Joe didn't argue, if only because, in one fluid movement peculiar to this very asymmetrical man, Willy Kunkle had launched himself from the car and was already following their quarry down the street.

Joe cranked the engine, eased into traffic, and drove to a second parking spot about a block ahead of John Moser. He waited, watching Moser approach in the rearview mirror, Willy quietly closing the distance behind him, before he, too, got out of the car.

"John Moser?" he asked the young man, whose face instantly froze. "I'd like to ask you . . ."

Predictably, he didn't get to finish. But he didn't have to break into a footrace he wouldn't have won, either. Moser spun on his heel to bolt and ran right into Willy's powerful right hand, which grabbed him by the throat like a farmer snatching a chicken.

"Be nice, asshole," was all Willy said.

"So, here's the thing," Willy explained to a scowling John Moser sitting on a metal chair in an empty borrowed room down the hall from the VBI office. "We've been working that robbery/assault on Chicken Coop Hill four days ago— the one where you wore gloves and a mask and thought you were so good your shit didn't stink—and guess what? We've come up with a solid case. In fact, the SA likes it enough that he thinks he'll run with it."

"You're full of crap," Moser said flatly.

Which was correct. Willy had only heard that Moser had committed the crime, and he'd read the victim's statement. But he didn't have a case. Not only that, it would have been a Brattleboro PD investigation to begin with. So Willy was bluffing twice over. He did, however, have two advantages: First, Moser wouldn't know how police jurisdictional tap dances got sorted out, and second, he had no idea, in this world of fantasy forensics, what a cop like Willy would be able to conjure up.

"I'm full of something, all right," Willy agreed, pulling a small plastic bag from his pocket. "Like a strand of fiber we linked to your ski mask."

Moser squinted at the barely visible thread, in fact something Willy had removed from his own jacket earlier.

"And this," Willy added, waving a randomly selected crime lab printout in the air so Moser couldn't read it. "You're too dumb to know this, but DNA doesn't just come from blood and semen. We can get it from almost anywhere." He leaned forward slightly. "Including saliva. Like the little drops of spit you spray when you're talking. Remember talking to the victim, John? You got right in his face and said some really ugly things to him. And every time you opened your big yap, you nailed him with tiny bits of DNA." Willy waved the printout again. "Which we retrieved from the poor slob's face. Amazing, huh?"

Amazing and impossible. Except that Moser's growing concern was becoming clear.

Down the hall, Joe sat leaning back, his feet up on the windowsill, chatting with a high-strung Jaime Wagner, who was perched on the edge of a folding chair as if it might collapse beneath him.

"You've got to know we've been watching you, Jaime,"

Gunther said in a fatherly tone. "Kid like you, in a rush to spend the rest of his life in jail. It wears me out. You know how many years I've been chasing guys like you?"

In the sudden silence, Jaime Wagner felt forced to murmur, "No."

"Way too many," Joe said expansively. "I mean, it's no skin off my butt. It's what I get paid for. But you know, every once in a while, I play it differently—try to be a little more supportive. Maybe it's because I'm getting older—beats me—but I like stirring things up now and then."

Wagner was staring at him as if he were speaking Chinese.

Joe swung his feet off the windowsill and placed his elbows on his knees, scrutinizing Jaime. "That's why you're here. I had you picked up so you'd know I'm making a special project out of you—something to make me feel better about myself. I figure if I keep you out of trouble, maybe God'll look kindly on me at the end, you know what I'm saying?"

Jaime Wagner had no clue. "I guess."

Joe smiled. "Great. I wouldn't want to do this without your cooperation, right?"

Joe stood up and took two steps forward, so that he now loomed over the teenager.

"Of course," he resumed, "I'd need a show of good faith from you so I know I'm not wasting my time."

Wagner licked his lips. "Like what?"

Gunther shrugged. "I don't know. Not much—barely anything, really. Just something to make me feel we're communicating. That you're going to be straight with me. I mean, I remember when we busted you for the Army Navy heist, you lied your head off, which kind of hurt my feelings, since we all knew you'd done it. See what I mean?"

Another awkward silence stretched between them. "What do I have to do?" Jaime asked in a near whisper.

Joe scratched his head, pretending to think. He'd spent half an hour interviewing the cop who'd dealt with Jaime most recently, learning how best to manipulate him. He suddenly snapped his fingers. "I know."

Wagner gave a small jump in his seat.

"You know John Moser?"

The young man's face closed down. "I guess."

Joe was smiling. "There you are. A perfect show of faith. I tell you what. This'll be like a small test. We've got John down the hall, being interviewed. All I want you to do is identify him—just tell me if the guy we've got is really John Moser—and then you're free to go."

Jaime looked confused. "But you know who he is."

Joe beamed. "Exactly. No risk to you." He leaned forward and helped Jaime to his feet by grabbing his shirt sleeve. "Look, it's like a positive reinforcement thing. I just have to feel you're with me on this. I gotta feel good about my commitment to you, okay?"

But Jaime was dragging his feet and shook his arm free. "Why're you talking to John?"

Gunther's voice hardened slightly. "That's not your concern. What you need to worry about is still being on probation and needing to make me happy." He gently but firmly placed his hand against Wagner's chest and pushed him up against the wall. "Tell me something, Jaime: What am I asking you to do here?"

The boy looked at him in surprise, groping for the right answer. "Name John?"

"Did I mention in what context? Or did I just say name him?"

"Just name him."

Joe leaned into him just a touch harder. "And what happens if you don't do that and only that?"

Wagner was starting to look seriously baffled. "I don't know."

Joe stepped back and smiled. "Right. And you don't want to. You ready to help me out now?"

Jaime's shoulders slumped in defeat. "I guess so."

Joe slapped him on the shoulder. "What're you worried about? You think John might get pissed? About what? You doing anything wrong here?"

"No." But he didn't sound too sure.

Joe didn't care. He knew from experience what Jaime Wagner's path was likely to be. Playing head games with him wasn't going to cost Joe any sleep. He therefore walked the youngster down the hallway and, just prior to opening another door near the end, asked him, "So, here's the sixty-four-thousand-dollar question: Is this John Moser?"

He knocked quickly and opened the door to reveal Willy Kunkle standing to one side of a small room, and Moser sitting in a chair, looking worried and straight at them.

"Yeah," Jaime confirmed, "That's him."

Joe closed the door and escorted Wagner outside.

"Uh-oh," Willy said to a surprised John Moser, who was still staring at the closed door. "That wasn't good. I forgot to mention we'd been grilling your little pal."

He placed his hand against his cheek thoughtfully. "Damn—now, on top of all the forensics, we got a witness. Too bad, John. Looks like you been tagged."

Moser was looking glum.

Willy had his hand on the doorknob when he paused, and added, "Unless, you have something that might smooth things out a little . . ."

*   *   *

Twenty minutes later, Willy Kunkle joined Joe in the VBI office. "I didn't know they still made 'em that dumb."

"You got what we're after?" Joe asked, looking up from what he'd been reading.

Kunkle sat down and rested his feet on Joe's desk. "And then some. The stupid bastard gave me stuff I didn't even know about. That's what took me so long. I had to give it all to Ron: dope deals, B-and-Es, a few smash-and-grabs. They ought to be able to get half a dozen busts out of it. Very sweet."

"And the gun?" Joe asked.

Willy smiled. "Oh, yeah. Moser sold it to Matt Purvis for seventy-five bucks. He paid twenty and some Ecstasy for it to one Derek Beauchamp, who said he found it under a floor he was sanding on some recent Yuppie rehab project."

He contentedly patted his chest with his hand. "Sometimes this job doesn't totally suck."

Chapter 9

"Hi. It's me."

Joe smiled at the phone, relief washing over him.

"Hey, Gail. How're you doing?"

He heard her sigh. "There's a question. You free right now?"

He was standing in his woodworking shop, a place he often retreated to when he needed extraction from the outside world. "It'll probably break some bluebird's heart to hear it, but yeah, I'm free. Where are you?"

Her voice was surprised. "You're building a birdhouse?"

"It's for my mother."

"That's sweet, Joe. I'm sorry I'm interrupting."

"Don't be. You sound like you're on a cell phone." He was slightly disappointed by that, suspecting that she was probably calling on the way to some official function.

"I am," she admitted. "I'm in your driveway."

He put down the block of wood he'd been holding and crossed to a window overlooking the front of his small rental property, actually a carriage house tucked behind a huge Victorian monster fronting Green Street. He saw Gail's car behind his own, her parking lights still on.

He waved at her through the window. "You want to keep talking like this, or would you like to come in?"

In answer, she blew him a kiss through the windshield and killed the engine.

He met her at the front door, having crossed the living room from the shop. They didn't say anything but embraced instead, surrendering to mutually shared lost time and frayed emotions.

Afterward, Gail pulled back just enough to say, "Damn, I was hoping I'd get to do that tonight."

He kissed her again, very aware of their bodies together, and feeling her hands running up and down his back.

"Can you stay awhile?" he asked, mumbling against her lips.

"All night," she answered, sliding one hand up under his shirt.

He nuzzled her neck and began lifting her sweater up over her head.

"Are you playing hooky?" he asked her later as they lay side by side in bed.

She curled one leg over his, her hand on his chest. "Oh, you bet. They'll survive one night on their own. After a while, everyone starts thinking the slightest detail will sink the entire campaign. There's no sense of proportion left."

"How do you think it's going?"

"Hard to tell," she said, her head finding a comfortable spot in the crook of his shoulder. "I'm so surrounded by enthusiasts, half of them convinced I'll fall apart at the first mention of bad news, that I'm having a hell of a time figuring out what the truth is. Susan's a brick, natch, but even she has an agenda. They all just want me to press the flesh and raise money."

"Ugh," Joe said. "That's gotta be fun."

"The pressing isn't bad. People are looking for hope. I'm happy to give them that. Fund-raising you can keep. The bigger the cats, the more obsequious they expect you to be."

"You need the money that badly?"

It was a pertinent question. Not only was Gail wealthy by birth, but she'd made a lot of money in real estate after retiring as a hippie, now quite a long time ago.

She didn't take offense. "I could fund it myself, but that would send exactly the wrong message, especially with Parker and the Republicans using Tom Bander as their personal J. P. Morgan."

"What's Bander's deal, anyway?" Joe asked. "Leo brought him up, and I didn't have a clue, aside from the money thing."

"Just a rich guy," she answered vaguely before pausing to add, "Actually, I don't really know. I met him at a ribbon cutting years ago—didn't make much of an impression. I didn't even know he was into politics until he came out for Parker. The grapevine has it that he keeps a low profile, gets really good people to do his deals for him, and basically reaps the benefits. Susan thinks he's backing Parker because he wants to step out a little—maybe join the mainstream now that he's made his bundle.

"Which is exactly why I can't be put in the same boat," she continued, back on track. "I've got to go out and raise money by tens and twenties. My own wealth is a liability, especially since right now I'm only running against fellow Democrats. That's the irony—it's members of my own party I have to playact for. Assuming I win the primary, it'll be much less dicey, even if it's a tougher race—what my handlers don't want me to know is that word on the street is, this whole thing is Parker's to lose."

She raised her head and looked at him. "You wouldn't be willing to help me out there, would you? Call on some of your buddies—tell them I'm not the Wicked Witch of the Far Left?"

"Sure," he said quickly, but he was instantly uncomfortable with the idea, even resentful. She knew that politics was something he worked to avoid. Now he'd been put between a rock and a hard place, having to lobby colleagues who were already leery about his new role with the VBI. It was going to be goddamned awkward, and he was angry at himself for not having said so immediately.

She seemed to sense his reservations without wanting to take him off the hook. She added, "It wouldn't be a lie. I know your guys can't stand all the environmental and education stuff, but you can assure them I'd be in their corner on law enforcement. I am an ex-prosecutor, after all."

He grunted assent, but was remembering that the "ex-" part of that had to do with her locking horns with her boss, the local state's attorney. The man was never happier than when she left.

"Maybe the Dover and Wilmington chiefs, some people at the police unions. That wouldn't put you in a bind, would it?"

Again, the opportunity to bow out. Again, ignored.

"No. I can do that."

She snuggled in again, kissing his chin. "God, it's nice being here."

He wished he could agree. But all he felt now was foolish.

*   *   *

Joe took Lester Spinney with him to interview Derek Beauchamp. The fourth and last member of Joe's squad, Lester was cranelike in appearance, the unit's sole family man, the only one to have come to them from the state police, and unique for his quiet, laid-back demeanor. It was this latter characteristic that had made him Joe's choice for this outing.

"What's your pleasure with Mr. Beauchamp, boss?" Spinney asked from the passenger seat as they drove north on Route 30 alongside the West River. He was reading the Oberfeldt file, which Joe had handed him in the parking lot, familiarizing himself with ancient crimes and procedures.

"I'm not looking for any problems," Joe told him. "I did a records check and found nothing beyond some recreational drug dabbling. He got into the usual mischief as a teenager, but he's mid-thirties now, on a second marriage with kids, and seems to get the high-end jobs, which must say something about his abilities. I phoned a contractor friend and asked him if he'd heard of the guy. He said Beauchamp was reliable and had a good reputation. He probably pads the bills a bit, overorders at the homeowner's expense, but that was it. No red flags."

Spinney glanced out at the passing scenery, a soothing blur of variegated green and sun-dappled water. "Reminds me of why I do all my own home improvements, regardless of how shitty they end up." He tapped the file with his fingertip. "According to John Moser, Beauchamp found the gun under the floorboards. That makes it a theft, doesn't it?"

"Technically," Gunther agreed. "We could use that if necessary. You want to be good cop or bad?"

Lester slapped his hand over his heart. "Oh, that cuts. With Kunkle available, you ask me that?"

Gunther conceded his point. "All right. You're the shining knight."

They were driving toward Newfane, some twelve miles northwest of Brattleboro, Windham's county seat and a village of almost pristine beauty. Joe had been told that Derek Beauchamp was working on an expensive remodeling job high on Newfane Hill, an area with a complement of very expensive real estate. Newfane was one of the towns Gail was counting on heavily, famous for its liberal leanings.

"How's the campaign going?" Lester asked, as if Joe had been speaking out loud.

"Fine, I guess," he answered, surprised by how little pleasure he found in the question. It saddened him that his best friend's greatest ambition to date should cause him to have such a reaction.

"I would find that tougher than hell," Spinney continued. "Having my better half running for office—everyone poking into her private life. You guys ever see each other?"

"Sure," Joe said shortly.

Spinney looked at him. "Ouch. Sorry."

"No," Gunther protested. "I saw her last night. It is awkward, though."

"The politicking or the gossip?"

Now it was Gunther's turn to take his eyes off the road. "What gossip?"

Spinney looked apologetic. "Jeez. I shouldn't have opened this can. I've heard mutterings that she's making hay off of being a rape victim. Shit like that."

"Oh, for Christ sake. Like there's a plus side to being raped?"

Lester held up his hands. "Hey, I hear you. That's why I asked if it was tough."

They were quiet for a while, each ruminating on how fast a conversation could deteriorate.

"She asked me to make some calls for her," Joe admitted as a way to apologize.

Spinney's reaction was upbeat. "That makes sense. You gonna do it?"

"I said I would."

Spinney paused and then added, smiling, "Well, I'm not the legendary Joe Gunther, but I'll help you do that, if you want."

Again Joe looked over at his partner's open, friendly face, feeling surprised and grateful. "No shit?"

Lester Spinney waved dismissively. "No shit, but it better count for some serious brownie points."

They saw Derek Beauchamp's van long before they saw its owner. A virulent shade of purple, it had a flamboyant yellow and red sign reading "The Sanding Sandman—Your Floor Is My Desire."

"Jesus," Spinney said as Joe parked among the standard construction site collection of battered pickups. "That's some sales pitch."

The building they were facing had once been a traditional Greek Revival farmhouse: two and a half stories, with the most ancient section standing at the head of a line of ever smaller additions, tacked on over the ages, which now trailed out behind it like a short row of diminishing train cars. As part of the present overhaul, it had all been reclad in bare cedar, topped with copper, and refitted with brand-new, triple-glazed gas-injected windows.

"Nothing but the best," Spinney muttered as they approached the entrance across a debris-strewn yard. "Must be nice."

They stepped through the open door into a wall of rock music and fine dust and the smell of fresh everything: lumber, joint compound, varnish, and new plastic. A man wearing a face mask and carrying a bucket appeared in a hallway opposite them.

"Can you tell us where Derek is?" Joe shouted to him.

The man pointed, still walking across the room. "Upstairs."

Following a broad path of taped-down protective kraft paper, they found a sweeping staircase leading up and proceeded through several grandiose rooms outfitted with built-in cherry cabinets, marble fireplaces, and other baubles. It was like stepping into a TV program of *This Old House*, minus the camera crew and the sycophant host.

Through it all, Lester kept muttering and shaking his head.

At the end of their trip, they slipped through a plastic sheet barrier and came to a large back bedroom/gym combination, filled not with the intended equipment but with a large, burly man wearing a mask, goggles, and ear protectors, who was pushing around a bulky, screaming floor sander. The air was opaque with sawdust.

Gunther, in bad-cop mode, walked across the room and stood in front of the machine, forcing its operator to stop and kill his mechanical beast.

The man tore off his protective equipment and glared at Joe in the sudden, echoing silence. "Goddamn it. If you made me fuck up this floor . . ."

Joe cut him off by flashing his shield. "You'll what?"

His mouth still open in midsentence, the man looked from Joe to Lester.

"Sorry about that," Lester said pleasantly, filling in. "Are you Derek Beauchamp?"

"Yeah."

"Then you won't mind if we ask you a few questions," Joe suggested, his face still grim.

"No. I mean, sure. What do you want?"

Joe went straight to it. "You sold a gun recently to John Moser. Where did you get it?"

Beauchamp paled so that the previously covered parts of his face matched the dusty ones. "I didn't sell a gun."

Joe stepped in close enough that their chests were almost touching. Beauchamp instinctively tucked his chin in.

"That is bullshit. You sold a gun illegally for twenty bucks and some Ecstasy. Moser gave you up so fast, we'd barely asked the question."

Just like in the movies, Lester now approached and held up his hand passively to Joe. "You mind? Just for a sec?"

Joe shrugged angrily and moved away to look out the dusty window at the scenery outside.

"Never mind him," Lester said in a near whisper. "Very bad day. Look, nothing'll happen here if you help us out, Derek. This is no big deal, okay? Just tell me where you got the gun."

"I found it," Beauchamp answered equally softly, as if their words weren't still bouncing around the cavernous room. "Under the floorboards at another job."

"How's that?"

"You have to prep the floors first," he answered. "Well, I mean, not here. This is all new flooring using old barn boards—really expensive. But over there it was more like the usual, you know? Just making what's already down look better."

"We get it, Derek," Joe growled without turning around.

"Right. Sorry," he said quickly. "Anyhow, you have to prep the surface, which means you have to go around and countersink all the nails so you won't tear up the machine. Well, that's when I found a loose board. It was wiggly, slightly warped. You gotta fix things like that, or it won't look right, so I pried it up to see what I could do, and that's when I found it."

"Just lying there?" Lester asked.

"Yeah. It was wrapped in a rag, like a towel, but there it was."

"Was there anything with it?"

"I swear, man. It was all alone. It looked old. For sure nobody knew about it, 'cause the homeowners had just bought the place, so I figured, you know, what the hey? Maybe I could get some money for it. I mean, I didn't want it myself. I'm not into that. But I didn't know it was illegal."

Joe reapproached, his expression still hard. "It's not illegal to sell a gun, stupid, unless it's stolen and the price involves drugs. Or are you going to pretend you didn't know that, either?"

Beauchamp actually hung his head. "Sorry."

Spinney glanced at his boss. The good-cop–bad-cop routine had ended when Beauchamp had confessed. This last outburst of Joe's had come from somewhere else.

Lester quickly moved to extract the last piece of information they needed. "Derek," he said gently, "where exactly was this job?"

"Dummerston Center," came the eager reply. "Just beyond the four-way intersection on the East-West Road, heading toward Putney. On the right, in the middle of that hairpin curve they got. Super-nice folks."

Beauchamp took a risk and looked at Joe. "I'm real sorry for what I did."

Joe's face merely darkened. "You little jerk. You're sorry we caught you at it, and you think dancing around like some ass-kissing five-year-old will get you off the hook. You and I know damn well that three seconds after we're gone you'll be calling us assholes to our backs." He suddenly stabbed the man hard in his chest with his finger. "Tell me I'm wrong."

Beauchamp didn't know what to say anymore. Spinney reached out and slowly lowered Joe's hand with his own. "We'll be heading out now, Derek," he said in a neutral tone. "But remember what happened here, okay? You are now on our radar. Call us whatever you like later, but if we ever hear of you screwing around like this again, we won't be coming around to chat. Is that crystal clear?"

During this speech, Spinney was steering Joe toward the door, talking over his shoulder.

Staring at them from his post near the silent sander, Derek Beauchamp still looked unsure. "So, I'm okay, then? This time?"

Joe swung around. "There's going to be another?"

Beauchamp backed up, tripping over the electrical cord behind him. "No, no. Sorry. Not what I meant. I get it. I mean, I'm cool. Everything's cool."

Gunther hesitated, as if pondering a choice of violent options. Finally, he turned on his heel, said, "Idiot," and walked away with Spinney in pursuit.

Spinney drove this time, allowing Joe to stare out the side window.

"You okay?"

Joe didn't answer at first. Didn't even move, until at last he shifted his gaze to the front and said, "You ever have those almost out-of-body experiences where you start doing something the rational part of your brain just can't believe? It's like being on autopilot and stamping on the brakes at the same time, getting nowhere."

"You know what pushed your button?" he asked.

Gunther sighed. "It's not like we don't deal with guys like that every day. Something just snapped this time. The futility of it, maybe. Damned if I know. I just stood there and got really pissed off—all of a sudden. I felt like smacking him." He altered his voice slightly in imitation. " 'I'm real sorry for what I did.' Jesus. Give me a break. I sometimes think we're just slightly more complicated than when we crawled out of the caves. We're sure as hell no better. Me want, me take, and screw you in the process."

Spinney didn't answer. Cops were ill disposed to think along such lines. It was almost guaranteed to undermine whatever satisfaction the job offered.

As Joe knew all too well.

"Sorry," he said a moment later. "Too much shit on my mind."

The house Derek Beauchamp had described was more in keeping with the area's norm for upward mobility. No Yuppie version of a rusticated mansion, this one was a straightforward salvation of a previously worn-down farmhouse: asphalt roof, economy paint job, a repaired foundation, and, they now knew, some refinished flooring.

Fully recovered, Joe pulled himself out of the car and smiled at the young woman who stepped from the house to greet them.

"Hi," he said, waving toward Lester. "Sorry to bother you. We're police officers from the Vermont Bureau of Investigation. My name's Gunther, and this is Lester Spinney.

We're just looking for some information—nothing bad," he added, to assuage the alarm he saw growing on her face.

As they drew closer, he stuck out his hand. "Call me Joe."

She shook it tentatively. "Margo Wilson."

Gunther indicated the house. "What a nice job. Just what the place needed."

Still flustered, Wilson turned and faced the house with them, as if they were all three admiring a mural. "Oh. Thanks. Did you know it before?"

"Just to drive by. But you can tell you've given it a shot in the arm. Actually, that's why we're here. It's sort of a historical fishing expedition. We're trying to find out who used to own it."

"The Zimmers?" she asked.

"Maybe," Joe said. "Depends on how far back they go."

Wilson looked doubtful. "Oh, I don't know. I don't think they lived here for more than a few years. Mrs. Zimmer turned out to be allergic to almost everything, and they ended up moving back to the city. That's why it was sort of run-down, and how we got such a decent price. Not that we haven't poured a small fortune into fixing it up," she added ruefully.

"They'll do that to you," Lester commiserated, clearly more kindly inclined toward this homeowner than to the unknown ones they'd just left. "You love them, but they are out to ruin you, day in and day out."

Margo Wilson began to relax. She pointed toward the still open front door. "Would you like to come in? I think I know where Edward—that's my husband—has squirreled away some of the old documents we got at the closing; maybe those'll help. Would you like coffee? It's fresh."

They entered together, she showed them around, and they made the appropriate flattering noises before settling down in the living room with the coffee and a small, messy pile of the aforementioned paperwork.

Spinney kept their hostess entertained while Joe began leafing through the offerings.

There were the standard items—surveys, legal correspondence, court papers, and tax records—but of most use to Joe was a copy of the town clerk's record of successive ownership. He went through the pages, deciphering the entries, keeping track of the years as his finger ran down the list.

Where he finally stopped short wasn't because of the date, however, but the name opposite it. He straightened and let out a small grunt of recognition, causing the other two to stop speaking and stare at him.

"You find something?" Margo Wilson asked him hopefully.

Joe closed the stapled sheaf and held it up. "I think so. Could I borrow this? Just long enough to get it copied? I promise I'll mail it back to you first thing tomorrow."

He stood up, still holding it, forcing the issue somewhat. Mrs. Wilson was gracious enough merely to smile and stand in turn. "Oh, sure. I doubt we even need it, to be honest, but sure—mail it back at your convenience."

She escorted them to the door, hesitating only as they were halfway across the threshold. "I hope this is nothing bad. I mean . . ."

Joe placed his hand on her forearm. "No. Absolutely not. We're literally just trying to track someone down—kind of like connect-the-dots. Where were they when? That sort of thing. Nothing to worry about. I promise."

Relieved, she let them go and waved as they backed down the driveway. Spinney waited until they'd covered about a hundred yards before saying, "Okay, Grumpy—spill. You look like you struck gold."

Joe smiled. "I don't know about that, but I found a familiar name. Thirty-two years ago that house belonged to Lawrence Clark. Remember that old case file you were reading before?"

Spinney's brow furrowed. "Yeah, but that name doesn't ring any bells."

"His sister, Katie, was living with Pete Shea when he vanished into thin air."

Chapter 10

After Peter Shea went on the lam, Klaus Oberfeldt suc-
cumbed, and Ellen slipped away forever, Joe began to do
some sliding of his own. He had hoped—even planned
on—the newly minted homicide to distract him, maybe
even afford him an emotional bridge he could use to distance himself from Ellen's death. But the frustration of
Shea's total disappearance, leaving behind no alternate
leads, ended up compounding Joe's sense of loss and lack of
direction. He became distracted, sleepless, and could find
no satisfaction in anything he did.

It was Frank Murphy who eventually gave him a hand-
hold at work. Without him, Joe always believed, he would
have hit the ropes just as Willy Kunkle did later, and maybe
worse. He'd never know for sure, fortunately, but that was
in some ways precisely the point.

It wasn't the first time Frank had come through, either.
After seeing combat as a young man and then dropping out
of college on the West Coast a couple of years later, Joe had
found himself rootless, restless, and without a plan. By then

back on the farm and attempting a fruitless return to a bygone life, he got a call from Murphy, an erstwhile older
neighbor and friend and now a Brattleboro cop, and went
down to take a look at what Frank was offering, as much to
prove him wrong as out of any true interest.

But interested he became. Now, several years later, Murphy again reached out and took Joe under his wing, inviting him over to dinner regularly, taking him fishing, and
making him one of his own family. Nurturing him, occasionally covering for his mistakes, Frank Murphy coaxed
Joe back to health, inspiring him in the process to be a better cop.

In many ways, that was why he continued to stick his
neck out for Willy Kunkle. There was a tradition at stake,
and it involved the saving of one's own, no matter how
obliquely.

Except that in Joe's own case, Shea was never found, the
Oberfeldt case was never closed, and Ellen's loss never fully
overcome. It took years before Joe could commit to Gail,
and then only because of her own interest in a completely
unconventional relationship.

Now, suddenly, these ancient wounds were being revis-
ited in odd ways—some through the distorted lens of
memory, others in light of confusing current events, but all
linked to names and actions Joe hadn't thought about in
decades.

"Okay," Joe asked. "What've we found out?"

The entire squad—Willy, Sam, and Lester—were convened at the VBI office, something that occurred with increasing rarity as the agency picked up more cases.

"I dug into the tax records and confirmed what Margo
Wilson showed us," Sam answered first. "Her place was

definitely owned by Larry Clark when the Oberfeldt assault took place."

"The same Larry Clark who then died of cirrhosis of the liver ten years later," Willy added. "Can't imagine how he came down with that, but that's when the house ended up on the market."

Joe ignored him—usually the best policy. "Any guesses on other family members, like Katie?"

Spinney held up a computer printout with a small flourish. "God bless the Internet," he said. "I tried every police resource we have, and in the end, it was one of those 'find your high school sweetheart' ads on the Net that finally worked. Katherine Madeleine Clark is listed as living in Orange, Massachusetts—assuming," he added with emphasis, "that she and your Katie are one and the same, which, given the common names, may be a stretch."

"How did you match them up?" Joe asked.

"Date of birth and where she went to high school. But like I said, Katherine Clark is right up there with John Smith."

"That's standing by your guns," Willy commented.

Sam threw a pencil at him, which he batted away. Out of the office, Sam and Willy formed a complicated couple, although so far, despite regular fireworks, they seemed to be lasting.

Joe had been sitting on the edge of his desk and now leaned forward to take the printout from Lester. "Can't hurt to give it a try."

"You going to check her out personally?" Sam asked.

"It's not far," he answered, "and if it's the same woman, I actually met her once. Plus, you've all got more than enough on your plates to waste much more time on this.

Chances are, even if I do get a fix on Pete Shea, he's been dead for years."

"Jesus, boss," Willy said, "you sure know how to sell a thing. You better not be writing that in your expense voucher."

Orange, Massachusetts, regardless of its own pride in self, is duplicated a hundredfold all across New England. Mill towns long ago, they are stamped as such by huge, hulking, soot-grimed architectural remnants of an era that once made the region a global industrial powerhouse. Nowadays they are crossroads with brick downtowns and Civil War memorials, their efforts to survive hanging on tourism, or on being attractive to part-time city dwellers, or on trying to cope commercially in a world that time and again proves it doesn't need them anymore. Often as not, they are the places people drive through wondering, "Why is this place here?"

Orange is healthier along those lines, what with its proximity to several recreational lakes, including the enormous Quabbin Reservoir to its south. About half the size of Brattleboro and also equipped with a river, it has a similar background of mills and factories.

Joe located the address Lester had given him, just off the town's main thoroughfare. It belonged to a heavy brick office building long ago converted into an affordably priced and severe apartment complex, right across the street from an oddly shaped, slightly forlorn park dedicated to local World War I veterans.

He parked his car and approached the building's front door, pausing when he heard music floating just above him. He glanced up and saw the back of a woman's head almost resting against a first-floor window, seemingly lulled by the soft classical notes emanating from her apartment.

He proceeded to the front lobby and studied the names above the mail receptacles. "K. Clark" was attached to the only apartment on the ground floor, clearly the one he'd noticed with the music and the apparently sleeping woman. Encouraged, he pushed the bell.

There was no answer. He hesitated, giving the lineup of names a second look to rule out any error. He rang again.

Still no response.

Leaving the lobby, he returned to the window and, standing tall on his toes, rapped on the glass with his knuckles.

In almost cinematic slow motion, the head above him stirred, swung around as if on a rusty hinge, and finally revealed the round, pale face of a woman who looked as if she'd just been shaken from a very deep sleep.

"Katie Clark?" he half shouted at the closed window, conscious of how people on the street might interpret this.

The face showed no change of expression. It was as if she didn't see him.

Maybe she's blind, he thought. He waved his hand at her and saw her grimace slightly, clearly in reaction. Reassured, he pointed toward the building's entrance and said, "I'll talk to you on the intercom."

Back in the lobby, he repeated his effort with the bell and again got no satisfaction.

He jogged back to the window, only to find it empty. She'd left, presumably to speak to him on the intercom.

"Goddamn Marx Brothers routine," he muttered, running back.

Once he got there, however, there was no voice on the speaker, and no answer to his third push of the button.

He stood motionless for a couple of minutes, wondering

what to do next, when suddenly, making him jump in surprise, an angry and exhausted voice inquired, "What do
you want?"

"Katie Clark?"

"Who's that?"

He'd thought about this moment, knowing the wrong approach might stop him from even getting through the door.
Now, God only knew where he stood. A little incongru-
ously, he tried keeping his voice upbeat. "My name's Joe
Gunther. From Brattleboro. You and I met more than thirty
years ago. I was driving through town, and I heard through
the grapevine you were living here. Thought I'd just take a
chance and see if you were in. I'm sorry about the confusion with the doorbell. I didn't mean to upset you."

"What was your name?" The voice had become no more
energetic or friendly.

"Joe. Joe Gunther."

There was a long pause, followed by "Did you say Brattleboro?"

"Yes. That's right. A long time ago."

"What was a long time ago?"

Joe looked at the intercom quizzically. "That we met," he
said, his voice trailing off.

The white noise of the speaker stretched out, eventually
followed by a weak "Oh, what the hell" and the buzzing of
the entryway lock to let him in.

He stepped into a hallway and turned left, toward where
he knew the apartment to be. He knocked on the only door
with a number on it.

"Come in," said the same weak voice.

Gingerly he tested the knob and pushed the door open.
"Katie?" he asked hesitantly.

There was no answer. He peered around the edge of the

door and saw a small, thin woman sitting on an upright chair in the short hallway before him, her back against the wall as if she'd collapsed there following some shocking news.

"Are you all right?" he asked, stepping inside.

She gave him a deadpan stare with hollow eyes and sighed. "Peachy. What do you want?"

"Nothing, really," he lied. "Like I said, I'd heard you were here. Actually, that was a while ago, but then, all of a sudden, I'm driving through town, and I remembered it, so I thought I'd drop by. Maybe not such a good idea, though, huh?"

"What?" she asked.

He approached slowly, looking at her, again caught off guard by her apparent confusion. "Maybe I shouldn't have bothered you today. You seem a little tired."

She looked at the floor and laughed weakly, doubling over with the effort. He feared she might fall off her chair.

"That's good," she almost whispered. "A little tired. Jesus Christ."

While she caught her breath, he asked, "Can I do anything to help?"

"You'd be the first if you could," she answered, and then went through an agonizingly slow process of standing up, using the wall and chair back for assistance, during which he fought the impulse to reach out and help, sensing that it would be poorly received.

The odd thing was that she looked fine. Nothing bloated or bent or altogether missing. She was just a slim woman in her late forties who moved like an ailing octogenarian. He remembered the lithe, attractive, quick-moving girl she'd been, and could still see the ghosts of all that, but in extreme slow motion.

He followed her into the apartment's main room, filled with soft music but also cluttered with magazines, newspapers, clothing, cast-aside mail, odds and ends, all looking as if it had been dropped in the midst of some military retreat. Dominating it was a chair by the window, overstuffed, crammed with pillows, and circled by small tables stacked with more junk. It made him think of the nest of some large flightless bird, reduced to being fed and cared for by others.

Laboriously Katie Clark worked her way toward this resting place, her hands slightly out to her sides like a tightrope walker's, her gait uncertain, as if negotiating a rain-slicked icy pond.

By the time she finally reached her goal and sank in among her pillows, Joe was as grateful as she appeared to be.

"Who are you, again?" she asked, squinting at him in concentration. "I know you told me, but I forgot."

He decided to keep it simple this time. "Joe, from Brattleboro."

She nodded thoughtfully. "Right. Brattleboro. Long time."

She didn't add anything to that, leaving him groping for a follow-up.

"Yeah. We actually met, you and I. Decades ago. You weren't even twenty yet." He was about to add that he was a cop and that their connection was Peter Shea, but then held back, deciding to let things evolve a little first.

She glanced out the window at a brief spurt of traffic, unleashed by the intersection's changing light. "Not even twenty," she murmured. "Christ, to be there again."

He sensed a small opening. "What happened, Katie?"

She turned to look at him, the exhaustion on her face ever more pronounced. "You ever hear of Yuppie disease?"

He nodded. "Chronic fatigue, right?"

She smiled bitterly. "Well, I'm one of the Yuppies who's got it. Yuppie, my ass. You know *that's* bullshit."

He grimaced his embarrassment. "Actually, I don't know much of anything. Just the name, really. I read about a woman with it who took several years to write a history book. That put it in the headlines."

Katie nodded. "Damned if I know how she did that. I change my sheets and it's lights out for the rest of the day. The name's crap anyway."

"What name?" he asked. " 'Yuppie disease'?"

She frowned dismissively. "Sure, and the other one. 'Chronic fatigue.' Makes it sound like we're a bunch of sleepwalkers. It's more than that. Sleep's a bitch, in fact."

"You don't sleep?" He was surprised.

"Not well. In fits and starts. We never feel rested. That's one of the . . . whatchamacallits they use to tell this from something else."

"Symptoms?"

"Yeah. Fatigue's only one. There's swollen glands, headaches, lousy sleep, achy joints and muscles, sore throat. You can't remember shit and you can't do anything right . . . fucking checklist. I've got it all and then some," she said regretfully. "You want to sound cool," she then added, looking at him sharply, "you call it CFIDS. Stands for something." She passed her hand across her forehead. "Whatever. I can't remember."

They both listened to the street sounds leaking through the windows for a while before he asked, "Are you in a lot of pain right now?"

"You bet your ass I am."

Gunther had expected none of this, and was at a loss how to proceed. Katie Clark was locked in a whirlpool of her own misery, which seemed to have consumed all her attention.

He decided to work backward.

"How long have you had this?" he asked.

She'd been gazing at him for a couple of minutes, and now continued doing so without any sign of having heard him.

He waited a couple of moments before softly saying, "Katie?"

She blinked. "What?"

"How long have you had this?"

She set her head back against a pillow and closed her eyes. "Twelve years."

"Do you know what brought it on?"

"Nobody knows. Some people think it's depression gone crazy; some say it's a virus or Lyme disease. One woman told me it was polio vaccinations we were given as kids. But everyone's clueless—don't know where it comes from, don't know how to get rid of it."

"How do you support yourself?"

"I don't. I'm on disability. I tried doing stuff a few years ago, but it didn't last. You can't keep a schedule. I feel it coming on, know I've only got an hour or two to reach home before I can't move anymore. People don't under-stand. Think you're faking it. I'd be better off if I had cancer."

Joe was caught off guard by the comment and had to bite back disabusing her of cancer's attractions. Instead, he kept her going, sensing he was making progress. "What did you used to do?"

Katie gave another of her short laughs. "Worked at a nursing home. Good, huh? Took care of old people sitting in chairs, drooling. Boy, I used to pity them."

It was like tugging a narcissist away from her own mirror. "You ever go back to Brattleboro?" he continued trying.

She tilted her head forward and looked at him. "Brattleboro? How did you know I came from there?"

He didn't miss a beat. "That's where we met, a long time ago."

She smiled, a lascivious glint in her eye. "Sorry. Guess you didn't make a big impression. I knew a lot of guys a long time ago."

He shrugged. "That's okay. There was a lot going on back then. Easy to get lost in the shuffle. Is there anyone in your life now?"

She laughed again. "I'd fight 'em off with a stick if I had the energy." Her face settled in upon itself again, revealing the sadness that defined her features. "I've tried it a couple of times. There's not much point. I have to sit down when I brush my teeth. That give you an idea how much fun I am in bed?"

He pressed on, determined to get something from her, as addicted to his elusive goal as she was to her chronic problems. "I remember a few other people from back then," he said. "Didn't you used to hang with Pete Shea? Wow. There's somebody I haven't thought about in a while."

She was giving him another of those strangely vacant stares. "What's your name again?" she finally asked.

He hesitated a split second, fearing she'd finally put the pieces together. "Joe," he answered simply.

She set her head at rest again. "Right. Sorry. Not good with names."

He didn't respond, waiting for her to react to his earlier question, before realizing she had no clue what he'd just said.

"Not a problem," he said. "I was wondering if you'd ever

kept up with Pete Shea. You were friends once, right? We all lost track of him."

"No shit you did," she acknowledged. "He got the hell out of Dodge. The cops were after him."

Joe nodded agreeably. "Nothing new there. Why this time?"

"They thought he murdered some guy. He didn't—he said it was a frame—but he took off anyhow."

Despite having heard variations on this before, Joe suddenly saw it in a completely different light. He'd always assumed that Pete had disappeared because they were interested in him from the thumbprint on the knife blade. Now, feeling foolish, he wondered for the first time how Shea could have known of that interest. When they'd set out to question him, he was already long gone.

"What made him think the cops were after him?" Joe asked carefully.

"They weren't," she explained tiredly, as if to a slow child. "Not yet. He just knew they would be. It was the gun that set him off."

"The gun?" Joe prompted after a pause, both puzzled and relieved that they'd finally reached his purpose for being here.

"He found it under our mattress. Had blood on it. The papers said the man had been beaten with a gun, and Pete somehow figured this was probably it. He'd put his fingerprints on it by handling it, so he knew he was screwed. That's why he ran. Good thing, too."

"Why's that?"

"He was right, wasn't he? They did come for him. Funny thing was, they didn't ask about any gun. It was all about that stupid switchblade he played with. Guess they found that, too. Sort of pissed me off at the time—the risk I took with that gun."

She took a rest, pausing to breathe as if she'd just sprinted up a set of stairs.

"What happened to it?" Joe asked quickly, not wanting her to lose this train of thought.

"I cleaned it up and gave it to my brother. He hid it under the floorboards of his house. Made me nervous as hell bringing it to him."

"And you never saw Pete again?"

She looked incredulous. "He lived here with me for a few years. Later on. Nobody had a clue. You'd think they'd put out one of those bulletins or something. Pathetic. Maybe they pinned it on somebody else and stopped looking. I guess that could happen and you'd never know it, right? There's something for you—be on the run your whole life and not know there's nobody after you. Kind of like *The Fugitive* in reverse."

Joe tried to keep the excitement out of his voice. "He lived here with you?"

She'd had her eyes closed through all this and now merely exhaled wearily. "Not here, here. In Orange. I live here because of the disability thing. This was before. Years ago."

"You guys split up?"

"Yeah. You drift apart. You know how it goes."

That he did. "You keep in touch still?"

"No," she said wearily. Her voice had been steadily losing whatever strength it had. By now she was almost whispering.

"That's too bad," Joe conceded, more truthfully than she could know. "I always liked him. What makes you think that he was innocent? The evidence seems pretty damning."

"You just know a guy," she answered simply.

"Wish I could look him up," Joe lamented.

"Can't help you. By the time we split, he was drinking every day. And then, all of a sudden, he was gone. Left everything behind, even his toothbrush."

Again she seemed to be purposefully tantalizing him with leading inferences. It was like water torture. "Really? That's weird. Must've been a bummer being stuck with all that."

"No. I threw most of it out."

Joe rubbed his forehead. Naturally. He looked at the woman across from him, her eyes shut, her body limp and draped across the chair's pillows as if she'd been poured there from a glass. He tried one more time, pushing a little since he had so little left to lose.

"Most of it?"

But instead of growing suspicious of all the questions, she merely smiled. "Yeah. Stupid, I know, but I kept his shot glass collection. Wherever we'd go—Maine, New York, wherever—he'd buy a souvenir shot glass. Funny, the things some people collect and other people hang on to, always for different reasons."

She opened her eyes then and slowly straightened her head, frowning at the exertion. Joe figured he had less than five minutes left before she passed out right in front of him.

"They're over there," she murmured. "On the wall."

He glanced toward the bathroom door and saw attached to the wall next to it a glass display case, its every shelf filled with small glasses, each one decorated with some image or motto or decoration. He rose from his seat and crossed over to it.

He scanned its contents, tracking the couple's travels all

over New England, again struck by the fact that Pete Shea had done all this with an open arrest warrant out on him.

The case had a door. He opened it noiselessly, seeing that Katie had once again settled down, and took a closer look. On one of the glasses directly before him, there was a fat fingerprint visible in the light slanting in through the window.

"You ever use these?" he asked.

In the answering silence, he turned to look at her again. This time it appeared she was fast asleep. He placed the glass gingerly in his handkerchief and slipped it into his pocket.

He crossed back over to her. "Katie?" he asked quietly.

She didn't stir.

He touched the crown of her head with his fingertips, as a parent might a sleeping child's after a long, hard day. "Take care, Katie Clark," he whispered, and showed himself out.

Chapter 11

What good's a print going to do?" Willy Kunkle asked Joe. "We already have his prints on file."

Joe was back in Brattleboro, staring at the shot glass nestled amid a small, ignored stack of pink call-back notes in the middle of his desk. It was his sole trophy so far in what was starting to look like a repeat exercise in futility.

"And didn't you say she'd moved since he split? That means she must've packed all that crap, touching each and every item. The print's probably hers."

Gunther shrugged. "It was something she said. She was impressed we never caught him, even though he was wandering all over New England. Made me think that if we'd missed something as obvious as his living with his old girlfriend, maybe we were missing something just as obvious now." He stood up, preparing to follow Willy out the door. "I'm going to run Shea's old prints through AFIS. We never did anything like that when we were looking for him, you know? Never sent them to the FBI, never circulated them anywhere. We just kept them here, relying on a physical description for the all-points." He scratched his head. "It was so long ago. It never crossed my mind he could've been busted somewhere else and his prints entered into the system. That would've waved a red flag right off the bat."

Willy looked at him. "Jesus, you're cracking up, you know that? Who says the guy's even alive, much less that he was printed someplace else? You're dreaming."

Joe walked out into the hallway with him, still distracted. "Maybe, but I never even thought of it. That's what's getting me. From the start, my head wasn't in this case."

Willy made for the staircase at the end of the hall, his meager counseling abilities exhausted. "You win some, you lose some. Shit happens. Get some sleep."

With a rattle of shoe heels on stair treads, he was gone.

Joe smiled and murmured, "In a while."

"You get what you were after?" the AFIS operator asked him an hour later.

Joe stared at the printout in his hands, incredulous. "You could say that."

The cell phone in his pocket chirped. He thanked the technician and moved out into the deserted hallway, only half visible in the after-hours lighting.

"Hello?"

"Joe. It's me."

He smiled at the sound of her voice. "Gail. Where are you?"

"I'm driving into town. I have to go from one something to something else, but I was hoping I could see you for a couple of minutes. Are you nearby?"

"The Municipal Building. Is everything all right?"

"I'm eating too much and I've lost track of who I'm meeting when or why sometimes, but I'm fine. It's something else. Can you stay put for five minutes? I'm almost there."

"Sure. I'll be in the parking lot."

She was faster than she'd thought, and drove up only ninety seconds after he'd stepped outside. He leaned on her door as she rolled down the window to kiss him.

"Come around," she urged him. "It's cold out."

He circled the car and waited while she cleared her passenger seat so he could slide in beside her.

"What's going on?" he asked after closing the door.

She reached for his hand, her face glowing from the dashboard lighting. "I have an apology to make."

He waited, confused.

Her words almost tumbled over one another. "I heard about the case you're working on—the one you had when Ellen died. I'm so sorry I didn't ask what you were doing. I've been so tunnel-visioned with this stupid campaign. It must be so hard for you, reliving all that."

He squeezed her hand. "Slow down. It's okay. How'd you find out, anyhow? Nothing's been in the paper."

But she maintained her manic pace. "In this town? You're kidding, right? 'Confidential' isn't even in the lexicon around here. Someone leaked it to Ted McDonald, so WBRT's been running it all afternoon, meaning the *Reformer* will have it tomorrow. I just couldn't believe it when I heard. You came by the house that night, probably to tell me, and I barely said hi. That was it, wasn't it? Why you came by?"

Joe was embarrassed, not to mention stunned by her revelation about the news getting out. He now had a pretty good idea what most of those unread call-back slips were about on his desk. "Oh, well, not really. Maybe a small reason. I just wanted to see you."

"And share a little of what was going on in your life," she finished. "Hardly a huge request, but too big for me." She leaned over suddenly and kissed him. "This thing has turned me into a total jerk."

He pulled back to see her better. "You're making too much of it. I would've mentioned it, sure, but I saw you were busy. And it's not like we haven't seen each other since. This thing's not as bad as it sounds. A lot of time has gone by. In some ways, it's like working any other case. It's just got some weird echoes attached to it."

That wasn't quite true, but he was touched by her concern, and didn't want her feeling any worse.

"What's McDonald been saying, by the way?" he asked.

"Just that the police have reopened an old murder case dating back thirty-plus years, based on some new evidence they won't discuss, and then a recap about Oberfeldt. How's it coming, anyhow?"

"Up to five minutes ago, not too well, but I just got some fingerprints out of AFIS that look pretty promising. How 'bout you? The primary's getting close. You feeling good about it?"

Gail made a face. "Not too good about some of the company I have to keep." She checked her watch. "I have to meet with Rene Charbonneau in ten minutes. Guy makes my skin crawl."

Joe looked at her in surprise. Rene Charbonneau was a county bigwig—a self-made man who ran a soft drink and beer distributorship and a small string of convenience stores and owned God knows how much commercial real estate.

"Charbonneau?" he asked. "What's that about?"

"Money. What else? He's the top Democrat in that category—a miniature version of Ed Parker's Tom Bander.

Sooner or later, everybody stands on his rug on their way to Montpelier, at least if they're coming from Windham County."

Joe was impressed by how little he knew of this world. "I've never even met the guy. No surprise there, I guess. I thought you were going after the tens and twenties of the unwashed masses."

She looked a little shamefaced. "I know I said that, but assuming I win the primary, I have to start planning for the next stage. Different game, with King Kong as an opponent. I play the same role—maybe a little more centrist—but I have to make sure the major movers are taken care of. I'm not after Charbonneau's money so much—more the support it represents. Parker's going to be really hard to beat." She paused to sigh wearily. "Christ, I can't believe what I'm saying. I sound exactly like all the politicians I used to hate."

He tried steering her away from such thoughts. "Is Charbonneau really bad news?"

"Oh, no. He's pretty progressive for a hard-core capitalist. He just sees himself as a ladies' man, and he gives me the creeps. Takes my elbow, pats my shoulder, guides me around by the small of the back. I wish he'd just grab my ass and get it over with."

Joe laughed. "That would be the end of somebody's career, sure as hell."

There was a momentary stillness, which she followed in a more muted voice. "That brings up something else, Joe."

"What?"

"It's the real reason for the apology. I did something I'm even more embarrassed about than having ignored you the night you came over. Have you started calling your law enforcement contacts yet, telling them about me?"

Joe felt his face get warm in the darkness of the car's interior. "No. I'm sorry. I talked to Lester about it, and he said—"

She put her hand on his arm. "Don't do it."

"Don't call?"

She looked out the windshield, avoiding eye contact. "I've been aiming at this campaign for a long time—a lot longer than I'll admit. I don't know if it's ambition or a need to be admired, or maybe, God forbid, because I actually believe in what I keep preaching about."

"Gail," he cautioned.

"No," she said with a quick smile. "It's okay. I spend so much time telling people what they want to hear, it's nice to just be honest with someone. Especially you." She took a breath. "Anyway, the point is that getting here has taken a lot of time and effort, and the actual campaign has rubbed my face in things I never dreamed of—like the allegations that I'm milking the rape for sympathy, or using my gender to advantage, or soaking my flatlander parents for money. It's all made me a little crazy, and turned winning the election into a kind of Holy Grail, especially against a guy who's starting to look damn near unbeatable. It's like a vendetta. I don't listen so much to all my friends and supporters anymore. I listen instead to the bastards who don't even know me and treat me like shit, and I want to win so I can shove it up their noses."

Joe didn't respond to any of this, recognizing not only its cathartic benefit but also that it probably reflected a much broader truth. He suspected that most politicians, if only in the secret recesses of their hearts, shared many of the same sentiments.

"Bottom line is," she continued, "that I sometimes lose sight of who I am and of what really counts in my life." She looked at him and took hold of his hand again. "In a more clear-sighted moment, it never would have crossed my mind to ask you to make those calls, Joe, especially while we were lying naked in bed."

She held up her hand to quiet the response she saw forming on his lips. "You would argue the point because you're a nice person, but I see what I did as emotional blackmail, and I don't want you to cater to it. So, promise me you won't make those calls, okay?"

He fought the instinct she'd already quelled twice, to downplay her words and make light of the perceived injury. Because in fact, she was right, and he was grateful for her perception and honesty. But despite his desire to, he still couldn't match her eloquence.

"Okay," he said simply. "Thanks. And don't worry. No matter how you're feeling now, you are the good guys. Don't forget that."

She leaned over and kissed him once more. "That's me— Wonder Woman. Oy." She rolled her eyes dramatically. "Would you be up for a late-night visitor in a few hours?"

"Absolutely," he said instantly, but just as immediately felt a renewed unspoken frustration. As he left her car and waved good-bye, he swore under his breath at his own weakness. Just as Gail had run roughshod over him because of her own ambitions, he'd just now shot himself in the foot so as not to hurt her feelings.

In fact, he didn't want company tonight. He wanted to be on the road. The AFIS printout in his pocket told him that Peter Shea's fingerprints currently belonged to a man named Norman Chesbro, and that Chesbro had been arrested for a chronic failure to pay parking tickets just two months ago in Gloucester, Massachusetts.

Once again, Joe found himself caught in tendrils of his own making.

He let out a puff of air in resignation and headed toward his car. What the hell. A few hours now wouldn't make that much difference.

Chapter 12

Gloucester, Massachusetts, is one of the grand old New England towns, as renowned in maritime history as Cape Ann—on which it is perched—was famous among vacationing artists of old. The same holds true for both places today, though mostly for sentimental reasons. Gloucester, while still fully functional as a fishing port, is but a pale glimmer of its past. And to Joe's jaundiced eye, Cape Ann's genteel and frugal Yankees were being overrun by Hummer-equipped megaconsumers seemingly bent on proving they had more cash than sense.

The population shifts reflect this latter aspect. From a year-round total of some 30,000 locals, the region bloats up to three times that number over the summer.

But he couldn't really blame either tourists or part-timers. Even if addicted to the latest trend in vehicle or cell phone, the most hopeless among them could only be impressed by Cape Ann's simple, breathtaking charm. It is a perfect commingling of history, good food, soothing scenery, and proximity to Boston. Despite the traffic, the boutiques, and a cheek-by-jowl crush of million-dollar homes, the whole place remains wedded to the basics preceding them: the gulls, the fishing boats, the smell of salt in the shifting air, and the huge, swelling, slightly ominous sea supporting it all.

Not surprisingly, there is a parallel arc of economic extremes, from the mansion owners spending most of their time away to the dock and fish-factory workers inhabiting Gloucester's ancient heart. It is the latter who continue the traditions of lore and trade and who occupy, in a feudal comparison, the role of peasants on whom the lords rely for food. Similarly, they also bear the brunt of a dangerous and unstable profession and are as exposed to the vagaries of the sea as their landlocked medieval forebears were to drought, disease, and foreign invasion.

In light of all this, it almost goes without saying that Gloucester is a hard-drinking town, run through with a steady stream of nameless people of no particular address.

An ideal place for someone on the run.

The Gloucester Police Department is perched along with the county's district court in a modern, largely windowless redbrick atop Main Street's modest humped back. Joe parked on the street, noticing as he did how the crest of the hill marked a social watershed of sorts, with the eastern slope leading toward the wharves, the older businesses, and some of the cheaper housing, and the western slope hosting more upscale, trendy shops and outlets. The majority of the pedestrian crowd, still clad in summer brights, was clearly weighted toward the latter.

Joe found the police department located off the building's lobby, in a dark room fronted by a bulletproof glass panel. He could just dimly make out what looked to be a dispatch center beyond. A phone was mounted to one side of the window.

"Hello? Gloucester Police."

"Hi. My name's Joe Gunther. I'm from the Vermont Bureau of Investigation, in town running a check on an outstanding warrant."

There was a pause from the other end, followed by "Hang on. A detective will be right out."

In three minutes, a barrel-shaped man in a polo shirt and khakis appeared at the far door. His expression was guarded as he stuck out his hand. "I'm Sergeant Wilkinson. May I help you?"

Joe reintroduced himself, presenting his credentials at the same time.

"Long way from home," Wilkinson said, opening the door wider and smiling thinly at last. "Come on back."

Joe followed him down a couple of dark, cluttered hallways and into a tiny office. For all its exterior clean lines and modernity, the building's innards seemed cramped and oddly designed. Wilkinson waved Joe to a guest chair wedged between his desk and a side table loaded with portable radios in chargers. Joe had to watch out for his knees as he sat.

"They told me you're looking for someone," Wilkinson stated.

Joe pulled an updated arrest warrant from his pocket and placed it before his counterpart. "Peter Shea. Suspected of homicide thirty-two years ago in Brattleboro, Vermont. I got an AFIS hit last night that you folks arrested him for unpaid parking tickets a couple of months ago."

Wilkinson's whole expression changed from reserve to bafflement. "You're kidding me."

Joe smiled. "Yeah—long story. Talk about a cold case. You have him in your files under the name—"

"Norman Chesbro," Wilkinson finished.

Just hearing the name out loud was a relief. After all this time and his own misgivings and self-doubt, Joe suddenly began to believe that the end might be within grasp. He wondered how it would feel to finally speak with the elusive ghost of half a lifetime.

"I guess you two met."

But Wilkinson was looking unhappy. "You could say that. We fished him out of the water early this morning. With a hole in his chest."

Gunther stared at him.

The Gloucester cop opened a file before him and slid a Polaroid picture over without comment.

Joe picked it up and saw a drenched man, his face pale as bleached rubber, lying on a stretcher on a dock. In one of those moments when shock calls out for distraction, he also noticed how the body was ringed by the tips of people's shoes, all caught in the margins of the photographer's frame.

"Sorry to ruin your day," Wilkinson said. "Was that your guy?"

Joe returned the picture. "I don't know. Last I saw him, he was barely twenty. His fingerprints checked out, though, right?"

"Yeah. And I was the one who arrested him for the tickets."

Joe sat back in his chair, struggling with the sheer mass of his disappointment. "Any idea when he was killed?"

"Must've been last night. He was seen alive around one this morning, at a bar—no surprise. He was a major-league juicer."

One in the morning, Joe thought. Long after when he would have been here had he chosen not to spend the night with Gail.

Unwittingly, Wilkinson then added exactly the wrong thing at the wrong time. "Too bad his prints weren't in the system. If I'd gotten a hit when I booked him for the parking tickets, I would've held on to him."

"That's true," Joe admitted mournfully. "It's always what you don't do that bites you in the ass later. Damn."

Wilkinson was looking sorry for him. "I wish I had some good news to balance the books, but we've got nothing so far. No clue on who killed him—or why, for that matter."

Joe rubbed his face vigorously with both hands and took a deep breath. "Okay, maybe there's some other angle. What was behind the parking ticket thing?"

Wilkinson made a dismissive gesture. "Like I said, he hit the bottle, hard and regular, along with a few hundred other people in this town. He had a car stolen a while back and claims he didn't know it was missing. It was being ticketed all over town; notices were being sent to Chesbro's address, but he never got them. That part, I half believe. He never collected his mail, including the final letter that told him to show up in court or else. I was the 'or else.' He was pretty surprised to see me. I'll give him that."

"Maybe more than surprised?" Gunther asked. "Did he act nervous you might find out he was flying under different colors?"

"I didn't notice it if he was," Wilkinson answered. "And we never did tumble to that. He had a license, a social security number. We were happy. It's still pretty easy to get a new identity in this country, especially if you're living low-profile."

"He have a job?"

"At a fish-packing plant. Don't ask; don't tell. We talked to them. Barely knew who he was. Just another face."

"Are you the investigator?" Joe asked.

"One of them. We have a team approach on these—one each from our department, the state police, and the DA's office. For all practical purposes, the state police take the lead."

Joe nodded thoughtfully. "I don't suppose there'd be any way I could look at where he was living? Check out his personal belongings?"

Wilkinson stood, taking his keys off the desk and pocketing them. "I don't see why not, assuming you fill me in on why you're here and what Chesbro meant to you. Could be we're after the same thing somehow."

Driving anywhere in Gloucester doesn't take long. It's more the traffic than any distance that usually gets in the way, and in this instance, neither was a factor. The place Pete Shea had been calling home as Norman Chesbro was a rooming house above a bar located only a couple of blocks down from the police department, on the "wrong" side of Main Street, assuming you preferred boutiques to dead fish. Joe barely had time to explain his interest in Shea before Wilkinson pulled his car over hard by the harbor and killed the engine.

"Home, sweet home." He gestured across the street at a largely windowless, stucco-clad blockhouse of a building, capped by two floors of a completely different type of construction. It looked as if a motel had been airlifted onto a warehouse, except that the warehouse in this case had a Budweiser sign decorating the door.

"He lived up there?" Joe asked.

Wilkinson hefted himself out. "Yup. The anonymous

Dew Drop Inn. People live there from half an hour to ten years, and nobody knows nuthin'. It's a cold fact that half the people upstairs and down are wanted for something somewhere, but anytime I step inside, they all pretend they're in a library." He pointed to a collection of moored fishing boats of various sizes and shapes. "That's where he was found this morning by a local fisherman about to head out."

"Any guesses on how he was killed?" Joe asked. "You said he had a hole in the chest."

"The autopsy's being done in Boston, as usual, but I'm guessing a knife—a big one. Looks like the killer caught him under the ribs and aimed straight up into the major vessels." Wilkinson squinted at him in the bright sunlight. "Anybody you know who might've wanted to get that up close and personal?"

Joe thought back to the morning's *Brattleboro Reformer,* which had run an article on the old Oberfeldt killing on the heels of the radio reports the day before. But all he could give Wilkinson was a hapless look. "It's all such ancient history."

The other cop nodded thoughtfully. "So, it's probably just a drunk getting knifed. Most of the people we find in that shape have a bad history—doesn't mean any of it played a part in making them dead."

He glanced across the street at the bar and waved to a man who'd just stepped out onto the sidewalk and was putting on dark glasses against the sudden light. Even at that distance, Joe pegged him as cop, from the shoes to the haircut.

"*Hey, Rick,*" Wilkinson shouted.

The man waved back and trotted over to them between cars.

"Rick Edelstein, from the state police. Joe Gunther from Vermont. Joe has an arrest warrant for the late Mr. Chesbro, known to him as Peter Shea."

Edelstein shook hands and arched his eyebrows, "Really? What for?"

"A thirty-two-year-old homicide," Joe admitted.

Edelstein's expression didn't change. "Moved right on that, didn't ya?"

Gunther hoped he was plugging into the man's sense of humor when he answered, "Well, you know how things pile up."

Edelstein laughed. "Shit. And I thought *my* desk was bad. Welcome to Gloucester. You have anything to add to this mess?"

Wilkinson answered for him. "Not a thing. He'd like to see the room, though."

"Sure," Edelstein said. "Right this way."

He led the way back to the bar, saying over his shoulder, "The place is barely full, it being so early in the morning."

He was only half joking. Gunther was surprised by the six or so people who were in fact sitting at the bar, grimly facing their first beer and shots. It was a dark, cavernous, ill-smelling place, its walls covered with a predictable chaos of photographs, mounted fish, maritime paraphernalia, and irreverent to crude signs. The lighting was poor and mostly supplied by battered brass fixtures along the walls, aided by a single wagon-wheel chandelier and a smattering of neon beer ads. The TV and the empty pool table stood ignored. The place was as quiet as a church on Monday morning.

"Stairs are over here," Edelstein said, still leading.

They climbed a narrow wooden staircase next to the bathroom and reached a dingy hallway running the length of the building.

"This is it," he announced, and knocked on a bruised hollow-core door. It was opened from within by a uniformed police officer, his face dulled with boredom.

"Welcome to chez Chesbro—or whatever. Crime scene people have come and gone, so feel free."

It wasn't much, and Joe couldn't help noting that its one window didn't even overlook the utilitarian harbor. The room was in the back, and the view was of the Dumpsters in the alleyway.

He glanced about. No surprises concerning cleanliness. The bed was a mess; clothes were strewn about in a dropped-as-you-stand fashion; the decor was minimal. The forensics team had been unusually delicate, leaving the place largely as he imagined they'd found it.

"No bathroom?" he asked, noticing that the only door led to a half-empty closet.

"Down the hall. Nothing of his there that we could determine."

Joe squatted down where he stood, not wanting to further disturb the spirit of the man who'd once lived here. The three other cops, instinctively understanding, stayed quiet and still.

Joe began absorbing the room, following Pete's habits by the clues he'd left behind: the single pillow, the way the night table's light was tilted over one side of the bed, indicating solitude. There were a few postcards taped to the wall, not of exotic places or naked women, but of Gloucester Harbor and the statue dedicated to those lost at sea.

Joe stood and crossed over to the small pictures. "You mind?" he asked the others, indicating his interest.

Edelstein said, "Go ahead."

Joe peeled a postcard from its mooring and looked at the back.

"'Dear Katie,'" he read aloud. "'It's beautiful here. Wish you could see it. I got a nest all ready and waiting for you to move in.'"

"Damn," Edelstein commented. "Hope she never took him up on that."

Wilkinson laughed. "Maybe she killed him after she saw this dump."

"No," Joe said quietly. "She can barely leave her apartment."

An embarrassed stillness greeted his remark, although that hadn't been his intention. He took down another postcard. Again it was to Katie, again sentimental, again unmailed. In the night table drawer, he found an old photo of Katie and Pete, heavily dressed and with their arms around each other, standing before a row of bare trees. They were smiling and dusted with fresh snow. Next to the photograph was a dog-eared Bible, several of its passages underlined in light pencil. Marking one page was a pamphlet from AA.

Joe pointed noiselessly at the single other piece of furniture in the room: a battered chest of drawers. Edelstein caught his meaning. "It's mostly empty. Forensics took a few things."

Joe checked its contents, finding nothing beyond a threadbare man's worn remnants.

He sat on the edge of the rumpled bed. "Not much to go on. How long had he been living here?"

"Here?" Edelstein answered. "Almost eight years. Before that, it's anyone's guess."

"Any friends or drinking buddies?"

Wilkinson answered that. "This was one of the most solitary guys I ever heard of. He worked; he drank; he came up here to sleep it off."

"Drank downstairs?"

"Mostly. We're still piecing it together, checking other places he might've gone, interviewing coworkers—the whole routine. I hate to say this, given what brought you here, but this may be history repeating itself, Joe—another murder with no solution. We've had that before. Guy kills a guy for a one-liner or less. It's hard to track when there's no motive. What about this Katie girl? He have anything to do with her not being able to leave the house?"

Joe rose to his feet. "No. He started drinking. They drifted apart. One day he was gone. At least that's her story. I have no reason to doubt it. She got sick later. Seems clear he was still thinking about her." Joe looked at the room appraisingly. "What strikes you about all this? I mean, generally speaking?"

"It's a dump," Wilkinson said.

But Edelstein got his point. "It's a hermit's cell."

"Yeah," Gunther agreed softly. "The cave of a self-exile."

Chapter 13

Joe returned to the bar that night. The place was utterly transformed—jammed, hot, and noisy. The voices were too loud, the laughter forced, the body language loaded with seduction, anger, or loneliness. Angling through the crowd, he watched the patrons enacting their rituals as he might have groups of wary animals circling a water hole.

He found a place at the end of the bar and prepared to wait patiently for the bartender to notice him amid the confusion. She was a tall, slim, attractive woman, probably in her mid-forties, dressed not provocatively but suggestively. From his vantage point, he could see her traveling the length of the bar, exchanging jokes, taking orders, replacing some drinks before she was asked to, and generally reading her customers like a good air traffic controller—separating the newcomers from the regulars, the easygoing from the boors, making sure everyone at least knew she'd seen them. It took her just forty-five seconds to look directly at Joe and gave him a one-finger be-there-in-a-minute salute. He nodded in response and then watched

her bend over the sink, facing her public, and quickly wash
a few glasses, giving every man within proximity a fast look
down the front of her carefully half-buttoned blouse.

This woman knew the game, the players, and the value
of the bar as barricade. Joe imagined she made great tips.

He'd spent the entire day in Gloucester, indulged by
Edelstein, Wilkinson, and finally the assistant DA who'd
shown up later, following them around as one or the other
of them, mostly Edelstein, interviewed a variety of Pete
Shea's acquaintances and coworkers. What they ended up
with was the portrait of a quiet loner who told no one of
his past, revealed little of his personality, and did his best
to stay clear of all groups, cliques, and organizations. In
one instance, when he'd worked at a place that was considering unionizing, he quit rather than get involved. In
fact, as far as they'd determined, he'd held a half-dozen
jobs on or around the docks, always doing menial tasks, always without comment or complaint, always turning down
any promotions.

By early evening, as Joe was seeking advice about a reasonable motel, his three colleagues were conceding that
they'd probably never find out who'd stabbed their man in
the chest. The assistant DA concluded by saying that he'd
be reachable by phone from then on, stimulating a dismissive sneer from Wilkinson, unseen by its target.

Unsurprisingly, due as much to his natural instincts as to
his personal investment, Joe demurred from agreeing with
them. In his gut, he knew there was something here far beyond a hopeless drunk pissing off the wrong guy at the
wrong time.

Sitting in Peter Shea's room that morning, seeing the
world Shea had inhabited for so many years, Joe had begun
exploring the possibility that this man had gone far beyond

simply ducking an antique murder charge. Over the years, Joe had developed a familiarity with the people who committed or aspired to commit such violence. It was that insight now that stopped him from putting Pete Shea in that category too quickly.

Unfortunately, there was no single rationale justifying his reluctance. It wasn't the Bible in the drawer, for example. Many murderers were religious fanatics. And it wasn't the sentimentalized affection for a love long out of reach. Nor was it the booze, the lack of social interaction, or the shiftlessness. In fact, the more Joe considered it, the more he began thinking it was the absence of several details that was making him rethink his long-presumed nemesis. There was no violence in the man's history, no acquisitiveness, no vanity or pride. He'd been a loner but not a sociopath, a drinker but not a bully. Pete Shea, Joe was starting to consider, might possibly have been a man who'd quite simply had the rug yanked out from under him, and forever lacked the emotional wherewithal to recover.

After Wilkinson and Edelstein called it quits for the day and Joe had politely turned down their offer of dinner on the town, he'd walked around Gloucester's streets for hours, touring the various neighborhoods while weighing several other long-held prejudices supporting the Oberfeldt case.

The focus on Pete Shea had not been capricious. He did have a history as a thief, his switchblade had been found covered with the victim's blood, his were the only prints found on the knife, his girlfriend, despite her best effort, had failed to supply him an alibi, and he had vanished as soon as he'd heard the police were interested in him. Finally, no single other candidate had fit the bill so well.

Additionally, as a foster child, Shea had been deemed

repeatedly "incorrigible," although Joe's search through those records had revealed only rambunctiousness, not violence. His run-ins with the police had been triggered by thievery, vandalism, and supplying minors with alcohol—never by any assaultive behavior.

And finally, there was Katie. Beyond telling Joe, back when he'd first met her, that Pete had been sweet and gentle, she'd added, "He's had a shitty life and I don't guess it's getting any better." She'd also ascribed his flight not to guilt but to his probably finding the entire situation "more than he could handle."

At the time, Joe had thought those claims predictable and weak at best. What else was a young girl going to say about the man whose bed she'd shared, especially to the cop hunting him? But what if she'd been right?

"What's your pleasure?"

Joe looked up, startled, into the face of the bartender he'd been admiring earlier. She stood with her hands flat on the bar, her expression pleasant and receptive, her eyes watchful.

"I'm sorry. Daydreaming," he explained.

"It's okay," she replied. "Not such a bad thing now and then."

He smiled and studied her more closely. She wasn't beautiful in Hollywood terms. She had a slightly crooked nose, lines around the eyes, and a hollowness to her cheeks that spoke less of glamour and more of hard times survived. She was handsome, he determined, in a way that only maturity and strength can deliver.

Which didn't make her hard, however. As she gazed at him in those scant few seconds, he saw something in her eyes that drew him in—a vulnerability he'd learned to watch for in hundreds of interviews with people doing their best to conceal it.

"Would you like something to drink?" she asked quietly, as if sensing the depths from which he was returning.

"Just a Coke would be great," he said.

She raised her eyebrows a fraction. "You boys find what you were after?"

He looked at her without comment or reaction.

"You are a cop, right?"

On impulse, he stuck out his hand. "Joe Gunther, from Vermont."

She took his hand in a firm grip and gave it a single shake—polite but noncommittal. "Vermont?"

"That's where the dead man was from."

"Really?"

Joe nodded. "A long time ago. Did you know him?"

Those eyes narrowed slightly. "I knew he was Norm, I knew he liked bottom-shelf Scotch, and I knew he lived upstairs. I'll get that Coke."

And she was gone. When she returned with his drink moments later, he merely nodded his thanks and was rewarded with the barest flicker of surprise.

Joe returned to his musings while still watching her work. Upstairs, he'd been struck by Pete's enormous sense of loss. There was little of the present among his paltry belongings, no hope for the future except what the Bible might have brought him, and only that one picture of Katie to tie him to the past. That and the wishful postcards that he'd tellingly never mailed.

In all his experience, Joe had never seen a killer with that particular kind of melancholy. It seemed to him that Pete Shea had been one of life's victims, not one of its aggressors.

But if that were true, then who had actually killed Klaus Oberfeldt? And, for that matter, Pete himself?

There was a small spike in the general clamor down the

bar. A self-consciously good-looking man—tanned, long-haired, tattooed, and tight–T-shirted—led a small group of buddies through the crowd and addressed the bartender. "Evelyn, you are a babe tonight. Damn. Could you fix these boys up while I admire the view?"

Surprisingly to Joe, she reacted not with the dismissive comeback she'd been handing out to others, but with an embarrassed smile and a tuck of the head, as if the compliment had been tender, gently delivered, and genuine.

His interest piqued, he watched her take the orders and line up the drinks, noticing as she did so that everyone paid except the man with the mouth, who merely winked as he swept the others away to the distant pool table. Her face slightly flushed, Evelyn glanced at the floor, composed herself in a split second, and got back to work.

I'll be damned, Joe thought. No figuring the people other people find attractive.

For the next several hours, and through a succession of Cokes that he knew would keep him up half the night, Joe watched the dynamics of the one place Pete Shea had used to escape. He didn't ask any questions, barely spoke again to the bartender, and didn't learn anything tangible about Pete Shea's fate. But by the end of the evening, he'd concluded not only that this bar was the one place with any hope of an answer, but that Evelyn the bartender—the casually watchful air traffic controller—was the person he should consult.

The trick would be in finding how to win her over.

Late the following afternoon, he was back on his perch at the end of the bar, looking just like one of the regulars he'd wondered about earlier. Except, of course, that he was still mainlining Coke.

Because of the hour, the place was almost empty. The same standard bearers were there, sitting before the same liquid nourishment, but otherwise the bar looked shabby and forlorn. Evelyn was back at her post, playing gin rummy with a small man who appeared to be a hundred and three, occasionally casting Joe a quick glance, seemingly caught between curiosity and irritation.

Eventually, with a laugh, the game came to an end. The old man stumbled off to the bathroom, and Evelyn sauntered down to Joe's end of the bar.

"You all set?" she asked, pointing at the glass before him.

"Yup. Thanks."

She nodded, hesitating, waiting for him to say more, before blurting out in a near whisper, "What're you doing?"

"Waiting to learn about Norm."

"How're you going to do that? You don't talk to anybody."

He shrugged.

She pressed her lips together, clearly thrown off balance. She turned halfway around, as if to retreat, and then challenged him directly. "Are you sure you're a cop?"

He smiled slightly. "You want to see the badge? They really went crazy with this one. Very flashy."

She smiled despite herself. "No. It would give heart attacks to the few customers I got." She shook her head. "You sure aren't like any cop I ever met."

"Not like the locals?"

She snorted. "Got that right."

"They give you shit?"

"They have their moments. What're you doing down here anyhow? What's this got to do with Vermont?"

Joe needed this woman to feel she was on the inside. He laid his cards on the table.

"There was a murder over thirty years ago. Norm came under a magnifying glass, so he changed his name and disappeared."

Her eyes widened. "Wow. I always wonder how many of these guys have done that." She swept a hand to include the near-empty room.

Joe caught her point. "It's not hard to do, even with all this Homeland Security stuff going on."

Intrigued, as he'd hoped she'd be, she leaned forward, resting her elbows on the bar. "What was his real name?"

He knew this was a test—an am-I-in-or-out kind of question. Again he didn't hesitate. "Pete Shea."

She straightened slightly. "No shit? Really? God, sounds like a little kid." She seemed to absorb that for a moment before adding, "So, old Norm killed someone."

Joe smiled, beginning to enjoy how this woman thought. She could have made a good cop. "I didn't say that."

She raised her eyebrows. "A drunk loser with no home and no ties? Seems like he'd be an easy hook to hang that on."

"I thought that way for a long time," he admitted. "And it may still be true."

She looked at him carefully. "Were you the cop when the murder happened?"

He merely smiled.

"Wow. This is just like the movies. You been after him for over thirty years?"

"If it were the movies, I'd have to say yes and that I'd sacrificed my health, my sobriety, and my family of three in the process."

Her expression was touched with a hint of sadness. "Guess not, huh?"

"No," he conceded. "We thought it was him, he beat feet,

we looked around for a better candidate, and then we gave up. It was only a new piece of evidence that got me going again. Otherwise, it would've been life as usual—fine health, no drinking, and no family."

For a split second, he wondered why he'd added that last bit, as if he'd wanted her to know he wasn't married.

She turned briefly to check on her other customers. The old guy had returned but still had half a glass to go. The few others seemed lost on distant planets. As her face was averted, however, Joe admired her from close up. Despite the hard-earned, well-carried miles stamped on her face, she was a very attractive woman.

Satisfied, she resumed her previous position, elbows on the bar. "So, what changed your mind? You thought he was the bad guy when he disappeared, and now he's not?"

He paused a moment, staring into his glass, getting his thoughts organized. "When the murder happened," he began, "there was some pretty damning evidence left behind. He didn't have an alibi, he did have a record of sorts, he disappeared before we could interview him, and there was nobody who looked better for the crime. He was it, almost by process of elimination. But nobody actually saw him do it, and nobody reported his flashing any cash around afterward, which was relevant since money was the reason behind the killing in the first place."

Evelyn nodded, clearly fascinated. "Sex and/or money, every time."

"Yeah," he agreed. "Along with anger, drugs, and alcohol. Anyhow, none of that's changed over the years, so I'm hard put to say why I'm suddenly rethinking it all. It was . . . Hell, I don't know . . . I was sitting on the edge of his bed yesterday morning, looking around, trying to get a feel for the guy, and somehow, I just couldn't connect the dots. The reality of that room didn't fit my picture of a killer."

He leaned back, stretched his shoulders, and took a deep breath, smiling at her with his head slightly tilted to one side. "Impressive, huh? Not the kind of thing I'd admit to another cop, but that's how I feel. Leaves me kind of empty-handed, in more ways than one."

There was some noise at the front door, and five men entered, talking loudly to one another. Evelyn straightened and glanced at them, assessing whether they would head to the jukebox, the pool table, the bathroom, or the bar, and then returned to Joe as they split up and did all but the last for the time being.

"Let me get this straight," she said, speaking more quickly now that their quiet was about to end for the evening. "For thirty-plus years, nothing happens with this case; then you get lucky, find out where Norm's been hanging his hat, but as soon as you get here, he winds up dead. Only now you're not so sure he was the right guy to begin with. Is that it in a nutshell?"

"Pretty much."

"You don't think there's something weird about that?"

He looked at her seriously. "I most certainly do."

"What're you going to do about it?"

He didn't respond. He just kept his eyes on hers.

"Right," she finally said. "You've been sitting here for two days waiting to talk to me."

"Hoping to talk to you," he corrected her. "I know the spot you're in—the credibility you need to keep working here. I'm not asking to jam you up."

She took a couple of steps backward. The men were beginning to sort out their priorities and were heading for the bar.

"How the hell have you stayed a cop for so long?" she asked. "Don't other cops drive you crazy?"

He smiled and shrugged instead of answering. That wasn't something he wanted to try explaining.

Turning away to tend to her other customers, she glanced over her shoulder and said, "I get off at two this morning. Meet me at the end of the pier directly opposite." She pointed at the bar's entrance.

"Thanks," he said, watching her shift gears and fire off a one-liner as she approached the first man to grab a stool.

Gloucester was still a busy town at two in the morning, at least in comparison to Brattleboro, so Joe sat thoroughly entertained on a strategically placed bench at the end of the designated pier. Across the narrow harbor, what he thought might be a packing plant was still open full throttle, its lights blazing and its mechanical heart throbbing deep within. On Main Street, traffic flowed periodically, often accompanied by boisterous shouts and the occasional horn blast. And in the distance, across the decks of several bobbing fishing boats, he could make out a man still working on some piece of equipment by the harsh light of a halogen lamp, the music from his softly playing radio barely audible on the gentle waves of a surprisingly warm, salt-flavored breeze.

And yet, there was quiet amid the groaning of docked vessels and the slap of taut lines against unseen masts— even an unsettling sense of isolation. It wasn't hard to imagine how easily a man could be waylaid, not a hundred yards from where Joe was sitting, and have a knife silently slipped into the center of his heart.

She emerged from the neon lights like a shadow detaching from the night, at first more a sensation than an actual outline, her footsteps covered by the soft lapping of the tide against the pier's pilings.

He smiled to himself as she drew into the feeble glow from across the water. Out of the bar's embrace, she was dressed in light sweatpants and a shirt, her physical attributes no longer available to any possibly good tipper.

She sat next to him without ceremony or greeting, stretching her legs out before her and sighing deeply. "God, it smells good out here, especially after eight hours in that dump."

"You come out here often after work?"

"Sometimes. It's a mood thing. There're nights it gives me the creeps just to walk from the front door to my car. Lot of strange people in this town."

"How was it tonight?"

She glanced at him, her expression covered by the darkness. "That's right. You left early. It was okay—average."

"I couldn't take two nights of straight Cokes in a row."

She liked that. "You on the wagon? Must be tough hanging out in a bar."

"No," he admitted. "I just gave it up. I never drank much to begin with, but I finally got tired of seeing what it did to people."

She grunted softly. "Christ. Got that right."

"You hungry?" he asked suddenly, offering her a small paper bag.

She straightened quickly and turned toward him, accepting the gift. "You kidding? Starving. I usually go to the diner after I get off."

He smiled. "I know—lobster roll and a strawberry shake. I heard you trading eating habits with your gin rummy partner."

Surprised, she tore open the bag and reached inside. "I

don't believe it. That's right." He saw the flash of her teeth in the gloom as she laughed. "You are too much. Thanks."

Without further ceremony, she took a large bite and settled back onto the bench, contentedly chewing, her eyes on the stars overhead. "God," she finally said, "that hits the spot. You want a bite?"

He held up his hand. "No, I'm fine. I might take a hit off the milkshake later, though. Big sweet tooth."

"Oh, right," she responded, diving into the bag again and extracting the waxy cup. "Take the first sip."

He did so as she ate more of her meal, and then placed the cup beside her. "How long have you been working there?"

"A few years—eight, maybe. Time flies. It's not my only job. I'm a freelance typist, too, and I do the books for the day-care center at the end of my block. I tend bar mostly for social reasons. It gets me out of the house without worrying about dates and all the mess that goes with them."

"The bar as safety net?"

She spoke with her mouth full. "Yeah. That sounds pathetic, doesn't it?"

"Maybe a little lonely." He hesitated and then took a gamble, adding, "I saw the small exchange between you and the guy with the hair and tattoos and the expensive taste in Scotch."

She stopped chewing abruptly, and he worried that he'd overstepped. But finally, all she did was nod several times before swallowing.

"You're pretty observant." She sighed again, this time less contentedly. "There's nothing going on there, needless to say. That's just Kenny being Kenny. And me being a total patsy, basically a wannabe lapdog."

"That's a little harsh," he countered.

"Yeah, well, maybe," she agreed. "The flip side to my being a bartender, I guess, is that I get to watch everyone doing what I don't have the guts to do myself. I can act superior and pretend that so-and-so's looking bad, and such-and-such is going to regret waking up next to *her* in the morning, but who's kidding who, you know? I'd trade places with any one of them in a shot. The closest I get is slipping Kenny a freebie to make him look good to his buddies."

"That might not be so dumb."

She rolled her eyes. "Don't I know it. I have a twenty-year-old daughter. Been there, done that, lost the T-shirt doin' it."

He joined her laughing, shaking his head at her unassuming directness. He liked this woman a lot.

She took a deep draw from the milkshake's straw and wiped her mouth with the back of her hand. "So," she announced, redirecting the conversation, "Lonely Norm Chesbro. Now, there's a man who makes me look good."

"Pretty solitary?"

"The loner's loner. Used to sit on the last stool, right up against the wall, and keep completely to himself, every night of the week. Never said a word to anyone but me, and most of the time that was just to order another one."

"Most of the time?"

"I gave it a shot," she admitted, "like I do sooner or later with all the regulars. Open them up a little, make them feel more at home. All I got was his first name."

"And nobody ever joined him?"

"They'd try. People from work would find him there and try to make conversation. He wouldn't have anything to do with them. It wasn't hostile," she added quickly. "It was pretty clear he was just really unhappy and wanted to be left alone, so in the end, that's just what we did. Who was he, anyway?"

"Who knows?" Joe admitted. "Foster child, early drinker. He was a thief when I knew him, which is why we thought he might've had something to do with this homicide, because of the money. But after he disappeared, I have no idea what became of him. I did find a woman he lived with for a while, but thirty years is a long time, and there's no telling what he was up to."

"I would say, nothing," Evelyn said quietly.

"Because of the way he was with you?"

She turned toward him. "This'll sound pretty stupid, but I think he had a broken heart. It's hard to get motivated when you have one of those."

For no reason he could determine, he took her hand in his. "That the voice of experience?"

He could just make out her sad smile. "I mentioned the twenty-year-old." She squeezed his fingers. "Her father's long gone."

"Right. I'm sorry."

She retrieved her hand to take another bite of lobster roll. "So was I, for a long time."

He nodded, taking her cue to move on. "Tell me about the last night you saw Norm."

"There was a stag party going. Having seen the place, you can guess how those go. They were holding it in the back of the room, around the pool table, and had the usual high jinks. You know, strippers, lots of screaming and yelling. Place was packed."

"Lot of new faces?"

"Oh, sure. People come off the street when they hear all the noise."

Joe stared off into the surrounding night, filling his brain with an image of the bar's layout. "That would mean Norm had his back to it all, if he was on his usual stool."

"And never turned around once. As if the whole thing wasn't happening. Not that I blamed him."

"You stayed behind the bar?"

"You bet. If ever that's my safety zone, it's during one of those parties. The girls do whatever they can to keep things going, including doing a little servicing in the bathroom afterward. It's no time for me to go wandering around the room."

"So, you had a clear view of the party in the back, Norm pretty nearby, and the comings and goings through the door." It wasn't phrased as a question.

Evelyn nodded thoughtfully, seeing where he was going. "Yeah, although Norm, as usual, might as well have been invisible."

"That's okay," Joe reassured her. "It's not him I want you to remember. Think back and tell me: Of all the people in motion, regulars and not, does anyone stick out who either approached Norm or seemed to take interest in him?"

She thought for a while, her eyes focused on some invisible middle space, and then she smiled broadly. "Yeah, there was one. As he was ordering, a guy asked me if that was Norm Chesbro. I didn't think of it till now, 'cause that was the beginning and the end of it, and like I said, it was super busy." Her eyes widened, and she put her hand on Joe's knee. "Is that who killed him?"

He smiled and this time left her hand alone. "Could be. Can you describe him?"

"About my height," she answered quickly, the trained observer brought to life. "Medium build. Light brown hair and a mustache, no beard. What else? Let's see . . . Oh, there was a scar on the hand that handed me the cash. Left hand, so he was a lefty, probably. The scar ran right along the back, dead center." She paused. "Is that enough?"

"That's pretty good," he admitted. In fact, better than he'd hoped. "Do you remember seeing him again that night?"

"I didn't serve him again. I know that, which is kind of unusual." She thought for a while longer. "No. He might've been there—for hours, even—I just don't know."

"How 'bout what time you served him?"

She straightened at first, as if to tell him how unlikely her memory of that would be, when she suddenly stopped short. "It was late. God, this is weird. I can see it like it was a photograph. I can see his face looking at me, and behind him, one of the strippers doing her whipped cream thing. They never get into that until they're almost out of tricks. The reason I remember is because at the time, only the guy with the mustache and Norm were facing me. Every other head in the whole place was turned toward the stripper. I remember thinking that was like noticing the only face at a tennis game not following the ball going back and forth. I saw that in a movie once. Never forgot it."

A small silence grew between them as Joe ran out of questions. "Well," he finally said. "I guess that's it, then."

"What happens now?"

"Nothing too exciting," he allowed. "I pass that description on to the locals, leaving your name out of it, of course, and then I go home—assuming they've never heard of Mr. Mustache—and I begin to put the computers to work. The scar will be handy, and the left-handedness. They collect details like that when they arrest people, exactly for situations like this."

"Unless he's never been arrested," she suggested.

He stood up. "Well, there's that. But at least we can try.

Plus, the PD here and the state trooper assigned to the case will be working on it. Maybe one of us'll get lucky."

She rose with him, crumpling the small paper bag and dropping it into a trash barrel beside the bench.

They stood facing each other awkwardly for a moment. "So, it's back to Vermont," she concluded for him.

"Yeah."

"Joe Gunther."

He nodded. "I never did get your last name, Evelyn."

She stretched up on her toes and kissed him lightly, her hand on his cheek. Her warmth mingled with the cool night air.

"Don't worry about it," she said, stepping back. "Take care of yourself, okay?"

"I promise," he replied. "You, too."

And he watched her vanish as she'd appeared, into the dark.

Chapter 14

The noise reminded him of the bar in Gloucester, except that, in every sense, this was as far from there as Joe could imagine.

People were happy, even ecstatic. It was now September, and Gail had just won her primary race. Two more months, and the die would be cast on whether she or Ed Parker got to hang their hat in the state senate for a couple of years.

Joe stood against the wall in Gail's converted living room, a plastic glass of cranberry juice in his hand. The furniture and computers and phones and faxes and all the rest had been shoved to one side, and everyone was milling around, exchanging hugs and talking loudly. "Send Gail to the Senate" signs were hung on the walls around the room, as they'd been adorning car bumpers and yard signs across the county for the past few months, although here they were accompanied by a few hand-lettered "Send Ed to Bed" ones as well.

"What do you think?"

Joe glanced down to his side. Susan Raffner, the epitome

of the satisfied campaign manager, was sharing the wall beside him, watching the crowd like a pleased raptor.

"It's a little odd," he answered honestly. "I am happy for
her."

Susan looked up at him silently for a moment. "That's
good," she said. "You should be. She worked hard to get
here."

He didn't respond. That was archetypal Susan: hard as
nails, as partisan as they came, and the kind of friend he
didn't think they made outside the Marine Corps.

"How are you doing?" she asked.

He smiled. And there was her saving grace. Once she'd
established where she stood, she was all heart. He knew the
question wasn't frivolous.

"Part of me's doing wonderfully," he told her. "The
rest . . ." he left the sentence unfinished.

She tilted her chin toward the milling crowd. "This have
anything to do with that?"

"Ah, yes. The political-widow syndrome, with a gender
twist. I guess a little," he conceded. "We sure don't have the
private time we once did, and I miss that. But there's something different gnawing at me, too—job related."

"That old case I read about in the paper?" she asked.

He nodded, still regretful that he hadn't gotten out ahead
of that story. He'd never contacted Ted McDonald even after
the news had broken on the radio, nor had he gone beyond
a traditionally bland general press release when the *Brattleboro Reformer* had followed up soon thereafter. "Yup. Lot of
baggage tied into that."

He didn't elaborate, and she didn't push.

"Look," she told him. "I can't help you there, but I've
been in politics a while. This'll settle down. You'll get her
back. Right now, she's like an outnumbered combat pilot in

a dogfight—all focus and adrenaline. What really counts doesn't matter, and what doesn't matter ruins her whole day. There's no perspective beyond the here and now. They all snap out of it after they win." She glanced at him one last time before heading back into circulation, adding with the grim determination of someone hoping a prayer will overcome reality, "And she will win."

Later that night he got a hopeful, pleasant taste of Susan's forecast after he and Gail had made love upstairs and were curled around each other in contented half sleep.

"I can't wait to get us back," Gail murmured.

Joe appreciated her choice of words. "You been missing us, too?"

She burrowed her forehead into his neck. "Like an ache I can't get rid of. November'll never be here soon enough."

"What if you lose?" he asked, not wanting to leave the question unasked.

"Either way." She then glanced up at him. "I won't be as much fun to be with if I do, but either way."

The next morning, the other problem he'd shared with Susan Raffner worsened. Stepping into the office, he was met by Sammie Martens, holding two documents in her hand.

"Hey, boss," she said. "I got bad news and interesting news. Well, I guess it's bad, too, but whatever."

He stuck out his hand. "Let's start with guaranteed bad."

"That's from the Mass State Police," she explained, handing it over. "A sort of after-the-fact advisory that almost got buried in the dailies. Katie Clark, the woman you interviewed in Orange several weeks ago, was found dead in her apartment."

Joe stared at the document. The date of discovery was one day after his visit.

"I was followed," he muttered. "That must be how they got to Pete."

"What?" Sam asked.

Gunther dropped the fax onto his desk and sat heavily in his chair. "I must've been followed from here to Orange and then preceded to Gloucester. Whoever it was probably got out of Katie what I didn't think she had, and went straight to Gloucester to kill Pete, all while I farted around playing 'twenty questions' with his fingerprints." And spending the night with Gail, he thought.

"How would anyone know you were going to Orange?" Sam asked.

"To quote Gail, ' "Confidential" isn't even in the lexicon around here.' As soon as that gun surfaced in the hostage negotiation, everybody and his uncle probably started trading tidbits on the latest developments. It's not like we kept it particularly under wraps ourselves. It was three decades old, after all. Or so we thought."

Joe propped his feet up on his desk and rubbed his face with both hands. "Shit. You dig into what the cops found out in Orange?"

He knew his colleague well. She retrieved a thin folder from her own desk. "I had them e-mail me the report. They're writing it off as a natural death, due to complications stemming from what they call a 'preexisting medical condition.' "

Gunther snorted. "She had chronic fatigue syndrome. That makes you feel like hell: it doesn't kill you."

"You want to give them a call?"

"Oh, I'll call them, all right, but I seriously doubt it'll change anything."

He stood up suddenly and stared out the window, anger and frustration sweeping through him. "Goddamn it."

Sam remained silent. This wasn't the only setback they'd suffered on this case. Following Gunther's return from Gloucester, they'd spent days searching every database they could think of, looking for any mention of a brown-haired lefty with a scar on his hand. They'd come up with nothing, making Joe a pain to work with. And the other piece of news she was bearing wasn't going to improve matters.

"I've rarely seen a person look so vulnerable," he finally said quietly.

"Who?" Sam asked after a pause.

"Katie," he answered tiredly. "She fell asleep in midconversation, she was so worn out. I probably could have killed her myself by just pinching her nose. I doubt she would've quivered. Natural, my ass."

"You want us to do something?"

Joe turned away from the window. "I don't know what else *to* do, Sam. We've put all our queries out on the wire. The only crimes we can point to happened in other jurisdictions. We're stuck with having to wait—just like we've been doing from the start. Only now we don't even have the suspect we thought we had. 'Cause I'll guarantee you one thing," he emphasized. "We were wrong about Shea, which means the Oberfeldt killing has just been kicked wide open again."

Sam didn't respond. Joe noticed the other sheet of paper in her hand. "Okay, keep the good times rolling. What's the next item?"

She gave it to him. It was a report from the Waterbury crime lab. "When you got back from Gloucester, you asked for Shea's DNA profile to be sent to forensics. It's taken forever, but they finally finished it. Those're their findings comparing his blood to the samples at the Oberfeldt crime scene—the ones you thought were the killer's."

Joe looked up from the report, his face grim. "I knew it. They don't match."

" 'Fraid not."

Four days later, Hannah Shriver parked her car in a sunlit field in Tunbridge, Vermont. It was warm for mid-September, a glorious late-summer day, and Hannah was feeling as upbeat as the weather. She got out, locked the door, and surveyed her surroundings. Hers was one of hundreds of parked vehicles glistening in the sun, spread out over eleven acres of precariously uneven pastureland, all sloping toward a flat floodplain beyond a small, rushing river called the North Branch. In the distance, thin and tinny spurts of canned carnival music swam against the air currents emanating from a man-made confection that was adorning the plain like the icing on a wedding cake—the Tunbridge World's Fair, one of Vermont's oldest and most cherished annual agricultural events.

Hannah paused to admire the view, positioned as she was like a scout atop a bluff. The basic, permanent blueprint of the place was simplicity itself: a half-mile-long oval dirt track, pinned in place along one side by a ramshackle wooden grandstand (with beer hall beneath the bleachers), a covered stage for live music facing it across the track's narrow width, and a large, open-ended pulling shed in the oval's center. That, year-round, along with a few low-lying cow, horse, and poultry barns, was all there was, along with a lot of open ground that in the old days was used to grow corn in the summer.

But every September, for the past 130 years, the place was transformed for less than a week—so filled with a

Ferris wheel, carnival rides, food stands, equipment trucks, show tents, and trailers that you couldn't even see the ground anymore. Over a span of four event-jammed days, up to 50,000 people came to the tiny village of Tunbridge— most of them Vermonters—to enjoy one of the last truly agricultural events left in the state. Hannah Shriver had been one of those people for forty-one years.

She smiled at the memory. No wonder she'd thought of this as a meeting place. It was one of the only upbeat constants in her life—a reliable album snapshot of happiness and goodwill where regular folks convened to have a good time each year before buttoning up for the winter. In more ways than one, in fact. When Hannah was a teenager, the saying used to be that you hadn't been to the fair until you left with a pint in your pocket and someone else's wife on your arm. Things had been so acceptably rowdy in those days that even the sheriff's department had sponsored a girlie show as a fund-raiser.

Naturally, everything was "respectable" now, and Hannah had to admit, she didn't miss some of the lechery she'd been a victim of at the hands of a few older drunks back then. As for the antics among her fellow teens, that was something else. She lost her virginity here, behind the racing sheds on the bank of the North Branch River, and despite the fumbling at the time, still recalled the moment fondly.

She set out downhill, aiming for a narrow, two-lane temporary footbridge that the fair staff had erected just for this event. The North Branch was fickle enough to have run riot over the years, so much so that all the barn doors were left open during the winter, allowing the spring floods simply to tear through the buildings rather than rip them from their moorings. Against fury like that, any so-called permanent footbridge would have been an exercise in futility.

All that seemed incongruous today. As she crossed the bridge, Hannah admired the river's peaceful gurglings around the pilings, empathizing with how the carnies always chose the curve of the tree-shaded bank just to the right to line up their mobile homes and trailers. She imagined that Tunbridge was one of the few venues they frequented where such sylvan gentleness was located so close to the frenzy of their jobs.

She stepped onto the fairgrounds proper and worked her way between the cow sheds before her. Here, farm kids by the dozen tended animals so curried and washed and meticulously trimmed that their hides took on the softness of brown butter. She'd loved hanging around here as a youth, not just for the boys but for the lowing beasts, too—their huge bulk and warm odors as inviting to her as the smell of fresh hay after a cutting.

She proceeded to the north end of the midway and melted into its crush of humanity, dense as any subway crowd at the height of rush hour. Here the smells were of boiling fat and fried dough, of sugar and beer and too many people, all things she found as appealing in their way as the ones she'd just left.

Basically, there was nothing that wasn't going to seem good to her right now, because today, as the saying went, was the beginning of the rest of her life.

Which could definitely stand improvement. Hannah, she'd come to believe, was one of those people whom good things avoided. A decent man, any children whatsoever, a home to call her own, a fulfilling job—even a car that worked properly—had all eluded her over a life filled with brawls, heartbreak, single-wide trailers, and a longing so deep, she thought it had no bottom.

Until she'd read that headline: "Cold Case Files? Cops Reopen Ancient Murder."

That's when she'd called T. J. to let him know she was still alive—and still equipped with a good memory. Not to mention a little something extra, in case the cops needed proof. Not surprisingly, she hadn't told him that part. That, she was keeping in reserve—her ace up the sleeve. After all, there was no point in revealing too much. He might come to see her as expendable, and she never wanted that to happen.

She smiled broadly to herself, weaving through the crowd. To think that a stupid job she'd held for a few months so long ago would suddenly become a gold mine— not once, but twice. She stopped at a fried-dough booth to indulge in a bit of celebratory excess.

The afternoon went by in similar high spirits. The harness racing was fun and profitable. She made ten bucks on a bet, which was clearly a good omen. She wandered by every booth, visited every tent, took the rides that wouldn't upset her stomach, including a tour on the Ferris wheel, where she caught a bird's-eye perspective. But as day yielded to night, and the sun gave way to the throb and blur of neon and flashing arcade lights, she did have to admit to a slow but steady building of second thoughts.

She knew she'd chosen the right place. She was familiar with every inch of it, both public and private. She was also secure in the context. Meet in a crowd—that's what the movies always said. She'd given clear and easy instructions—contact at the entrance to the bingo hall at ten p.m.—and had even thought to tell him to watch for the woman wearing a cowboy hat and a red blouse, an unusual outfit to compensate for how much she'd aged and for the number of people that were sure to be milling around her.

She'd covered everything. And couldn't stop worrying about what she'd left out.

By the appointed time, all the fun had evaporated. She was back where she usually was, convinced it would go wrong and that she'd get the short end of the stick again. She stood by the bingo hall entrance, feeling stupid in her hat, drawing bemused looks from passersby.

Ten p.m. Ten-fifteen. Ten-twenty.

"Nice hat, Hannah."

She whirled around at the proximity of the voice, right by her ear, and came face-to-face with a bland-faced man with brown hair and a mustache.

"Who're you?" she demanded, her voice high with tension.

"The man with the money."

"Where's T. J.?"

"Busy. He sent us."

Us? She glanced around nervously. In the swirl of passing bodies, she saw three others standing still at various distances from them, all looking at her.

"Why so many?"

The brown-haired man smiled. "It's a lot of money."

"Do you have it?"

He ignored her. "He wants assurances this will be the last time you call him."

That angered her. "The last time? I haven't called him in over thirty years. What's he complaining about?"

"So, this is it, then?"

It was an interesting question. She hadn't actually thought that through, that this could become a steady source of income. "Sure," she lied.

His smile widened. "Good. That's all we needed to hear."

"Fine. You got it?" she repeated.

"Yeah. Follow me."

She stood fast, her arms straight by her sides. "I want it here. Now."

He looked at her quizzically. "It's in a briefcase, Hannah. I left it in the car. No point lugging it all over the place." He then added as a joke, "It's not like it's a check."

Still she hesitated. He didn't seem threatening, and what he'd said made sense. But where was T. J.? And why were the others here if the money was in a car?

"I'll wait," she said. "Bring it to me."

The smile faded. "Hannah. T. J.'s doing you a favor here. Did he complain when you called? He said he'd help you out right off the bat, didn't he? Don't be a pain. Come get your money so we can all go home."

She looked around again, now feeling almost panicky. "I don't know."

The man shrugged. "Fine, call him tomorrow and work something else out." He motioned to the others and turned to go.

"Wait," she blurted.

He paused.

"Okay."

He seemed to relax and leaned toward her in a conspiratorial way. "Great, and you know what I said about this being the only time?"

She had to strain to hear his near whisper in all the surrounding noise.

"Well," he continued, gently taking her arm and beginning to walk her south, parallel to the midway and toward the parking lots below the fairgrounds. "I'm just an employee, and T. J.'s a real easy touch. I wouldn't take that part too seriously, if I were you."

She didn't like being held that way, but he did seem to be on her side. "Really?"

"Sure. Give it some time, and then maybe talk to him about being put on a kind of salary. God, you read about that sort of arrangement all the time, don't you?"

It was true, she guessed, but her mind was still in a whirl. She remained anxious—almost skittish. It wasn't what she had planned. It was becoming complicated, and it was slipping from her fingers. Just like always.

To give herself a little breathing room, she jerked her arm free of the man's grasp. In that split second, she both saw his face flash with anger and sensed one of the men right behind her suddenly moving as if to head her off.

It was all she needed.

She pretended to shift left, toward the midway and the solid column of people there, and then cut right as her escort went for the feint, pushing the off-balance brown-haired man out of her way as she cut into a narrow alley between the two buildings beside them, tipping over a large trash barrel behind her as she went.

It worked. She reached the fence separating the alleyway from the racetrack and climbed over it before the men behind her could clear away the barrel.

Opposite her was the covered stage, facing the grandstand to her left. She cut away from the music and the bright lights and ran north as fast as she could, making for the entrance of the track's central oval. She heard a fair attendant yelling over her shoulder at the men climbing the fence in pursuit.

The inner oval combined all of the fair's offerings. There was a second midway, complete with rides, tents, and booths, and a second crowd of people. On its far side, near the river, was also where most of the vehicles and trailers belonging to vendors and other personnel were parked in near-total darkness. As kids, that was often where Hannah and her friends ended up to indulge in some of their more private activities.

She quickly glanced back as she passed through the gate. All four men were coming on at a run.

Now convinced her life was at stake, she plowed heedlessly into the people before her, at once desperate and hopeful that her actions would cause problems for her pursuers.

She was right. Slipping by the initial shouts of angry surprise, she was aware of a secondary outburst being triggered by those in her wake. Risking a second backward look, she saw them being slowed and blocked by the protesting crowd.

Except that now there were only two of them.

Hannah kept struggling west toward the darkness. Like a passing fog, the crowd abruptly melted to a few stragglers as she passed the entrance to the second midway and headed for the horse barns barely visible in the gloom. If she could reach the far gate, leave the oval, cross the track, and work her way between the barns and the riverbank back toward the bridge and her car, she might still get away. At which point, she thought bitterly, old T. J. wouldn't know the meaning of the word "misery."

A man's shadow suddenly appeared out of the night, blocking the gate and her planned route.

She veered right, still inside the oval, running toward the lights of a small circular clearing lined with some secondary food booths. A thin cluster of people and their kids were milling around eating French fries and cotton candy.

She slowed slightly, tossed her hat away, and headed for a knot of two large families debating what to do next.

Startled, they made way for her as she knifed through their midst, closing behind her like a body of water. Hidden for just a moment from anyone following, Hannah ducked and slipped in between two booths, again aiming for the railing separating the oval from the surrounding track. She was now facing north. On the far side were the cow barns, filled with people as before, and beyond them the bridge to her car. She could almost make out the steep parking lot in the night sky above the low-slung wooden buildings ahead of her.

Stealthily, in the blackness of the narrow space between the two booths, she leaned over the railing and checked the track in both directions.

Nobody.

Shaking by now, sweating and near exhaustion, she climbed the railing and jumped.

She heard footsteps running from her left, the same direction of the man who'd blocked her exit earlier. Bolting in blind fear, she sprinted for the distant fence, climbed it at a run, missed her footing, and fell sprawling on the far side, twisting her wrist and skinning her face on the grass.

"You okay, lady?" a young voice asked from near one of the dimly lit barns.

She didn't answer. Didn't think to seek safety among the people caring for their animals. Didn't think of all the deputies that she'd avoided with scorn as a teen. She'd been reduced to one mindless goal: to get to her car.

Stumbling, in pain, she set a straight course now, directly between the barns and toward the footbridge beyond, unaware and unconcerned about what might be happening behind her.

The bridge loomed into view, empty of people, poorly lit. Here, suddenly things were quiet again, on the fringes of the fair, with shadows cast long and deep by the bright lights behind her. She stopped abruptly, caught up in the contrast, a sense of foreboding catching in her throat.

Her target within sight at last, she moved only hesitantly toward it, her ears tuned to the slightest anomaly. But all she heard was the canned, repetitive music, the hum of the distant crowd, and the sleepy lowing of an occasional cow.

Hannah tentatively placed her hand on the bridge's handrail and stopped a final time to look around. One last dash should do it, up the hill to her car and gone. She reached into her pocket and removed her keys.

Again, the dark outline of a man appeared before her, this time blocking the far side of the bridge.

"Hannah."

The voice was quiet, almost otherworldly, coming not from ahead but seemingly from the night itself. She spun around, saw another silhouette approaching from where she'd come. She stared wide-eyed at the gap between the two barns she'd used earlier upon arrival, when she'd been feeling so upbeat and hopeful. A third outline stood there, waiting patiently.

On sheer impulse she ran east, upriver, where she knew very well there was no outlet. The bluff overlooking the flood plain pinched together with the river and eventually formed a sheer drop into the water. But it was the only way clear.

The fourth man—the one with the mustache—appeared so fast right before her that she actually fell into his arms, like a lover yielding freely. She didn't feel the knife go in, but merely her legs going limp, as if from simple exhaustion.

Which wasn't so unreasonable. She was very tired, after all, in all senses of the word. She looked up into his face, saw the gentle eyes, and wondered why she'd put up such a fuss. Now that they were together at last, he didn't seem so bad.

He carefully lowered her to the ground by the rippling water, moving with her as she lay down. The familiar sound made her smile. So many years ago, that young boy fumbling with her clothes. Such a peaceful, endearing rite of passage. A moment of pure innocence.

A time to remember.

Chapter 15

Joe knew he was fixating. Fully conscious that he'd caused the deaths of Katie Clark and a now presumed-innocent Peter Shea—but ignorant of why or precisely how—he'd tapped every resource to reopen the original investigation. His desk was piled high with files, reports, Internet printouts, phone message slips, and letters, some of them yellowed and worn with age, all relating to people who'd been peacefully hibernating in the boxes he'd retrieved from the basement weeks earlier.

He knew as a virtual certainty that somewhere in the midst of it all was someone, deemed unremarkable at the time, who now had good reason to keep the past where it usually stayed.

But finding that someone was proving to be difficult.

He entered the VBI office carrying more documents from downstairs and was only slightly surprised to find Sammie Martens hard at work, even on a Saturday. So far, Joe had been tackling the Oberfeldt case alone, not wishing to add to anyone else's load. Since the only new activity related to this had occurred out of state, Joe had been hesitant to officially assign anyone to help him out.

"Just got a call about a murder in Tunbridge," she commented, looking up from her paperwork.

He stopped in midstride. On average, there were about seven murders in the state every year. Hardly a bloodbath by New York standards, but as a result, any homicide was a real topic of interest up here.

"At the fair?" he asked, as aware as most locals of this regional tradition.

"Yeah. They found a woman's body this morning in the river. She was tangled up in the footings of a pedestrian bridge. That's what the report said, anyhow. I have no clue. Fairs aren't my thing."

Joe smiled and continued to his desk to deposit his files. No, Sam would be more inclined toward a good, competitive paintball battle, he thought.

"Who's on it?" he asked.

"VSP's the lead, but we have a couple of our guys from the Waterbury office there."

"By invitation?" he wanted to know, sitting down.

She gave him a look, knowing all too well the VBI's cardinal rule of engagement. "Yes, Mother. We're doing the usual, offering money, manpower, and expertise," she added. "And this time we got invited from the get-go."

He nodded with satisfaction. "Nifty."

That was a first, and an important one. Where the state police went, others often followed.

"Usual sex-and-liquor falling-out?" he asked her, sitting behind his desk.

"A whodunit," she replied. "Guy used a knife. Caught her under the ribs and sliced her descending aorta, according to the ME's office—unofficially, that is."

Joe stared at her, speechless.

"You okay?" she asked.

He held up his hand. "Wait a second." He began rummaging through the piles before him as she watched keenly. This man had been her boss in two different jobs by now and could safely be considered her mentor. The times when she despaired of her abilities the most were those when she feared she'd never acquire his sixth sense. Saying negative things about Joe Gunther was ill advised in her presence. Which was where she and Willy Kunkle sometimes clashed, among other places. Despite the fact that Gunther had saved Willy's job countless times, Willy was not a man to play favorites, although, to be fair, he treated Joe with a tiny bit more respect than he did everyone else.

Gunther finally extracted a copy of the medical examiner's report done on Pete Shea in Massachusetts, and read aloud, "Trauma was apparently inflicted with an approximately seven-inch-long, single-edged blade, administered in a single thrust, completely transecting the descending aorta at the T-six level."

He placed the report carefully down before him. "How old was the victim in Tunbridge?"

Sam felt a tingling at the back of her neck. "Mid-fifties, I think."

He raised his eyebrows. "You up for a drive in the country?"

The Tunbridge Fair ran for four days, the most heavily attended being Saturday, which was, naturally, when Joe and Sam headed its way. Joe poked along the narrow two-lane road off of Interstate 89 in a Boston-style traffic jam, enjoying the late summer weather rather than using his lights and siren to save time. Despite the surge of adrenaline that he'd experienced hearing the method of this woman's death, Joe had been around long enough to distinguish between a real emergency and his own excitement.

Sammie Martens, true to her nature, was disposed altogether differently. Sitting unhappily in the passenger seat, she stared glumly out the window, occasionally cursing under her breath at the drivers ahead.

When they finally did draw abreast of the uppermost fairgrounds entrance, however—blocked by sawhorses—Joe did pull out his badge to demand entry. The young man at the gate, overwhelmed by the number and variety of police vehicles already allowed through, barely gave the badge a glance.

Joe parked on a grassy strip behind a string of cruisers, a mobile command truck, and the crime lab van, and walked down toward the low-slung cow barns to the right, casting an eye over the swarm of people roaming the floodplain below him.

"I can't believe they're still running this thing," Sam commented.

"Better that than send everyone away," Joe said. "At least this way, some witness may still be around to be interviewed." He pointed ahead. "There they are."

He led the way to the area near the footbridge, by now cordoned off with yellow tape. A young state trooper approached them as they neared.

"Agents Gunther and Martens," Joe told him. "VBI. Is Paul Spraiger here?"

The trooper studied their credentials, more out of curiosity than protocol, Joe thought. Word was out by now, especially among younger officers, that to join the VBI was to reach a law enforcement pinnacle. This may not have been the view of its many sister agencies, but Joe got a kick out of it nevertheless. Getting this far had not been easy.

Returning their badges, the man lifted the tape so they could pass under it, and pointed upstream along the bank. There they could just see a small grouping of men in plain-clothes.

"Hey, Paul," Joe called out as they came within earshot.

The group opened up; handshakes were exchanged. Not surprisingly in a state so thinly populated by police officers, those within the even smaller tribe of investigators all knew one another well.

Paul Spraiger, a scholarly man fluent in French, who'd once teamed with Joe on a case in Sherbrooke, Canada, filled them both in.

He pointed to a small disturbance in the mud by the water's edge. "Looks like this is where she was knifed, and probably died, given the wound. Not sure if she was then pushed or just rolled into the river, but she ended up hung up among the bridge pilings."

"So we heard," Joe said. "You have a name yet?"

"Hannah Shriver," intoned the lead VSP detective, a lieu-tenant named Nick Letourneau with whom Joe had also worked before. "D.O.B. 5/16/49. Lived in Townshend."

Joe glanced at him, wondering if his having answered for Spraiger meant his nose was officially out of joint. The ad-dress he'd mentioned, however, was of special interest. "Just outside Brattleboro. For how long?"

Letourneau gave him a blank look. "I don't know. Why?"

"I'm working an old open case, and someone directly re-lated to it just got knifed the same way in Massachusetts. I'm thinking there might be a connection."

Letourneau's response caught him pleasantly off guard. "Well, that probably makes this one yours, too."

Joe stammered slightly in answering. "Oh. No. That wasn't what I meant. We're not horning in here . . ."

"I know," he replied with a small smile. "Paul's made that crystal clear. But we've been kicking this around since dawn, and I've got a gut feeling it's going to cost a fortune in overtime. What with all the bitching upstairs about money, my ass'll be grass if I turn down free help. So I'd just as soon hand the whole thing over. Happy to assist," he added, almost as an afterthought, "within reason."

Joe smiled in appreciation. "Okay. Well, we still don't like hogging the trough, so I'll take you up on that—within reason—and we'll still make you look good at the end."

"Assuming it works out," suggested Letourneau meaningfully.

Gunther laughed. Too much, he thought. "Gotcha. We end up with zero, we take the heat, despite VSP's best efforts to make us look good."

The implied irony of the last comment had no effect on his counterpart. "Great," he said. "It's a deal."

Next to Joe, Sam let out an impatient sigh and walked off toward the bridge, clearly pissed off.

Joe, on the other hand, was genuinely happy. This was one case he definitely wanted to control. He didn't give a damn who collected the credit later—or the blame. And he had to admire Letourneau's pragmatism.

"How'd you find out who she was?" he asked, moving on.

This time, Paul was allowed to answer. "Her car. At daybreak, it was all by itself in the lot across the river." He pointed off into the distance, and Joe could see a hole in the sea of cars on the opposite slope, ringed by more yellow tape and filled by a single vehicle guarded by another trooper.

"We ran the plate, had a photo ID e-mailed to the command vehicle, and matched it to her. Then we broke in. Didn't find anything of interest, but with your old case, maybe you'll think different."

"I'll take a look later," Joe told him. "What else?"

"We've tried figuring out when she got here yesterday and who she might've met with. Her photo's being circulated all over the fair right now, mostly among the vendors and staff. So far, no luck beyond a fried-dough guy who says he noticed someone like her around the bingo barn last night, but he couldn't be sure, since the woman he saw had a cowboy hat. He thought the shirt matched, though—bright red."

"The Ferris wheel operator remembers a cowboy hat, too," Letourneau added, "but he couldn't swear to the shirt or even to it being a woman. He just focused on the hat because he was afraid it might blow off and he'd get the blame. Said it had happened before."

"You ask lost-and-found for the hat?" Gunther asked.

In the ensuing awkward silence, both men revealed not having thought of that. "I'll check it out," Paul said softly.

"What about her family or friends?" Joe continued. "Any luck there?"

Letourneau was clearly happier with that. "We've got people chasing it down. So far, just a mother near Brattleboro, in a nursing home. Last I heard, no one had talked to her."

"And friends?"

"I had someone check her place in Townshend. Looks like she lived alone, kind of in the sticks. A rental house on some out-of-stater's property. Looks like a custodial deal, maybe, where she got a discount for keeping an eye out in general. We've asked the Connecticut State Police to contact the owners and have them call us."

Joe nodded. It certainly looked like the basics were being covered. "Did you get anything out of her house? Bank records, letters, a diary?"

Letourneau pursed his lips before answering. "Not enough manpower. I just have a trooper sitting on it till we can get an investigator there."

Gunther immediately thought of Kunkle, who, despite his impatient personality, had a paradoxical affinity for painstaking house searches. "I'll get someone up there."

He glanced around. "I saw the crime lab van. Have they figured out how it happened?"

"They have a theory," Paul Spraiger confirmed. "Not much to go on, though, what with thousands of people walking all over the place. Because of where she ended up, they think she may have been corralled out here. At night it's pretty dark, even this close to the bridge. Since she was parked on the other side, it's possible she was heading back to her car when she was cut off."

The radio on Letourneau's belt chattered briefly. He pulled it out and exchanged a few words, finally replacing it and telling them, "They found a couple of more witnesses who maybe saw her. They're at the command post."

The three of them picked up Sam on the way back to the VSP's mobile office. Standing outside it, looking slightly nervous, were two men, one dressed in a fair official's dark blue vest.

A uniformed officer made the introductions to his boss, ignoring the rest of them. "Hi, Lieutenant, this is Rick Manelli. Operates a bow-and-arrow booth near the National Guard display inside the oval. And this is Fran Dupont, who sort of backs up security."

"I'm a roamer," Dupont clarified, shaking hands all around. "We do a bit of everything, wherever we're needed."

Gunther started with him. "And you saw something we might be interested in?"

Dupont didn't look that confident. "Maybe. It didn't have anything to do with the lady you're looking for, though. I don't know about her."

"That's okay. What did you see?"

"Four guys. They were jumping the fence separating the track from the midway area, between the bingo hall and the grandstand."

"That's unusual?"

Dupont shrugged. "No. Happens all the time. Sometimes even when the races are on. Back in the seventies, some woman, high on pot, just walked right out there to wave at the guy in the starting truck. He faces backwards, see, so he can know when all the horses are lined up, and then he operates the fence on the back of the truck and swings it in so they can really open up. It's really kind of neat to watch. Anyhow, this woman just walked out . . ."

Joe had silently placed his hand on the man's forearm, stopping him cold.

"Sorry," Dupont resumed. "Anyhow, they weren't like that—they were serious. Plus, it's not like it's a good short-cut or anything. Takes some effort to climb, you know?"

"What do you think they were doing?"

Dupont finally got to the point. "Chasing someone. I could tell. It was real obvious. They were pretty mad and pushing each other to climb the fence faster. I yelled at them but they just ignored me. It didn't really matter 'cause nothing was going on and they moved off fast. Ran, in fact."

"Did you see who they were chasing?"

"No, sir, I didn't."

"I did, maybe," Rick Manelli spoke up, sounding left out.

Joe ignored him temporarily by asking Dupont, "Can you describe the men?"

That seemed to stump him. "Describe them? You mean, what they looked like?"

"Sure. You could start there."

He shrugged. "I don't know. Regular."

"Any of them have a beard or no hair at all or anything distinctive?" Letourneau asked.

Dupont looked confused. "Like a bald man? I don't think any of them was bald. 'Course, one of them mighta had a hat."

"What kind of hat?"

"I don't know. What kind are you looking for?"

"What did you see, Mr. Manelli?" Joe asked, turning to the other man.

Manelli's eyes were bright with eagerness. "That woman you been asking about. I saw her run by. She looked bad. Scared. And she threw her hat away. That's why I remember her. I couldn't figure that out. Nice cowboy hat."

"You have it?"

"Nope. Gave it to lost-and-found."

There was a telling stillness among several of the police officers.

"Did you see anyone following her?" Joe asked quickly.

But Manelli was very clear about that. "Nope. I looked, too, because that happens sometimes—women being hassled. I try to look out for stuff like that. Don't like it."

"But there was no one?"

"Nobody I saw, like I said. That doesn't mean he wasn't there. See, after she ditched the hat, the woman stopped running and tried to walk normal, like she was pretending. So maybe the guy did the same and I didn't notice."

"Anything else?" Joe asked both of them.

They looked at each other and remained silent. Joe thanked them, and Letourneau made sure they could be located later if needed.

The four of them were watching the two men walk away when Joe suddenly asked, "People take a lot of pictures when they're here?"

"I guess," Letourneau replied.

"It may be a stretch, but I wonder if we couldn't get some of the folks who were hanging around here last night to help us out. Circulate it in the papers and on the radio that we're looking for any and all photographs taken at the fair on Friday night that have any crowd shots whatsoever, even if they're in the background."

Nick Letourneau grunted softly. "Good idea. I can get that going."

Joe eyed the command post. "And if it's all right, I'd like to make a phone call and get somebody started on Hannah Shriver's house. If we're lucky, she may still have something to tell us."

Chapter 16

It was a full day before Joe got to Townshend and Hannah Shriver's small house in the woods above the village. Willy had recruited Lester Spinney to help him out and, in his own manic fashion, had been driving them both relentlessly since getting the call to check the place out.

By the time Joe arrived, he was greeted by Lester at the front door of the mudroom and given the look of a man fresh from the desert eyeing his first glass of water.

Joe smiled at his expression. "Been having fun?"

Usually ready with an upbeat response, Lester could only say, out of Willy's earshot, "Been having fun seeing a man prove he's a total head case, is more like it. Can I go home and catch some shut-eye?"

Joe let him go and wandered deeper into the house. It was a log cabin, old and bruised, probably uncomfortably cool in the winter, with a rusty woodstove at its heart, a sleeping loft over half the diminutive living room, and a bathroom and kitchen to one side. In many ways, not much different from what a similar home would have looked like two hundred years earlier, apart from the plumbing and electricity.

Joe glanced up toward the loft at the sound of someone moving around out of sight.

"That you, Willy?"

"Jesus, save me," came the muffled sarcastic reply. "It must be Sherlock Holmes."

Gunther sighed and climbed the sturdy ladder. As his head cleared the level of the floor, he saw Willy on his hands and knees, half buried in a three-foot-tall storage closet cut into the knee wall abutting the sharply angled roofline. He resisted further comment and merely finished his ascent, settling on the edge of a mattress lying directly on the floor.

Waiting for Willy to finish up, he looked around, getting his bearings, much as he had in Pete Shea's room in Gloucester.

It was a threadbare home, filled only with the necessities, most of those either secondhand or with so many miles on them, he guessed they'd come through several generations. But it wasn't a hovel. The sofa below him was tastefully covered with shawls and blankets to hide the rips and worn spots. Odd pieces of discarded junk—a rusty saw, a few old bottles, some plates—hung on the wooden walls as decoration. The few pictures of sunsets and tropical islands alongside them, clearly cut from calendars or magazines, were carefully framed and mounted behind glass, and there were plants and dried flowers on the windowsills and on the rickety table that Gunther guessed had been used as a place to dine. There was no TV set, only a radio by the sofa.

Joe had been in some isolated houses before, running the gamut from trailers in need of a bulldozer to rustic mansions of millionaires wanting to "get away from it all." More often, however, they'd been places like this one: modest, well-cared-for homes, lived in by people whose independence meant more to them than the ease of modern conveniences.

There was something odd about this one, however. The more Gunther studied it, the more it looked almost imperceptibly disheveled, as if everything, from the wall hangings to the pillows, to the one rug in the center of the floor, had been recently moved and not quite replaced to its original position. It was as subtle an anomaly as someone wearing a hairpiece. Willy and Lester had been both thorough and tidy.

"Thinking of buying it?" Willy asked, having emerged from the closet, flashlight in hand.

"You could do worse."

"Place is a substitute rubber room—be like putting a rat in a box and watching it go bananas."

"That what she did?"

Kunkle made an equivocal expression. "From what I've dug up so far, I don't think she was certifiable, but I figure she had a few fuses blown, living in a dump like this. It's a half mile from the closest neighbor, for Christ sake."

"Lot of people live that way in this state."

Kunkle snorted. "I rest my case. Fuckin' crackers."

Despite the years he'd lived up here, Willy was a born New Yorker. Joe moved on.

"You find anything interesting?"

Kunkle sat in a rocking chair in the corner, the only other piece of furniture in the loft besides a small chest of drawers and the mattress on the floor. His response was unusually philosophical. "Interesting in terms of her death? Not off the bat. Interesting in terms of a life lived on the margins, making ends meet, and maintaining some dignity at the same time? Yeah."

Joe smiled at him. "You like her."

Willy frowned. "I understand her. She did what she had to do, or so it seems."

"Which was . . . ?"

Willy sat back. "Well, it's not like she had her life cataloged and waiting for us, but from what I found, she tried her hand at teaching, bookkeeping, secretarial work, housecleaning, dispatching for a trucking company, and even did a stint as a court secretary or whatever it is where you use those goofy-looking typewriters you see in Perry Mason movies."

"Court reporter," Joe said, his interest sharpened. "They're called steno machines. When did she do that?"

"Beats me," Willy answered. "All that's here is the machine and a bunch of the paper rolls that come out the far end of it, all bundled up. Looks like Sanskrit."

"What about family, husbands, boyfriends, anything like that?"

"A few pictures, some letters. Nothing recent, though. No diary I could find. No address book." He paused and then added, "Off the top of my head? I get the feeling of somebody whose batteries were running low. She kept the place up, did her laundry, washed the dishes, made sure the bathroom was clean, but that's about it—maintenance-level stuff. That's the dignity I was talking about. But three years from now, I wouldn't have been surprised to hear a 911 call for a suicide here."

"A life of quiet desperation?" Joe asked, gazing about, struck by his colleague's insight—the very thing that kept Joe playing interference for the man.

Willy covered with a dismissive laugh, probably worried

that he'd revealed too much sensitivity. "Shit, no. That's me. This broad was just going crazy."

Joe nodded quietly, allowing Willy his pretense. "Well, if you think you're done, let's collect what we'll need and move it to where we can work on it. I better beg the PD for their basement room—set up a data center. I get the feeling that before we're done, this'll just be the tip of the iceberg."

Willy stood up and stretched his one good arm, looking oddly like a man hailing a cab. "Sounds like a pain in the ass to me."

He then paused and fixed his boss with a pleased expression Gunther had grown to expect. "There is something else."

"Ah—I was wondering."

Kunkle's smile broadened. "The place was tossed before we got here—very carefully."

Gunther stared at him. "I thought that was the two of you. I was going to compliment you on being so neat and tidy."

Willy was clearly insulted. "Neat and tidy? Shit, if I'm left on my own, I guarantee you'll never know I was there. These guys weren't that good. If you did notice something—assuming you're not bullshitting me—it was the people who came before us."

"You think they found what they were after?"

Willy was back to looking superior. "What did I say? No diary, no address book."

Gunther waited for the standard premeeting chatter to peter out. They were in a windowless room in the basement of Brattleboro's municipal center, designed to serve as an emergency command post when needed, and thus equipped with phones, copiers, computer hook-ups, and the rest. It was used only sparingly, and mostly during drills or serious storms. For the VBI, with its one office upstairs, it had come in handy more than once as a conference or training room.

Joe watched as the stragglers got their coffee and dough-nuts at a table lining one wall and searched out an empty chair. In attendance were his three squad members, Paul Spraiger and two more from up north, several BCI officers from the state police, and a couple of Brattleboro's finest, Ron Klesczewski and J. P. Tyler, both of whom had worked for Gunther when he was chief of detectives.

"I'd like to thank you all for coming," he said as the last chair scraped into position. "I think everybody knows everybody else, if only by reputation."

"Guess that covers Willy," Spraiger said to general laughter.

"Some of you," Joe continued after a pause, "are here be-cause of the death of Hannah Shriver in Tunbridge. Others because of a thirty-two-year-old Brattleboro homicide. What connects them is an old gun that surfaced during a hostage negotiation several weeks ago here in town, along with the recent deaths of a woman in Orange and a man in Gloucester, Massachusetts, both of whom, like Hannah Shriver, were living in Brattleboro years ago when a shop-keeper named Klaus Oberfeldt was beaten to death and he and his wife were robbed of their life savings."

Gunther gestured to Ron. "Could you fire up that pro-jector?"

The room's lighting dimmed, and the white screen beside Joe became one of the black-and-white images he'd studied upon first revisiting this case.

"The Oberfeldt store, taken from the entrance looking to-ward the back room. You'll note the large bloodstain on the floor, belonging to the victim, who died of his injuries six months later, and a small string of droplets heading toward the rear exit. The working theory, then as now, is that during the beating, the assailant was also wounded and left those smaller bloodstains behind on his way to the storage room, where he removed the money from under the floorboards before escaping out the back door."

"Were samples collected of both?" J. P. Tyler, the PD's forensics expert, asked from the darkness.

"Yes," Joe answered, "and they both still have viable DNA, one matching the victim, the other unmatched to date. There was also blood on . . . next slide."

The shop was replaced by a close-up of the knife.

"This switchblade," Joe continued, "which matched Mr. Oberfeldt's. It also had a thumbprint on the blade, the only solid clue we managed to get at the time. The print belonged to a young repeat offender—primarily a thief—named Peter Shea. We went after this kid for the robbery-assault—Mr. Oberfeldt hadn't died yet—but Shea had already left town, we think because of this." He nodded to Ron, who brought up a slide of the Blackhawk.

"According to Shea's girlfriend, Katie Clark, Pete found this under his mattress in the apartment they shared. The papers at the time were told that Oberfeldt was pistol-whipped, but not about the switchblade, so Shea apparently figured that the gun, covered with blood when he found it, was the one we were looking for. Already being a penal system graduate, he assumed we'd connect the gun to him and throw away the key. So he ran."

"Wasn't he right?" asked one of the troopers. "If the knife was his and the gun was under his bed, didn't that make him the bad guy? Did he have an alibi?"

"No," Joe conceded, "which is why we liked him, not to

mention that the blood type of those droplets matched his, as they did most of us in the pre-DNA days. But you'll see the real problem in a bit. This takes a little explaining. Next, Ron."

This time the slide was of Katie Clark, looking fast asleep, just as he'd left her. Except that this was a medical examiner's photograph.

"This is the girlfriend I mentioned—Katie Clark—found dead a few days ago in her apartment in Orange. So far, she's been ruled a natural, although obviously I have my doubts. In any case, after Pete left Brattleboro, Katie gave the Blackhawk to her brother, who hid it in his Dummerston house, probably forgot all about it, and then died a few years later. In the last couple of months, a young couple bought the place and began fixing it up. During that process, a floor refinisher found the gun, stole it, and sold it, indirectly, to the guy who died in that hostage negotiation. That's how it resurfaced. It had been so well preserved over the years that the lab was able to match the blood on it to Klaus Oberfeldt's."

Joe paused to let everyone absorb what he'd told them so far, before resuming, "Now here's one of the first problems I mentioned: if Katie told the truth, and Pete did find the gun planted under his mattress, who planted it? One of you already suggested it wasn't planted at all, implying Katie was covering for her boyfriend. That's fair enough—God knows we've seen that before—but a second problem then presents itself. Next slide."

This showed a body floating in the water at night, wedged between a boat and a dock piling. "This is the late Peter Shea, who'd been living under an assumed name in Gloucester for several years. He was murdered just hours before I could talk to him, just as Katie Clark died one day after I spoke with her. Needless to say, if Shea was Ober-feldt's killer, then who killed him and why? And here's the kicker: The knife wound that did in Shea is a carbon copy of the one the ME found in Hannah Shriver."

Predictably, there were a few muted comments ex-changed among the audience.

"All right," Joe went on. "Let's allow for several explana-tions, the first being that Shea was good for the Oberfeldt killing, that Katie lied about his finding the gun under the mattress, and that he died the death of any number of drunks who hang around the rough part of town. That would also mean that Katie did in fact die of natural causes and that Hannah Shriver's wound looking a lot like Pete's is pure coincidence."

"Right," Willy commented caustically.

"Another explanation," Joe said, "is that Shea was framed, like he claimed, and that the recent resurfacing of the gun had the effect of pounding a fist on a chess table and rearranging the pieces. The person who framed him was forced to cover tracks he didn't think he'd ever have to worry about again."

"Isn't that a bit of a reach?" asked Tyler. "The evidence still points to Shea."

"Yes and no," Joe answered. "The circumstantial case is the same, but now, with DNA analysis, we know that those blood droplets, although of the same group, aren't actually his. To my mind, they represent the one unplanned aspect of this whole thing. You could see someone stealing Shea's knife, which he did say he'd lost; you could see the same person planting the gun on Shea later. But who could pre-dict that Oberfeldt might land a lucky punch as he was being beaten? It's the spontaneous nature of those droplets that gives them credibility."

There was a moment's silence as everyone considered the point.

"You can hit the lights, Ron. Thanks."

They all blinked in the sudden brightness as Joe continued. "Okay, for the time being, I'd like you to just tuck this away—an old anomaly needing closer scrutiny. Our primary job right now is the murder of Hannah Shriver. If nothing else, it's a spanking new case, which should help. Let's not forget, though, that she was roughly the same age as Katie and Pete; she lived here the same time they did; she died pretty close to when they both died, and precisely the same way Shea did. In addition, for what it's worth, Willy's pretty sure her house was searched before we got to it. We have no idea what may have been taken, if anything, but whoever did it was thorough and tried covering their tracks."

He rose from where he'd been sitting on the edge of a desk and began pacing before them. "My proposal is that we divide and conquer, concentrating on Hannah now and on Hannah thirty-two years ago, 'cause if I'm right about there being a connection between these three people, Hannah is officially the wild card. It's looking like Pete was framed for the murder; Katie was definitely his girlfriend, helped ditch the incriminating gun, and might've been killed because she knew of his whereabouts. But Hannah? Who knows? If we really dig into her history, both recent and past, my instinct tells me we'll find the common denominator that pulls everything together."

He motioned to Sam, who stood up and began distributing packets.

"This is what we've got so far. You'll find photos, crime scene sketches, witness interviews, an inventory of Hannah's house contents, and anything else we thought might be helpful. The top sheet outlines everyone's assignments and responsibilities. As you proceed with your separate investigations, there will be daily briefings down here at four p.m. unless or until an alternate time is announced. I would like to stress that if any of you uncovers something clearly fitting someone else's job description, please make sure that person gets the information ASAP. Sam will be the designated gathering point for everything, and she will be apprising me on a continual basis. Also, if I'm unavailable, she will run the daily briefings. Are there any questions?"

He waited for a slow count of five while they each studied the cover sheets before them, no doubt judging their own ranking in the perceived pecking order of assignments—territoriality being the incurable rash that it is—before he concluded, "All right. Thank you all, and best of luck."

Chapter 17

In fact, Joe was as guilty of being as territorial as anyone else. The assignment he chose for himself—after scrutinizing the employment timeline that Willy had reconstructed from Hannah Shriver's files and financial records—was to analyze her activities at the time he'd been trying to solve the Oberfeldt robbery-assault. Despite his statement at the meeting that Hannah's murder should take priority over all else, there was no doubt in his mind that every aspect of this recent mayhem was rooted in that ancient case.

Willy's timeline was by no means complete. Some of the documents removed from Hannah's place were helpful—old tax returns, copies of résumés where she'd outlined her professional history, and a few pieces of correspondence. But Willy had shown his mettle by also digging into the town clerks' offices in both Townshend and Brattleboro, checking tax records, property transfers, and the like, and filling in a few additional holes.

To Joe's relief, however, the few remaining gaps fell outside his scope of interest, if just barely. At the time of Klaus

Oberfeldt's assault, Hannah Shriver was working as a self-employed court reporter, although by six months later, she'd apparently moved on to something else as yet unknown.

His biggest problem was in how to proceed. So much elapsed time was going to be difficult to backtrack. Hannah's contemporaries would be middle-aged at best, possibly far afield, and probably have only vague and faulty memories of her. And that was if he found them. He'd brightened when he first heard of the court reporter job, hoping that such a connection to the judiciary, however vague, might hold some promise, but a trip to the county court building revealed that reporters' names weren't indexed to the jobs they'd completed, and that locating any such past efforts would require a case-by-case review of everything in the archives. An onerous effort, which, even if successful, still wouldn't address any jobs she might have done for the various private attorneys across town. The term "court reporter," after all, wasn't restricted to the people Willy alluded to when he'd conjured up his vision of Perry Mason. Reporters functioned in all sorts of capacities, transcribing depositions, sworn statements, and any conversations where the participants wanted a full and accurate rendering of what was said. The fruits of their labors weren't always filed with the court.

If Hannah Shriver had been killed because of something related to her job, it was going to be a neat trick finding it.

There was another possible avenue. At the Tunbridge Fair, Nick Letourneau had mentioned that Hannah had a mother residing just outside Brattleboro, who hadn't yet been approached for questioning. Generally, Joe liked having such conversations with more facts in hand, but it was clearly time to start hoping for a little dumb luck.

Natalie Shriver lived at Pleasant Acres, a sprawling complex south of town. Part home for the elderly, part straightforward nursing home, it was the only such facility of its size in this entire corner of Vermont, its brethren having been mauled to death in the never-ending and always changing struggle among the powers of Medicare, Medicaid, the health care industry, and the state.

Mrs. Shriver, he happily discovered, lived in the independent wing, meaning, he hoped, that she might be more helpful than he'd feared upon first learning of her address. On the other hand, he knew that she'd learned of her daughter's death by now, and while he'd never had children, Joe had witnessed the grief of parents outliving their youngsters. Such misery was hard to imagine, even after his own experience with loss.

A cheery LPN escorted him down a series of hallways, eventually delivering him to the open doorway of a large, bright room overlooking a gently sloping lawn and some manicured trees. Sitting by the large window, looking out, was a small, slight woman with a full head of white hair, who turned toward them as the nurse gently knocked on the door.

"Natalie?" she said gently. "You have a visitor."

The old woman merely watched them with a vacant expression.

"It's okay," the nurse whispered to Joe. "Just sit with her awhile. She needs the company."

In a louder voice she added, "Okay. I'll leave you two alone. If you need me, you know how to get me coming."

Joe waited until she'd left before entering the room a few feet. "Mrs. Shriver? Is it okay that I'm here? I don't want to disturb you. I know you've just been through a huge shock."

Natalie Shriver tiredly waved a hand toward the other chair by the window. "It's all right."

Joe sat opposite her. "I'm a police officer, Mrs. Shriver."

"Natalie. Everyone calls me that."

"Okay. I'm Joe. I'm really sorry to bother you, but I'd like to ask you a few questions about Hannah."

Natalie's tired, pale blue eyes studied him as if searching for salvation. "That would be fine."

"Before we start, is there anything I can get for you, or would you like to ask me about what happened?"

She blinked a couple of times, he thought perhaps translating his words into something she could decipher.

"No."

"Okay. If you don't mind, then, I'll be direct, only because I don't want to drag this out more than I have to. But if anything I say upsets you, or if you want to stop at any time, please just tell me. Times like these are tough enough without people like me making them worse."

She continued looking at him, and finally acknowledged his speech with a barely perceptible nod.

"All right," he began, unsure of what to make of her silence. "Do you know of anyone who might've wished Hannah harm?"

"No." The answer came after a moment's reflection.

"Did she mention that she was involved in anything or with anyone that might've been even slightly risky, or which might've caused you concern?"

"No."

"How about just the reverse? Did she seem upbeat lately, perhaps excited about something good coming her way?"

"No."

Gunther paused to rethink his approach. There was

nothing hostile in the woman's responses. Her voice was thin but steady, her expression open.

It dawned on him where he might have gone wrong. "When was the last time you saw your daughter, Natalie?"

This time there was a slight frown. "I'm not sure. I think it was about five years ago, but it might have been longer. Time isn't quite the same when you reach my age."

Joe couldn't resist smiling a little. God knows, time had been a little confusing to him, too, lately. "I may be gaining on you, then," he said. "If it's not too personal, were the two of you not close, or was your daughter just very busy?"

This time the small smile was hers. "You have a nice way of putting things. Do you have any children?"

Whether it was the directness he already sensed in this woman, or simply a decision to set the mood by opening up first, he chose to answer her honestly.

"I wish I did. I wanted to, a long time ago, but my wife died of cancer and I never had the heart to try anything like that again."

Natalie nodded thoughtfully and gazed out at the peaceful sylvan view. "That's the struggle, isn't it? Not to have kids and to mourn their absence, or to have them and be forever concerned about their fate."

Joe stared at her. A startling aspect of this job was how often people defied expectations. Before coming here, he'd worried about this person being mentally capable. Now he knew he was dealing with someone whose brains and verbal competence were several notches above the norm. He was grateful he'd broken the ice as he had.

"Was Hannah a challenge along those lines?" he asked.

"She was willful, independent, stubborn, and proud," her mother told him. "All the makings of a corporate tyrant.

Unfortunately, she was also lazy, hedonistic, impatient, and arrogant."

Gunther felt a small chill. He didn't doubt the portrait's accuracy, but he would have expected it from someone other than the subject's own mother. It was almost clinically detached. The image of grief-stricken parent was undergoing serious revision.

"Sounds like she might've been a handful now and then," he commented blandly.

Natalie shifted her gaze outdoors once more. "I suppose so. It's a shame you never had children, in a way. They're quite fascinating to watch. You can learn a great deal. The concept that they mimic their elders is quite hopeless, obviously, beyond certain speech patterns and behavioral twitches. Fundamentally, they set their own course pretty early on, which I think is why so many parents become baffled and anxious when the child acts so wholly differently from their memories of themselves."

She stopped. Joe waited, unsure if that constituted her answer in full, or if she was warming up to an entire treatise on children as lab rats.

But she was done.

"You've given it a lot of thought. I'm guessing you've had training in some of this," he suggested, by now ready for anything.

"I was a psychologist at Tufts for thirty years," she answered. "Research work only, of course," she added.

Of course, he thought. Probably a good thing, too— might have cranked up the suicide rate otherwise.

"Did her father play much of a role in her upbringing?" he asked.

She eyed him appreciatively. "You are good. Were we divorced? Yes, early on. His name was Howard, and after we broke up, he moved to Vermont—Norwich. Hannah spent most of her summers with him. After I got her back each fall, it would take me weeks to undo the bad habits he let fester."

Joe opened his mouth to ask the next obvious question, but she anticipated him with, "He died almost fifteen years ago."

He nodded and pretended to consult the notebook he'd pulled from his pocket. At least he was no longer concerned about her falling apart. "She had a lot of different jobs over the years. Why was that, do you think?"

Natalie sighed—not impatiently, Joe chose to think, but perhaps with a touch of melancholy. "Hannah was one of the perpetually discontent. She aspired to wealth, respect, and being admired, but she never worked hard enough to earn them. In purely structural terms, you might say she was too eager to operate at the uppermost tiers to bother constructing the scaffolding that could have gotten her there. She never seemed to either understand that dichotomy or to stop hoping that some shortcut might render it moot."

"Did she ever marry or have any boyfriends?"

She looked straight at him. "Same disability with the same results. No one ever measured up. She tried enough times, but again, with absurd expectations."

"Anyone recently that you know of?"

"I knew little of her life during these last ten years. She grew distant. Perhaps my increasing lack of vitality proved discouraging—too much of a reminder of what she would be facing soon herself."

Joe could have thought of a variety of other, more plausible reasons for Hannah to distance herself from Mom. Lack of warmth, for one. For that matter, Joe was beginning to think that adding vitality to the woman before him might be a horrible idea.

"When I was looking into Hannah's background," he continued, "I noticed she worked as a court reporter for a period. Do you recall that?"

Natalie Shriver nodded slowly. "About thirty years ago. She went to Champlain College in Burlington for training. Took her a couple of years or more. I was quite impressed at the time. I didn't understand the interest, but she seemed very taken with it. Perhaps she thought it would lead to an easy entrance to the legal world and all that might entail. I never asked much about it, because I was afraid she'd take such questioning as interference and quit."

"But she did quit, didn't she, not long after starting?"

The woman's brow furrowed. "Yes. I never understood that. It was an odd period in her life, generally—I suppose as it was for so many her age. Society in a turmoil, the country running without a rudder. Her behavior was quite erratic."

"Can you go into a little more detail?" Gunther asked, at this point milking the professional viewpoint for all it was worth.

"Not really. One of her patterns then was to be quite secretive. At one moment she was working as a court reporter, complaining as usual about how difficult it was to get ahead, and the next she was footloose and fancy-free, not working at all and living like a bohemian. That lasted about a year before she settled down to yet another job."

Joe's interest sharpened at this. "How did she support herself during that year?"

"I don't know. I assumed she'd either saved up or done something lucrative enough to once again short-circuit her potential."

"But in either case, she acted as if she'd come into some money?"

"I don't know that I'd put it that way, but she had no job that I knew of." She sighed once more. When next she spoke, her voice was higher, more distressed. "Poor child never seemed able to get a grip. Do you know what I mean?"

She'd closed one narrow, angular hand into a fist and was looking at him again in that pleading way he'd mistaken for heartbreak at the start.

But now, to his own surprise, he was no longer so sure he was wrong. In her detached, academic way, Natalie Shriver appeared to be genuinely grappling with the abruptness of her daughter's death—not just the news of it, but with the unexpected effect it was having on her. It was as if the scientist was trying to understand why emotion was interjecting itself in the midst of an analysis.

"Natalie," he asked softly, "when Hannah was working as a court reporter, did she do any jobs that affected her personally—something she mentioned to you?"

Natalie spoke to her hands. "It was so long ago. You tell yourself that everything your child does will be locked in your memory forever. It comes as such a shock, that first time you discover it isn't so. Shouldn't there be a special capacity there? An exception that places a son or daughter apart from everyone else you meet?"

She glanced up, and he could see that at last her eyes were moist. "The first time Hannah left me for any period of time," she continued, "was to live up here in Vermont with her father for a few months as a teenager. Not for the summer, as before, but to finish out the school year. We'd had a falling-out, and we all three thought a short separation might help. And it did, to a degree. At least the arguments abated. But when she returned, I remember looking at her face once, as she was reading and unaware, and thinking to myself that for the first time in her life, things had happened to her on a daily basis that I would never know about. Influences, encounters, thoughts, even a fragment of evolution I'd never share with her. It struck me with such force, it almost made me cry on the spot."

She was trembling. Embarrassed that he'd so misread her, Joe slipped off his chair to kneel by her side and hold her hand in his own.

"I didn't recognize that moment as just the beginning," she said, "Nor did I realize that it would lead to a time when her entire life—everything she'd ever experienced as a living human being—would be as void as what existed before she was born. A mere figment in my mind."

The tears were flowing freely as she added, "Once she was only the dreams and hopes of a young and happy childless couple. Now she's now a patchwork of memories to an old, tired, and childless woman. How fair is that?"

"It's not," Joe could only agree. But he added, hoping it might help, "Is there any chance you could spend some time with a relative, even for a few days?"

She took a deep breath. "They're all gone. There weren't many of us to begin with, and longevity is not our strong suit. I envy them," she concluded after a pause.

Sensing there was nothing he could say or do to lessen her pain, Joe rose helplessly and murmured, "I'm sorry I've put you through this, Mrs. Shriver. It was not my intention."

Her eyes met his one last time. "Don't apologize. It actually felt good, getting it out. I've become such a closed box of all I've known. Without someone to share it with, what good is it finally?"

He nodded and moved toward the door, ready to take his

leave, when he suddenly turned and asked her, "Would it be all right for me to visit you again?"

She'd produced a handkerchief from her sleeve and was wiping her eyes. She stopped and gave him a surprised look. "To ask about Hannah? I don't know how much more—"

He interrupted her with an upheld hand. "No, no. Just to visit."

She paused to consider the offer before smiling slightly and saying, "Thank you."

"Okay," he told her. "I'll see you later, then."

The offices of the *Brattleboro Reformer* occupied a flat, bland, modern building adjacent to the interstate at the far north end of town. This was a shame, in Joe's opinion. He remembered when they used to be on Main Street, on the first floor of one of the cluttered, ancient redbrick behemoths that made of the town's heart an architectural museum of a bygone era. Before the move, it seemed to him, there was more of a sense of the reporters and editors belonging to the town's social fabric. It was understandable that cramped quarters, lousy parking, and occasionally iffy electricity had proved too much to bear, but ever since the paper's relocation to Brattleboro's outer fringe, Joe felt that a vital though intangible connection had been severed.

It had become a hard-luck place, too. Changes of ownership had taken a toll, and staff turnover was so routine, he'd all but given up remembering who worked there. Also, arching over all, money was such a continual grind that it had become a more frequent topic between him and the paper's editor, Stanley Katz, than the crime rate, politics, and the state of law enforcement combined.

That hadn't always been so. Katz had been the courts-

and-cops reporter when Joe had run the PD's detective squad, and as such, he'd only been contemptuous of the paper's own management issues. His sole mission in life then, it had seemed to Gunther, had been to pester the PD like a cold sore. Katz had always had integrity, though, had never been spiteful, and, now that he was finally inhabiting the editor's chair, had even mellowed in his dotage.

Of course, it also didn't hurt that Joe had left the police department behind. Nowadays he rarely had cause to deal with the *Reformer* except as just another Vermont press outlet.

Not this time, however. As he pulled into the paper's large parking lot off the Black Mountain Road, he had a very specific idea in mind, which definitely played to the *Reformer's* strength.

He opened the building's front door, passed through the glass-enclosed antechamber—reminiscent of an air lock—and stepped into a large, open room full of desks and filing cabinets and service counters, a room vast enough to make the ceiling look low and oppressive. He glanced around, briefly thinking of how many times he'd been here over the years, usually on the brink of some sparring session with Katz or his ilk, before he set off for the corner office of the man himself.

Looking older and more worn than Joe remembered, Stanley was sitting, elbows on his desk, staring through half glasses at a pile of financial reports. He looked up wearily as Joe tapped gently on the doorframe.

He removed the glasses and smiled. "Joe Gunther. My God."

He rose and circled around to shake hands, escorting his guest to a chair and then choosing one next to it. Joe had never been so warmly greeted before.

"How the hell are you? It's been a dog's age."

"I'm doing well, Stan. You keeping out of trouble?"

Katz laughed. "Don't I wish. I never thought I'd actually look forward to retirement, but there are days . . . and I have years to go before qualifying. Goddamned depressing."

He took a breath and added, "Pretty exciting about Gail, huh? Finally going for the big leagues—relatively speaking."

Not being as glib with such comments, loaded as they were with double meanings in his own mind, Joe merely stammered, "Yeah. Well, we're all keeping our fingers crossed."

Katz looked at him for a moment, pretending to be caught off guard. "Come on. She's got a decent chance. If she totally nails Marlboro, Newfane, Putney, and Brattleboro, and works overtime to paint Parker as Bander's lapdog, she could pull it off. It also wouldn't hurt if every Republican in the county came down with the flu on election day, but still, if I were her, I'd make room for some champagne in the fridge. Hey," he added with the cynical lift of an eyebrow, "she's got our endorsement, after all."

He waited for a response and got only a half smile in return, followed by "Nice try, Stanley."

Katz shook his head. "Such a hard-ass. Well, you've never been so desperate you came here just to shoot the shit. What're you hoping to squeeze out of me this time? Or am I about to hear some spin on a screwup we don't even know about yet?"

Gunther let out a moan and held his forehead. "Jesus, Stan, do you practice that in the shower? The lowly press as Christian martyr, suffering for the public good?"

"Not with my last name, I don't," the newsman hedged. "I do think we fulfill a service, though."

Joe held up his hand. "All right, all right. Let's not go there, especially since I am about to ask a favor."

"That old case you're working on?" Katz guessed.

Joe nodded. "Very good. The showoff gets lucky. You know the details?"

"No thanks to you people. Old man Oberfeldt, a thousand years ago, took six months to die from an assault and left a cold case with a vengeance. There was blood, a bullet hole, and the mechanism of death was a pistol-whipping. You had your suspicions, but nothing ever came of them. That much," he added with an upraised forefinger, "is what you gave my predecessors. I doubt things were any different then than they are now, so I'm assuming you kept as much or more to yourselves."

"The gun disappeared at the time," Gunther admitted, "and now it's resurfaced. That's what got me going again."

Katz was clearly interested. "When? How?"

"The hostage negotiation that went bad. Same gun. It'd been hidden under some floorboards all this time, discovered by accident, and put on the secondhand market. That's how Matt Purvis got hold of it. It still had some blood on it. We got lucky—the ballistics matched."

"You do a DNA match as well?" Stanley asked, all management woes behind him now.

"We ran a profile, but no hit."

"So, you're stuck again?"

"Maybe, but I'd like to try a long shot."

Katz smiled broadly. "Which is why you just fed me all that. I better be able to use it."

Joe nodded. "Oh, yeah, and I'll follow it up with some more, within reason, but for the moment, what I'd like to do is have a picture run in the paper of a woman who may have been connected to it all."

"Who?"

Joe figured that the name alone would be enough. "Hannah Shriver."

Katz whistled. "No shit? The Tunbridge woman?"

"We don't know how or why—to be honest, we don't even know *if*—but I'm thinking she played a part in the Oberfeldt case, although maybe just a small one. If we could find out what that was, it might open things up."

Katz nodded, leaned forward, and pushed the intercom button on his phone. "Get a reporter in here," he ordered. "Preferably Alice, if she's around."

He sat back and gave Joe an appraising look. "You got yourself a deal."

Chapter 18

The next few days were filled with forging through a thickening blizzard of information. Between the search for photographs from the fair, responses to Hannah's picture in the paper, and collecting and collating reams of witness interviews concerning both Hannah's death and Pete Shea's, Joe had all he could do to find a few hours' sleep. Now it was he and not Gail who had a hard time returning phone calls or e-mails. In truth, her entire campaign all but slipped from his mind as he spent most of his time in the Municipal Building's basement room, like a commander under attack, hoping for a break not just in the relatively new Shriver case but also in the one that had become as intimate as a lifelong ailment.

And that wasn't all. Reliving Ellen's death, hearing his mother's take on why he'd remained single and childless, and comparing it to Gail's current disappearance into her campaign had made him ponder his past—even amid the present chaos—and consider what might be waiting in the near future.

If Stanley Katz was right about Gail, and she did pull that rabbit out of the hat, then Joe would soon be involved with a high-profile politician. Not because being a state senator amounted to that much—Vermont had a citizen legislature that worked for only a few months of every year—but because Gail would treat her new post as the proverbial bully pulpit. Becoming a senator would mark only the beginning of her ambitions. She wouldn't be lost to him forever, as Ellen had been, but he sensed that they might undergo a permanent change.

For that alone, he saw his present workload as a blessed distraction.

The biggest logjam was the photographs of the Tunbridge Fair. Considering both the popularity of the event and the egregious nature of the crime, the publicity surrounding Hannah's death had become statewide and constant, creating yet another pull on Joe's time in terms of daily press conferences and endless phone calls in which nothing new was ever revealed.

Pictures came in by mail, were dropped off in person, or arrived via e-mail, and covered the gamut from professional near masterpieces to barely discernible snapshots. Sizes varied, too. The standard four-by-fives and five-by-sevens made up the majority, but added to them in surprising numbers were tiny thumbnail shots in the form of miniature stickers, produced, Joe was told by a savvy Lester Spinney, by the latest teenage rage of point-and-shoot camera. But however they came, and in whatever format, there were thousands of them, each one demanding the utmost scrutiny.

The response to Hannah's picture in the *Reformer* was an entirely different matter. Joe had made sure that the photograph was roughly contemporary to the era in question, but perhaps as a result, both the command center and the *Re-former*'s letters-to-the-editor column were quickly filled with any number of reactions—as much to her as to other young women who might have simply resembled her. To a startlingly large number of people—despite her name being printed right under the photograph—the smiling girl in the quaint hairdo served as a substitute for loved ones now long gone.

It wasn't all for naught, however. As the days slipped by, Joe began to construct a mental home movie of Hannah Shriver as she practiced her newly learned profession, found an apartment on Main Street, and began integrating herself into the community after her two years of schooling in Burlington.

Lawyers, friends, a landlord, a bartender, an old lover—all began adding their own brushstrokes to the portrait begun during Joe's conversation with Natalie Shriver. What emerged was a more detailed version of the elderly woman's recollection, given more immediacy by many of the portrayers' having been of Hannah's age.

Lou Boxer was one of them. A quiet, serious, bespectacled man given to extensive pauses between sentences, he came by Joe's office one afternoon and confessed in a muted monotone that he and Hannah had once been lovers.

"Was this when she was working as a court reporter?" Gunther asked after offering him a seat and a cup of coffee.

Boxer turned down the coffee as he settled into a chair. "Yes. Not that she did that full-time."

"Oh?" Joe asked.

"She was a freelancer. Little tough to find jobs right out of the starting gate."

"That's reasonable," Joe conceded. "Did things improve over time?"

"A little. Never to the point where she made a living."

"How did she pay the rent, then?"

Boxer smiled wistfully. "She got people to help her out. Like me. Hannah could be persuasive."

Gunther raised his eyebrows. "Interesting comment. Tough relationship?"

The other man considered that before asking, "Aren't those two words synonymous?" He fell silent for a moment and studied the ceiling in contemplation. Joe let him think.

"Those were different times," he finally said. "We worked harder at being cool and detached, trying not to be possessive."

"She had other lovers."

Boxer nodded silently.

"You know who any of them were?"

"Oh, sure. That was part of it, wearing those kinds of things on your sleeve. Very countercultural."

"Sounds like you've gotten a little cynical over time."

Boxer sighed. "I shop at the Co-op, protest against the government, and always vote pro-union. Let's just say I've either gotten wiser or too tired to cover much beyond the basics. Right now all the posturing we indulged in sounds as self-focused as anything the movie stars do in the tabloids."

Gunther moved on. "How soon after Hannah hit town did you two hook up?" He pulled a calendar from a file of the right year. "Maybe this'll help nail down the date, more or less. Anytime around then?" He flipped to the month Oberfeldt was attacked.

Lou Boxer glanced at the calendar. "About two weeks earlier."

"Pretty good memory."

Boxer reacted to Joe's doubtful tone. "Not really. I celebrated my birthday with her shortly after we met." He reached out and tapped a date with his finger. "Then."

One day after the attack. "You recall how she was that day, since it's clear in your mind?"

Boxer looked at him quizzically. "How she was? Meaning what?"

"Was she nervous, distracted, in any way unlike herself?"

Again the nostalgic smile. "No. What little I do remember is pretty pleasant."

Joe changed his approach. "Do you remember reading about an assault on a storekeeper around that time?"

"Yeah, vaguely. That may be because it's been in the news, though. You guys are supposed to be looking into it again. Is that connected to Hannah?"

Gunther answered him truthfully. "We don't know, but we're looking at everything right now. Did you and she ever talk about that case?"

Boxer shrugged. "God, I don't know. Some things I remember better than others—chitchat isn't one of them."

Which at least meant it hadn't been a major topic of conversation. "All right," Joe continued. "Let's step back a little, then. How long were you two an item?"

"About half a year, give or take."

"Okay. So you met, you hit it off, had some good times, did all the right cool things. Then what? A falling-out? What changed?"

"She did," Boxer answered, without hesitation for once.

"Could you elaborate?"

The other man removed his glasses and rubbed the bridge of his nose. "I'd fallen in love with her. I knew it was a bad idea. Hannah was a free spirit—*there's* a phrase from the old days. Groovy. Now I guess I'd call her flighty and selfish and maybe a little cruel. It was pretty much her way or the highway. At the time, I saw it as feminism and free expression and all that other crap, but it was what it was. In hindsight, or maybe just because I *am* more cynical now, I don't think she ever gave a damn about the feminist cause, or any other cause, for that matter—just herself."

"So, she gave you your walking papers because she wasn't ready to commit?" Joe asked.

But Lou Boxer was clearly still struggling to define a specifically sharper memory. "Partly. There was something else, too. She wouldn't own up to it, but it was almost like I was suddenly superfluous—like she'd caught a sudden gust in her sails and I was just slowing her down."

"Suddenly?" Joe repeated, struck by the word. "What do you think happened?"

Boxer replaced his glasses carefully. "I don't know. She dumped the whole court reporter thing right afterward, so maybe it was tied to that."

"After two years of study," Gunther mused, remembering Natalie's mention of the same thing. "Makes you wonder why. She come into some money?"

"She didn't tell me one way or the other. I didn't get hit for any more financial favors, but I assumed that was because I was old news."

"So, she wasn't living high on the hog that you could tell?"

"She might've been," he admitted. "I wouldn't have known. To be honest, I took this pretty hard. Wandered off to lick my wounds. Lived in California for a couple of years. I never heard from her again. Not," he added ruefully, "until I saw that photo in the paper. That was a real shock."

Gunther let a moment of silence pass before asking, "You mentioned you knew her other lovers, or at least some of them. You remember any names?"

Lou Boxer scratched his forehead. "So long ago. One of them was named Travis. I never knew his last name. Another . . . Jesus . . . Bob comes to mind. That's useful, right?" He sighed. "I'm not going to be much help there. They were faces to me, you know? Rivals. I didn't want to know who they were. It was bad enough they existed. I was never as cool as I pretended. Just a middle-class kid undercover."

Gunther nodded sympathetically, but with visions of Hannah and Pete Shea and Katie Clark and even himself as a young man in his head, he was thinking that there was quite a bit of pretense taking place back then.

Slowly and sporadically, another piece of the puzzle that was Hannah Shriver fell into place from her incoming transcriptions. Task force members started uncovering old documents from the court archives, and a couple of law offices pitched in with yellowed depositions and other interviews. It was haphazard and erratic, done by the private lawyers only in the hope that it might curry favor with law enforcement, but even so, it resulted in a tremendous pile of reading. Transcribed conversations average one page per minute of dialogue, depending on how they're typed up, and every "uh," "ah," and "you know" is faithfully and excruciatingly recorded. Staring at page after page of vacuous meanderings, baffling phrasing, and—in Hannah's case—a stunning number of typos and misspellings helped Joe understand why she might have left the business so quickly, and why she'd been hard up for work while she lasted. Considering many of her efforts as professionally produced documents almost seemed ludicrous at times.

On one such day of overexposure, he was leaning back in his chair, pressing the heels of his hands against his aching eyes, when Sammie Martens walked in from downstairs.

Finding the windowless basement claustrophobic, Joe had temporarily fled to his top-floor office.

"Got something that may be a total dead end," she told him, dropping yet another transcript onto his desk. "But the date in it is the same night Oberfeldt got whacked. I figured you'd want to see it. I marked the section."

Joe straightened and picked up the document, leafing to the page with the yellow Post-it note.

Sam continued speaking. "It's a deposition Hannah typed from someone named Sandy Conant. He was a coworker of a guy named Mitch Blood, whose wife claimed she was being abused and had been beaten in front of Conant, making him a witness. Problem was, Sandy claimed ignorance and had an alibi to back him up. He was collecting his mail in the lobby at exactly the same time the wife said she was being clobbered across town."

Joe focused on the words before him.

MR. CONANT: I pick up my mail same time every day, right after I get off work. 9:30 on the dot. Been doin' it for years.

MR. JENNINGS: I understand that, Sandy, but without corroboration, we only have your word. Did any . . .

MR. CONANT: Corra-what?

MR. JENNINGS: We need to know if anyone saw you doing that. Getting your mail.

MR. CONANT: T. J. was there. Came in just as I opened the box.

MR. JENNINGS: Does T. J. have a last name?

MR. CONANT: Sure. Everybody does.

MR. JENNINGS: And what is T. J.'s last name?

MR. CONANT: Ralpher. T. J. Ralpher. I have no
clue what the T. J.'s for, so don't bother askin'.
MR. JENNINGS: Did you and T. J. talk?
MR. CONANT: Nope. We're not like friends. He
said hi, I said hi. We live in the same building.
That's about it, but he could vouch for me. I
don't know shit about Mitch and that cow he
calls a wife. Never seen him lay a hand on her,
and if she says different, well, then she's full of it.
MR. JENNINGS: Thank you, Sandy. I think we
get the idea.

Joe turned the page, but Sam interrupted him. "That's
really it. A little more about where he worked and what he
knew of Mitch's marital problems, and then it's over."

Gunther closed the transcript and returned it. "Any
alarms go off?"

She shrugged. "I called the lawyer who gave us this—
Jennings. He didn't remember the case, but he had one of
his slaves look it up for me. It never went anywhere. I guess
it all hinged on Conant being a witness, so once he faded,
that was it."

"You look up T. J. Ralpher?" Joe asked. "That rings a
faint bell."

Sam equivocated. "I ran him by VCIC on the computer.
Some ancient stuff, dating to back then. After that, nothing.
Like I said, I only showed you this because of the timing."

"What about Sandy Conant?"

"Yup. Checked on him, too. Died an alcoholic about ten
years ago."

Joe cupped his chin in his hand and gazed at the wall a
moment. "How 'bout the other stuff Willy and I found at
her house? All those paper rolls from the steno machine.

Do we have one that matches this?" he held up the document.

"Yeah," she admitted. "But you'd have an easier time reading hieroglyphics."

The phone rang beside Joe. He picked it up and answered.

"Joe," Lester said. "You might want to come downstairs. We found something in the Tunbridge pictures."

The basement room had lost the neat and tidy appearance of its inception. The squared-away tables equipped with phones and computers were piled high with paperwork, the floor was strewn with debris, and the air was close and vaguely unpleasant. Men and women either sat at their stations drinking coffee and squinting at screen or page or wandered back and forth comparing notes. A low buzz of continuous conversation, both face-to-face and on the phone, filled the air like a mechanical hum. In one corner, Lester Spinney had commandeered two folding tables he'd lined up catty-corner and covered with folders and piles of photographs that had fallen to him for analysis. In the center of it all was another computer, designated solely for e-mail downloads. This is where Joe and Sam found him sitting.

He looked over his shoulder as they approached. "It ain't like in the movies, but it's still pretty cool."

They peered at the screen. Before them was a slightly blurry picture, enlarged as far as it could stand, of the fair's interior midway, the one enclosed within the racetrack. It was a crowd shot, with a smiling child in the foreground holding an enormous cotton candy, his cheeks already smeared bright pink.

Lester tapped the screen, where his two colleagues were

already looking. "That's her, moving fast, so she's out of focus and almost out of the picture, but look at this guy."

Framed by the entrance gate and still clearly in mid-stride, the person he'd indicated appeared to be directing two men to go elsewhere, while a third continued after Hannah. Their expressions were grim, in stark contrast to the child's, and there seemed no doubt that they were staring straight at the woman in the cowboy hat and bright red shirt.

"What do you think?" Lester asked.

Joe studied the leader. Medium height and build. Brown hair and mustache.

"I think I better drive back to Gloucester."

It was early evening when Gunther stepped through the bar's door. The usual hangers-on were still there, seemingly unmoved since he'd left them—in fact, barely looking alive. The one exception, as before, was back playing gin with Evelyn, both of them chatting quietly. Out of deference to the place's clear traditions, Joe took his own usual seat and gazed down the length of the bar at the woman he hadn't been able to chase from his mind as easily as he'd hoped.

She cast him a smiling glance, slapped down a final card, patted her old rival on the shoulder, and slowly walked in Joe's direction, pausing only long enough to draw him a Coke. She placed it before him with a napkin and leaned on the bar.

"Couldn't keep away, huh?"

"Don't I wish," he said, taking a sip.

She pushed out her lips slightly. "Interesting answer. Could go either way."

He laughed. "No, no. Don't take me wrong. I'd love to be back here for pleasure only."

"That would suit me, too."

Even with the kiss she'd given him last time, her response came as a surprise and made him blush. Sammie Martens had asked if he wanted company on the trip, and he'd turned her down, citing the enormous workload confronting them all. That was true enough, but he knew in his heart that efficiency had played no role in his wanting to travel alone.

And now that he was here, that knowledge was making him feel awkward.

Nevertheless, he heard himself say, "You on a full shift tonight?"

She nodded slowly, watching him carefully. "Yup. What were you thinking of?"

He smiled, hot and uncomfortable. "Just a question. I know you don't like me acting like a cop in here."

She raised an eyebrow. "That what you want to do? Act like a cop?"

He knew she was enjoying herself—self-confident behind her bar—which had the funny effect of lessening his embarrassment. In that way, he started feeling he could trust her, regardless of where this led. Which was comforting, given his own confusion.

"I have a photograph to show you. It might be the guy who asked you about Pete Shea."

"Norman," she reminded him.

"Right—Norman."

But he didn't pull the picture from his pocket.

"I could save this till later," he said instead, still torn.

"Another late-night rendezvous by the water, with lobster roll and milkshake?" she asked, teasing again. "What would people say?"

He took another sip, grateful for the cold coursing down

his throat. He wiped his mouth with the napkin and conceded, "You're right. Bad idea."

"No," she said, suddenly looking quite sad. "Just a badly
timed one—for you, I think."

"That obvious?" he asked.

She merely looked at him kindly.

His gaze dropped to the polished bar between them.

"Show me the picture," she said gently, the regret in her
voice a combination of empathy and support.

Reluctantly, thrown off by how at odds he felt, Joe did as
she requested, and placed the photograph of the man with
the mustache before her.

She looked at it for a long time before saying, "That's
him."

"No doubts?"

She gave him a funny half smile. "I'm as sure of that as I
am of never seeing you again."

He studied her face, using it as a mirror to better see his
own inner turmoil finally settling down.

"You're very good at this," he told her.

"I've had a lot of experience."

He collected the photograph, slid off his stool, and gave
her hand a quick squeeze. "Well, thank you for sharing it
with me."

She nodded. "It was a real pleasure. Take care of yourself."

Chapter 19

Alvah Jordan was Putney's town constable, a position considered by some in law enforcement to be the very first rung—or the lowest, depending on your prejudice—on the profession's ladder. An ancient role, dating back to Vermont's birth, it had fallen on hard times with the passing years. Most every town had one, and sometimes more, but the job ran the gamut from truly fulfilling a police function, as when the next closest officer of any stripe was more than half an hour away, to merely being a post the selectmen were forced to fill. In one of the latter such towns, the constable had actually been bedridden for four years before being replaced, with virtually no one the wiser.

Jordan fell between the extremes, as did most of his fellows. He took care of animal complaints and minor neighbor disputes and generally handled items of little or no interest to the sheriff, who was therefore only too happy to pass them along. This was an arrangement of unspoken mutual consent, because, in fact, Alvah Jordan had made the effort to become a certified part-time police officer, complete with a week's training at the academy in Pittsford, many hours of continuing education, and some field training alongside a designated deputy sheriff. The town hadn't required this of him, although some did of their constables. He'd taken the extra step because he'd thought it the right thing to do. That kind of thinking had pretty much directed him throughout his life.

And his life so far had been full and satisfying. He was married, had four kids and three grandchildren, and owned his own house, a dump truck, a pickup with a plow, and a backhoe, the last three of which he put to creative use to generate income. He was, like many Vermonters, a man given to solving problems—his own and those of his many customers—with a combination of common sense, hard work, good humor, and an instinctive rapport with mechanical objects.

Tonight, however, that good humor was being tested. On the sliding scale of regular calls, noise complaints were his least favorite, perhaps because, in most cases, the complainant rarely bothered telephoning the offender—whom he might not even know, much less dislike—preferring to use the constable as an ax handle instead. That bothered Alvah Jordan. He approached life directly and would never have asked someone else to act on his behalf, especially over so trivial a matter. Nevertheless, as often in the past, he'd left his family again tonight to do the bidding of others.

Perhaps it was time to think of retirement.

He pulled up the dirt driveway of the address he'd been given, killed his engine, and stepped out of the car. It was now full into fall, the leaves were turning, and the earth smelled of moisture and decomposition. The chill in the night air foretold winter poised on the threshold.

Alvah hitched the gun he always carried on calls to a more comfortable position. He wasn't in uniform. It wasn't that formal a job. And the gun's holster was a clip-on model, so he could take it off as soon as he was done. Many constables didn't even carry them, but he figured he ought to, as a matter of form.

Closing his truck door gently, he grudgingly had to admit that at least this time, the complaint had merit. The music throbbing from the small house ahead of him was loud enough to fill the surrounding woods, and certainly the neighborhood up and down the road. Why did people think their favorite pastimes should be community property?

He stepped up under the porch light and pounded on the door.

Blessedly, the music died down almost instantly, footsteps approached, and the door swung back to reveal a man of medium height with brown hair and a mustache.

"Yes?" he asked pleasantly enough.

"Sorry to bother. I'm Alvah Jordan, the town constable. Could I have your name?"

"Gabe Greenberg. What's the problem?"

"I received a complaint about the noise and have to ask you to keep it down."

The man smiled regretfully. "I should have known. I am sorry. I was in a good mood, felt like celebrating a little, and got carried away. Living out here, I kind of forget there're other people around, you know? Am I in any trouble?"

"Not if you don't do it again."

Greenberg put his left hand on his chest in a gesture of contrition. "I promise. And tell whoever complained that I'm really sorry."

It was the scar that did it, deep and vivid and running down the back of the man's hand. Jordan prided himself on being a part, however small, of the law enforcement community, and so kept up with the bulletins and alerts that regularly made the rounds. Days ago, he'd received a BOL e-mail, a so-called be-on-the-lookout, featuring a man with brown hair and a mustache who was wanted for questioning in a homicide. The photograph hadn't been great, and the guy had looked pretty ordinary. But the BOL had stressed both the scar and the man's left-handedness.

Jordan knew instinctively that he was staring at the one they were after.

Unfortunately, Gabe Greenberg noticed Jordan's interest. His eyes narrowing slightly but with his voice still light, he waggled the hand before him. "Nasty-looking, isn't it? I suppose I should get some plastic surgery or something. I've just had it so long, I don't hardly notice it anymore."

Jordan stepped back, intent on getting to a phone as fast as he could. "Didn't mean to offend. Well, I'll leave you be."

Greenberg also moved, following Jordan out onto the front stoop. His voice was less upbeat as he said, "Most people ask me how I got it."

"I figure that's your business."

"I don't mind. It was a dog bite, when I was a kid."

Jordan nodded, still backing away. "Tough."

Greenberg kept coming. "Yeah. My dad sicced him onto me."

"Don't say?"

"You seem a little nervous, Constable. You know something I don't?"

It was one of those critical moments, usually missed, which—if you survive—you forever refer to as a miracle. Alvah Jordan's plan A of heading for a phone was clearly over. Plan B was to try to save his hide and live with the embarrassment of possibly being wrong.

Without another word, on instinct alone, he threw himself at Greenberg.

That timing saved his life. As Jordan suddenly closed in, Greenberg was drawing a knife from the back of his belt, but by the time he'd swung it around to use it, he was already off balance, and Jordan had inadvertently blocked the blow with his body.

Both men careened backward, smacking against the door frame. Greenberg's head made contact with an audible crack, distracting him long enough for Jordan to pull his gun free and use it as a hammer on the other man's left wrist.

Greenberg let out a yell of pain, the knife fell to the ground, and Jordan completed his string of lucky breaks by bringing his knee up sharply into his adversary's groin. As astonished as if he'd just been watching the past three seconds on video, Alvah Jordan saw Greenberg crumple up and collapse, both hands on his testicles.

After a moment's stunned hesitation, he bent over, quickly removed Greenberg's belt, rolled him onto his face, and strapped his wrists together, checking to make sure the knife was out of reach.

Then he stood, already shaking with adrenaline, and asked as calmly as he could, "You have a phone I could use?"

Greenberg's only response was, "A fucking constable—Jesus."

The VBI was still threadbare enough that it depended on sister agencies for everything from copiers to jail cells. Gunther's official bailiwick extended solely to the one office with four desks, and all across the state the situation was roughly the same. Personally, he didn't mind it. It heightened his own sales message that VBI was a support team to every other cop out there. There were moments, however, when the level of dependence stretched credibility. One hour after local constable Jordan had arrested Gabe Greenberg, Joe was watching what was technically his prisoner through the one-way mirror of the Brattleboro police department's tiny interrogation room—marking the first time anyone from the VBI had even heard of this latest development in their very own investigation.

Ron Klesczewski stood beside Joe, watching the man sitting alone and now properly handcuffed, next to a rickety card table.

"How's he been acting?" Joe asked.

"Pretty much like now: cool and calm. He asked to see a lawyer once, and he's been a clam ever since."

"You run him through the system?"

Ron handed him a thin file. "He exists. That's about all you can say. He's either been very careful or very lucky."

Joe noticed the touch of doubt in his former subordinate's voice. "Or he's innocent."

Ron looked at him. "Is that possible? Does make you wonder."

But Joe had only been playing devil's advocate. "I don't think so. The bartender in Gloucester had no doubts, we have the pictures from Tunbridge, and he did go for the constable, from what I hear. That's enough for a warrant. Once we tear his house apart, we'll probably get more. If we're really lucky, we'll even match his knife to the wounds and/or blood types of both Shriver and Shea." He stopped, ran all that through his mind once more, and added, "I'm betting this is the guy."

It was an odd sensation, despite his having watched hundreds of other suspects through similar windows over a lifelong career. Looking at this nondescript man, he felt an emotional pulling in his chest connecting Greenberg to his own entire past history.

"You going to talk to him?" Ron asked.

Joe hesitated. The temptation was great, even if the likelihood was slim that it would yield anything.

"You have, right?" he asked Ron.

"Yeah."

"What did you think?"

Ron pursed his lips. He didn't enjoy being put on the spot. He was a detail man, devoted to reports and analyses. But he knew what Joe was after, and owed him a response. "I think he's guilty as hell and not about to say a word, no matter what you lay on him."

Joe waved the file in his hand. "So, when I do, it better weigh more than this." He left the tiny viewing cubicle and stepped into the hallway outside, adding, "Let's feed him his lawyer, lock him up, and do some homework."

Joe slipped his arm behind Gail's bare shoulders and cradled her more comfortably against his chest. She let out a contented sigh and placed her hand on his stomach.

"I like coming over to your place," she murmured.

"Too crazy at home?"

"Too crazy, too big, too empty or too full, depending. It's gotten to be like an office. Not a place to escape."

"How's it coming? Katz told me you should consider making some room in the fridge for champagne."

She laughed, making his chest tickle. "What a bullshitter. Bet he hoped that would open you up. What did you tell him?"

" 'Nice try,' I think. He let it go. Not the persistent mutt he used to be."

"I hope he's right," she said reflectively, "but I have my doubts. I still haven't connected with so many people—the truck drivers and farmers and regular working stiffs. Sometimes it feels like they all see me as a threat, not realizing I'm more in their corner than Parker'll ever be. But he plasters the county with all those signs and ads and waves around all that red-white-and-blue crap, pretending that if you're pro-choice or against war you're anti-American, anti-Christ, and anti–everything else. I end up looking like Fidel Castro, when the first thing he'll do is come down on every program we've got for the poor and the working class, and try to gut the economy, pushing for sweetheart deals with big business—anonymous Tom Bander megamoguls nobody knows anything about."

"Whoa," Joe told her, patting her shoulder. "I'll vote for you—promise." But what she was saying cut straight to something he'd learned late this afternoon, and which had been preying on him ever since.

"Sorry," she said. "But I'm really getting nervous about him. I don't think people realize just how powerful Bander could be. Charbonneau is just a grab-ass happy boy with too much cash. According to Susan, Bander's got connections everywhere, and he's completely untouchable—never run for office, no publicly traded businesses, and he has a bunch of flunkies standing in for him on every occasion. He's like a woodchuck Howard Hughes. I just have this awful feeling that come election day, all the headway we've been making in this county for the past couple of decades will be suddenly walking the plank. Bander and his types will come out of the woodwork big-time."

It was against every rule, but Joe couldn't not share what was so much on his mind, even if he did think Gail's comments were approaching paranoia. "I may have an extra monkey wrench to add to that."

She lifted her head to look at him. "Joe, what's wrong?"

"I'm not supposed to tell you this, especially given that you're running for office, but I don't feel I really have a choice: the guy they just caught—Gabe Greenberg? The one in the news, who killed Hannah Shriver? He works for Bander."

Gail sat up, her eyes wide. "What?"

"We searched his house. In fact, we're still processing what we collected—it'll take days—but the connection to Bander is solid. Canceled checks, phone records, a bunch of stuff."

"What does he do for him?" She was clearly stunned by what he was saying.

"We're still piecing that together. He's lawyered up, and we haven't wanted to talk to Bander yet. I just thought you ought to know—political ramifications and all."

He watched her. She made an incongruous picture, the thoughtful strategist figuring the angles while completely naked. He felt suddenly more sentimental toward her than he had in months.

Gail and he had worked so hard to establish such an unlikely relationship that he hadn't noticed the simple truth: that theirs was a union unusual only on the outside. In fact, they *were* a pretty conventional couple, and they did make allowances for each other all the time. He'd been wrestling for some elusive answer to his recent discomfort, naively equating his loss of Ellen to losing Gail to politics, selling short in the process that since Gail was still alive, so was their love for each other. In itself, a new job wasn't going to end that—although any number of emotional missteps based on that assumption well might.

Gail finally gave a small shiver and slid down next to him again, pulling the sheet up over them. "No shit, political ramifications. I guess I can't worry about it, though—not officially, anyhow. Do many people know about this?"

"No, but it's bound to get out."

"This'll sound pretty bad, so I apologize beforehand, but do you think that'll be before the election?"

He couldn't repress a laugh. "That is pretty bad. I don't have the slightest idea, but if you're the one to leak it, it could come back to bite you."

She sounded grim. "I'm not sure I have much to lose. There're a lot of people out there already blaming me for everything bad, including the weather." She added, as if to pacify a protest he hadn't even uttered, "I know, I know. You've stuck your neck out a mile. I won't even tell Susan about this. But, Christ, what a potential bombshell. Can you imagine?"

"From Greenberg to Bander to Ed Parker?" Joe suggested.

She straightened again to stare at him. "You saying that's true?"

He pulled her gently back down. "No, not that I'm aware of. I was just floating a possibility. But keep in mind that Greenberg surfaced just as Bander was throwing all his weight behind Parker for what was looking like a shoo-in. One reason I just told you this is because people might turn it around and somehow point the finger at you."

She wrestled free again. "What? That I planted a hit man in their camp to make them look bad? That doesn't make any sense. I already have a snowball's chance in hell of winning this damn thing."

He was amused by her outrage. "I'm just saying it's a loose cannon on a tossing deck. It could injure anyone and everyone. Who knows what's going on here? People do the damnedest things to win elections—or to stop other people from winning them. Assuming this has anything to do with politics. Greenberg may have been acting entirely on his own."

Gail settled down before musing, "This is so bizarre. Normally, I'd just be horrified that someone had murdered somebody else. Now all I can see is how this might affect my chances. I'm starting to wonder what this is doing to me."

Joe briefly returned to his own thoughts along similar lines. For the moment, though, he merely comforted her. "You're fine, Gail; being realistic doesn't diminish your integrity. It's not like you made this happen."

She burrowed in more comfortably, clearly struggling to dismiss the matter for the time being. "Okay," she said in an artificially light tone, "I think I'll just wait and see. Thanks for the heads-up, though."

"Sure," he said, his mind already stretching ahead. He didn't believe for a second that Gabe Greenberg had acted on his own, and he knew for a fact that the present political race was but one aspect of all this. Greenberg was just a button man. The trick was to find out who'd pushed him—and why.

The next morning, Sammie Martens met Joe in the Municipal Building's parking lot as he was getting out of his car. It was cold, but in her enthusiasm, she'd come out in her shirtsleeves only.

"Hey, Sam," he said, collecting paperwork from his passenger seat. "What's up?"

"I couldn't sleep last night, so I did some extra poking

around on the computer, taking a closer look at all the players we have going."

He smiled at her eagerness. "Don't tell me. You found something interesting."

"Laugh all you want, boss. I did a background check on Tom Bander."

Gunther paused. This wasn't what he'd expected. "And?"

She cocked her head slightly to one side. "He changed his name thirty years ago."

Now he straightened to stare at her, his paperwork abandoned.

She continued, "It used to be Ralpher. Sound familiar?"

"Yeah," he said softly, the word forming a thin cloud as it hit the cold air. "T. J. Ralpher—he was Sandy Conant's alibi in the deposition Hannah recorded. The same night Klaus Oberfeldt was beaten into a coma."

Gail's earlier concerns about Tom Bander suddenly came back to him in full force. And he'd thought at the time she was being paranoid.

Chapter 20

Kathy Bartlett was the VBI's prosecutor, attached to the attorney general's office but permanently assigned to the Bureau or, as Kunkle was fond of saying, "for as long as this turkey can fly."

Kunkle wasn't along on the trip Joe took to Montpelier to meet with her, however. Willy wasn't among the VBI assets Gunther liked to trot out for review, especially to a no-nonsense person like Kathy, who'd been dealing with hardheads long enough to have lost all sense of humor about them.

Instead, Joe had brought Lester Spinney. A completely different sort from Willy, both physically and temperamentally, Lester had also once worked as an investigator for the AG right after leaving the state police, and therefore knew Kathy Bartlett personally. There was no particular strategy in having Spinney there, but Joe was of a mind that the larger the number of friendly faces around a table, the better.

All the more so when the topic to be discussed was a political hot potato.

After offering coffee, exchanging pleasantries, and otherwise settling her guests in, Kathy leaned back in her office chair and eyed the two of them watchfully. "So, right now, Mr. Greenberg's under lock and key for assaulting a police officer, possession of a lethal weapon, and other assorted junk, correct?"

"Yes," Joe concurred. "The local SA figured that would hold him in place until a better plan was cooked up."

"Yeah," she dragged out. "I talked to him on the phone. Seemed pretty eager to unload this one. That got my antennae quivering. You got an explanation?"

Spinney and his boss exchanged looks.

"Cute," Bartlett commented. "What've you handed me this time?"

"Right now," Joe answered, "it looks like Greenberg works for Thomas Bander."

"Okay," she said, holding up a finger. "That's money."

"Who's working overtime," Joe added, "to finance Ed Parker's campaign for the senate."

"That's politics." She held up another finger.

"Whose Democratic opponent," he continued, "is Gail Zigman."

Bartlett stared at him in silence for a split second before saying, "That's awkward. And it explains the SA's cold feet, since Gail used to work for him. Big-time conflict."

Spinney smiled and held up a finger of his own. "Don't quit yet."

Joe sighed and explained, "Bander was born T. J. Ralpher, who was a Brattleboro bad boy when I was starting out. I've got a pretty strong notion that Ralpher grubstaked both his name change and his new life with the twelve thousand dollars he stole from a mom-and-pop store after beating pop to death with a pistol."

Kathy's eyes widened. "Jesus Christ, Joe. What the hell is this?"

"I *think*," Joe said, emphasizing the word, "it's two killers and three murders, one of which happened before you left grade school." He removed a file folder from the briefcase he'd arrived with and laid it on her desk. "Those're the basics. I didn't want to send them to you without being here in person."

Bartlett let out a sigh and reached for the file. "How thoughtful."

She flipped it open and leafed through a few pages, getting a feel for its contents. She then glanced at them and said, "It's a pretty day—fall in Vermont. Why don't you two go out and catch the sights for an hour? Let me dip my toe into this mess."

It was a pretty day, the air sharp but not too cold. Kathy's office was directly adjacent to the capitol building and the sloping expanse of slightly weather-beaten grass surrounding it. The bright, cool sun made the capitol's golden dome sparkle like an oversize Christmas ornament, complemented by the bowl of surrounding hills burning with the vibrant hues of a New England fall.

"You gotta admit, it is going to be complicated," Spinney commented as they walked the grounds.

"And that's just on the surface," Joe agreed. "Tack on the possibility that Ed Parker is even vaguely inside the loop, and you've got something with real teeth on it."

"Does Gail know anything about this?" Spinney asked reasonably enough.

This was potentially explosive—pillow talk indiscretions that could end a career. Wisdom and self-preservation dictated silence or evasion right now. As was his style, however, Gunther chose neither. It wasn't the kind of precedent he wished to set, especially with a trusted colleague.

"I gave her a heads-up. She said she'd keep it to herself."

Spinney took the confidence in stride. "I can see that. She must've been surprised."

Gunther remembered the moment in more detail than he would ever share with Lester. " 'Stunned' might be a better word."

When they returned to Kathy Bartlett's office an hour later, they found her standing by her window, looking down on the same scene they'd just left.

She faced them as they entered. "How solid are you on Bander being Ralpher and Ralpher being good for the Oberfeldt thing?"

"Very on the first, still putting it together on the second," Joe told her.

"What about Greenberg?" she asked. "I saw you have the bartender's ID, a gas charge receipt from Gloucester dated the day Shea was killed—presumably as Greenberg was leaving town—the photo of him at the Tunbridge Fair, the witness statements about how Hannah Shriver seemed to be running from him and his pals . . . By the way, any luck rounding them up?"

Spinney answered, having been assigned precisely that. "We've got some names—haven't put our hands on anyone yet, but I think we're close."

"What else?" she asked rhetorically. "How 'bout the knife he was found with?"

"At the lab right now," Joe said.

"And how's he connected to Bander?" she continued, gaining steam. "What was his job?"

Joe glanced at Lester. "Full-time staff," Spinney answered, "complete with health and bennies—listed as head of internal security. His job description, from what we've put together, was to coordinate the security at all of Bander's various enterprises, meaning everything from hiring rent-a-cops to getting buildings wired against break-ins, to running checks on employees. A sort of generalized Mr. Fix-it."

"I bet," Kathy commented. "He have any kind of record?"

"Military background, some fancy training there and a few comments about being prone to violence, but either he kept out of trouble as a civilian or nobody ever caught him."

Bartlett pulled on her earlobe. "Okay," she said. "We've got a mishmash here. I know you think everything's connected, Joe, and I won't argue with that. But right now we have one strong case—Greenberg—which looks like it'll only get stronger, and a second, much older one—Bander/Oberfeldt—that still needs a lot of work. I suggest you look at these two the way I am, and divide and conquer."

"I see what you're saying, Kathy," Joe replied. "But I'm not sure I can nail down the older without cherry-picking from the newer. The connection is Greenberg's motive. I know you guys don't like to mess with that, but I'm almost positive Shriver and Shea—and Katie Clark, for that matter—are all dead because of the Oberfeldt killing. If we only hang Greenberg for Hannah's death, we'll be missing the bigger boat."

"I'm not saying that's what we will do, Joe," she countered. "I'm saying I want at least one guaranteed bird in hand. If we get that, I'm not opposed to casting a wider net. For one thing, I wouldn't mind using Greenberg to roll on Bander."

But Joe wasn't ready to so quickly give second billing to a case that had played such a big role in his life.

"I'd like to get hold of some of Bander's DNA—try matching it to the drops of blood found at the Oberfeldt scene," he said almost stubbornly. "There are ways I could do that without him even knowing it—people leave their DNA all over the place."

Kathy surprised him by turning his proposal around, a good example of her practical thinking. "All right, then, try this on: If you go after his DNA, don't go sneaking for it—hit him straight on. All you need is reasonable suspicion for a judge to sign for it. You pull that off, it might put a little extra heat under him from an unexpected quarter. Trick is, you have to satisfy that judge. Can you do it?"

Joe had been pondering the same problem, and hoped he'd come up with a possibility. "I think so."

"Good luck on getting Greenberg to talk, much less roll over on anybody," Lester commented, still on Kathy's first topic of interest. "So far, he hasn't said a peep."

"I wouldn't have, either," she agreed. "His lawyer's probably told him to sit tight and wait to see what we'll spring. What I'd like to do, assuming we get enough ammunition, is to threaten him with the death penalty and then bargain down."

Gunther and Spinney didn't immediately respond. Vermont had no such penalty, nor did Massachusetts for the moment.

"You want to go federal?" Joe asked.

Kathy smiled. "Maybe. Mostly I want his lawyer to know we've got the urge and the ability. If I and the Massachusetts DA and someone from the U.S. attorney's office all show up to that first meeting together, the message should be pretty clear."

"Does that mean we build our case using federal rules?" Lester asked. The question had merit, since the feds allowed for much broader latitude with rules of procedure.

But Kathy looked at him sharply. "I'm only threatening federal. No cutting corners here, okay?"

Both cops nodded in response.

"Good," she concluded, pushing herself away from the window ledge she'd been leaning against. "Go round up some ammunition."

"That sounded pretty good," Spinney said later in the car, clearly sounding out his silent boss.

"Yeah."

Spinney hesitated, pretending to watch the multihued panorama of trees painted across the string of low mountains of the valley they were traveling.

"You want us to do a full-court press on Shriver, then? Nail that down so Kathy can use it to squeeze Greenberg?"

"Yup."

Lester nodded to himself. "Right. Like she said, better that than digging around ancient history."

Gunther remained silent.

"Or maybe not?" his partner suggested.

Joe blinked a couple of times, as if trying to pay attention. "No, that's right. That's what you should do."

Spinney smiled. "While *you* dig into ancient history."

Joe cast Lester a rueful look. "Yeah."

The younger man smiled. "I thought so. Could I ask you a personal question?"

"Sure. You can ask."

"This is like a private thing, right? The whole who-killed-Oberfeldt deal."

Gunther didn't answer at first, and Lester thought for a moment that he wouldn't, that it ran too deep.

He was wrong.

"You know my wife died while I was chasing that case?"

"I'd heard that," Spinney said cautiously. In fact, he'd heard Willy ranting that Joe had become a "fuckin' Ahab" on the matter.

"That was a bad time," Joe continued. "I was earning my spurs as an investigator, coping with my wife's cancer, struggling to do my best as a cop and a husband, and feeling like I was failing at both." He paused, as if witnessing it all over again. "And I did fail. Maria Oberfeldt told me so."

Lester opened his mouth to ask the obvious question. He wasn't up to speed on the Oberfeldt case.

"The wife," Joe explained, cutting him off. "She rode us like a tyrant while her own husband was dying down the hall from where Ellen was doing the same thing. She'd call, drop by the PD, even bushwhack me in the hospital corridor."

"Jesus," Spinney muttered. "That's pretty tasteless. Didn't she know what you were going through?"

Joe nodded, but only with sympathy. "Sure she did. All the better, as far as she was concerned. I more than anyone should have shared her pain."

"I don't see *that*."

"I did," Gunther told him. "I did then and I do now. We were both on a death watch, but where cancer was killing my spouse, she didn't know who'd killed hers. It wasn't fair, and it was up to me to level the playing field."

Spinney's response was gently put. "Isn't that being a little unrealistic? On both your parts?"

Gunther thought about that for a moment before admitting, "That *was* our reality. I doubt either one of us was ever able to let go of it."

A mile fled under the car's wheels before Lester suggested, "So, you'll be trying to connect Bander to Oberfeldt while the rest of us go after Greenberg."

"Yeah."

Chapter 21

Kathy Bartlett had asked Joe if he had anything against Tom Bander—born T. J. Ralpher—beyond his past history as a bad boy and the fact that his rags-to-riches story had been born following Klaus Oberfeldt's death. Instinctively, he thought he did, and that it also connected the past with the present. But his hoped-for evidence, unlike Poe's in "The Purloined Letter," wasn't hidden in plain sight. If he was correct, it was the only thing actually missing from plain sight.

Upon returning to the VBI office that afternoon, he called the one contact he had in an arcane and much misunderstood profession.

"Court Reporters Associates," the woman answered on the other end.

"Hi. This is Joe Gunther, of the Vermont Bureau of Investigation. Is Penny Johnson there?"

Court Reporters Associates was a well-known Burlington-based firm with employees who worked all over the state. Joe's knowledge of them had been peripheral at best until he'd met the current owner, Penny Johnson, at a party thrown by the Windham County state's attorney several years back. For some reason, they'd both ended up in the same corner of the room and had passed the time trading résumés. It was a habit he'd practiced for as long as he could recall, and one he was blessing right now.

"Joe, how are you?" Penny's voice eventually said on the phone. "It's been quite a while."

"We haven't been wallflowers together in quite a while. Guess we both need to get out more."

She laughed. "After my average workday, the closest thing I want to see to a human being is on TV. What can I do for you?"

"I have some questions about your profession, actually. During a search recently, we came across some old . . . I don't know what you call them . . . the things that come out the end of your steno machines."

"Paper tapes," she said. "Is it indiscreet to ask who typed them?"

"Someone named Hannah Shriver."

"Oh." A shocked silence followed her reaction.

"Did you know her?" Joe asked, hardly believing his luck.

"No," was the slightly stammered reply. "But I read the papers, Joe. She was the poor woman killed at the fair, wasn't she?"

"Yes," he said, disappointed.

"And she was a court reporter?"

"Used to be, over thirty years ago. That's how far back these tapes go."

"Oh," Penny repeated, but this time he could hear the relief in her voice, as if by placing Hannah in a time long past, he'd also put her at a safe distance.

"I wanted to ask you how those tapes are produced," Gunther continued. "They're completely verbatim, right? Word for word?"

"That's correct."

"Just like the typed transcription that follows? Every 'ah' and 'um' included?"

"Every one, yes, painful as it is to read sometimes."

"So," he surmised, "if the typist chose to leave something out of the tape, then there's no one who would know it had ever been said, unless they were asked to recall the conversation from memory."

"No," she said.

Joe was taken aback. "No, what?"

"No, she wouldn't leave anything out. It doesn't work that way, Joe. It's not like taking minutes at a meeting, where you select the relevant parts. We're on autopilot, sometimes typing two hundred and sixty words a minute. Our fingers bypass our brains, in a way, and connect only to our ears. It's so much that way that sometimes I can actually daydream while I'm typing. It would be a real feat to interrupt that flow and start picking and choosing what to write down. In fact, I'm not sure it's even possible. I certainly couldn't do it."

Joe furrowed his brow, thinking of alternatives. "The same typist writes the transcription?"

"Yes, especially back then. Now, with computers, it's a little different, but if you weren't exaggerating about the time frame, then the whole process was very personalized, especially in how the tape reads. Each reporter had her own way of doing things."

"I thought it was basically shorthand," he said. "Once you know how to decipher it, it's like reading a regular language."

She sounded embarrassed. "Well, yes and no. We all come up with our own shortcuts, and they sometimes get pretty hard for other people to figure out."

"Meaning you might not be able to translate what's on a tape?" He couldn't keep the disappointment from his voice.

"It could be difficult," she admitted apologetically. "Although certainly feasible. It would just take a long time. Where was she trained?"

"Hang on," Joe said, and pawed through the files on his desk. "Champlain College," he finally announced, holding a sheet of paper before him.

"Oh, that's great," Penny said, relieved. "My old school. We probably know the same tricks. That'll help a lot. I'm assuming you want me to try to read her tape?"

"Would you mind?"

"Not at all. It will take a while, though, like I said. It's not the same as in the movies. It's more like solving a jigsaw puzzle without the box top."

"I have the transcription," he said hopefully.

"That'll help."

"And I even know the exact place I'm curious about."

Her reaction dispelled all his earlier concerns. "Oh, good Lord. Well, then, I should be able to do something pretty quickly. When can you get it to me?"

"Today," he answered. "By courier."

The ringing phone dragged him out of a deep sleep, making him wonder at first where he was. His dreams, as so often lately, had been of ancient history, while the faces populating them were from everywhere and every time.

"Hello?" he asked sleepily, automatically checking the clock by his bedside. In fact, it wasn't that late. He'd just gone to bed far earlier than usual, yielding to a weariness that he'd been staving off for days.

He half hoped it would be Gail again, maybe even calling from his driveway.

It was not.

"Joe? It's Katz. You sleeping?"

"Trick question, right? What do you want?"

"A statement. We're going with a story that VBI is investigating Tom Bander for murder."

Gunther sat up. "What? That's bullshit."

"On the record?"

"Whoa. No. Just a minute. Jesus Christ, Stan. What kind of high school stunt is this?"

"I didn't think you'd be asleep," Katz said defensively.

"So you call me three seconds before press time? Give me a break. This is an ambush."

"So," Katz drawled, "no comment, is it?"

"Up yours. Tell me what fantasy you and your *Deformer* crew have cooked up this time."

"I have a solid source telling me you guys are after Tom Bander. You denying that?"

"You said we were investigating him for murder. If that's your story, it's a bald-faced lie."

Katz was enjoying himself. "Interesting answer. Very precise. So, maybe not for murder, but you are chasing him for something."

"Good night, Stanley."

"No, no. Wait, Joe. Don't hang up. I'll tell you what I got. You arrested a man named Gabriel Greenberg for the murder of Hannah Shriver."

"That's public record," Joe said, feeling his face warm with anger. Couldn't keep a lid on a goddamn thing around here.

"The same Gabriel Greenberg who works for Tom Bander."

Joe remained silent. He had no idea how Katz was getting his information. So far, none of this was the deep, dark, secret stuff being shared among investigators, for which he was grateful. That probably meant Stan was just making good use of his standard contacts inside the PD.

"Right?" Katz insisted.

"You asking?"

"No, I'm not asking. I'm looking for a confirmation."

"No comment."

"All right, fine," Katz said heatedly. "Fuck you, too. We're going with this, Joe, whether you comment or not."

"Going with what, Stanley? You haven't told me anything, yet."

"That you busted one of Bander's employees for murder and that you're tearing into all of their backgrounds."

Joe began feeling slightly better. "That's it? How do you go from there to our going after Bander for murder?"

He could hear the reporter sigh with exasperation before Katz asked, "How's Gail taking the news?"

Gunther didn't answer.

Katz perked up. "Uh-oh. Hit a chord?"

"Stanley, you are such a jerk. I haven't talked to her about this. I have no idea how she's taking it."

"You're kidding. Bander is Parker's money bag—the power behind the throne. If he gets mired in this shit, Parker can kiss his ass good-bye."

In Joe's continued silence, Katz followed that with, "Come to think of it, that could get Gail in trouble, too. I mean, here you are, busting the guy who's backing her opponent and all but giving her an election she would've been hard-pressed to win otherwise. Talk about a conflict. Wow. You have any thoughts on that?"

Gunther hung up the phone.

At home the next morning, at about the time he imagined the first papers were being delivered, Joe got a call from Susan Raffner. Her opening line substituted for any conventional greeting.

"What the hell were you thinking, talking to that asshole? I thought at least you were a professional."

Gunther hesitated, struck by his own forbearance. There was a time when he would have let her have it right back. Now he was surprised how little impact such words delivered.

"Good morning to you, too, Susan."

"To hell with that. I am royally pissed off at you, Joe. You sleep with this woman, goddamn it. The least you could've done was make a phone call."

"Is this making you feel better?"

"You think this is a joke?"

Again Gunther hung up the phone, this time hearing the tinny voice struggling out of the earpiece all the way down until he severed the connection.

Clearly, he needed to read the paper—and leave his house.

In fact, Katz's article didn't say much. It mentioned names, drew a few vague connections, and made much ado about the senate race and the fact that the VBI wasn't talking, as if that implied a Watergate-size scandal in the making. Joe was unhappy to see a passing reference connecting him to Gail, but he had to admit that only the context was painful. Their relationship was widely known. The bottom line, as he interpreted it, was that the article was as harmless for the cops as it was clearly explosive politically. For that, he felt sorry for Gail. She and Parker and Bander were going to be grilled in the media, and it wouldn't just be local. But for the short run, he could most likely remain safe behind a barricade of "no comments."

Thus comforted, he was prepared for the reactions he got on entering the basement command center. He waved his hand placidly at the few alarmed or angry faces bearing outrage at a so-called renegade press, and issued a couple of the verbal bromides he'd been telling himself during the car trip over here. No big deal. Just keep on track.

Seeing Willy Kunkle approaching fast, however, as he was setting his coffee on his desk, made him brace for the worst. Willy placed a faxed report beside the coffee mug. "I always knew sleeping with her would get you in trouble," he said.

"Very tasteful, Willy. What're you doing up so early?"

"Thought I'd bring you a little good news to balance the bad," he said.

"Oh, yeah?" Joe picked up the fax.

"Yup. The lab matched not one but two samples of blood on Greenberg's hunting knife. They extracted them from where the blade meets the guard and at the bottom of the 'Made in USA' stamp at the base. Looking at it with the naked eye, you couldn't see a thing."

Joe stared at him, a smile slowly spreading across his face. "You going to tell me, or do I have to read it?"

Willy waggled his eyebrows. "Perfect matches to both Shriver and Shea. I love it when bad guys don't ditch their toys."

Chapter 22

Joe Gunther pulled into a parking space and shivered slightly as both he and Kathy Bartlett emerged into the crisp fall air from their heated car. "You know what Harvey drives?" he asked, looking around the lot.

"No clue," she said grumpily, turning up her collar. Dan Harvey was her federal counterpart from the U.S. attorney's office in Burlington, and one of the two people they were hooking up with before meeting with Gabe Greenberg. The other was someone from Massachusetts neither of them knew, a Nick Kennedy, from the Essex County DA's office.

Having gotten directions earlier on how to proceed, Joe set out for a small gate cut into the chain-link fence.

This was not the entrance most visitors used. It was more discreet, and out of sight of the prison's general population. Meetings between inmates and prosecutors were not something the former liked witnessed by their brethren—it was an excellent way to be labeled a snitch and earn a proper pounding at the first opportunity. As a result, the Joe Gunthers of this world and their lawyerly associates had long ago opted for having such conversations off-site. Kathy didn't need her bargaining sessions hindered by the man opposite her checking over his shoulder every five minutes.

The brand-new Springfield facility had been built with that in mind, however, allowing her and Joe to enter and depart without undue notice. The decision to meet here, though, had been largely because of Harvey—he had the farthest to travel and the tightest schedule and, if things worked out, would have the least to do.

They met with both Harvey and Kennedy ten minutes later, after negotiating the prison's security, and then filed as a group into a closed, featureless room where Gabe Greenberg and his lawyer, a thin young man with a permanent scowl, named Randy Nichols, were already waiting.

Nichols smirked as they milled about taking off their coats, opening their briefcases, and choosing seats.

"No choir to back you up?" he asked.

Kathy Bartlett ignored him, making introductions instead. "Okay, Mr. Nichols," she finally said, "wisecracks aside, we're here both at your request and to show you that we're not blowing smoke up your skirt. The States of Massachusetts and Vermont and the federal government are all on board with a death penalty case here, so what you're offering had better be good. We're ready to go to trial right now with what we've got."

Greenberg was sitting back in his chair, as unruffled as ever, looking like a bored accountant, despite the nature of Kathy's comments. By contrast, Nichols leaned his elbows on the table, his expression darkening. "I want assurances that the death penalty not only disappears, but that the whole federal route does, too." He pointed at Harvey and Kennedy in turn. "This becomes a Vermont case only."

Kathy smiled, not bothering to glance at the other two

attorneys, having anticipated this demand earlier. "Any deal depends on what you tell Special Agent Gunther here. You ready for that conversation?"

Greenberg stirred himself enough to whisper into Nichols's ear.

"All right," the attorney conceded.

"Great," Kathy said brightly, rising to her feet, as did the mute Harvey and Kennedy. "We'll be outside."

Joe waited until the three of them had filed out so he could begin the next phase of the minuet. Absurd as it sounded, just as it was necessary for all three legal entities to be present today, it was just as important that none of them fall into the trap of becoming a defense witness because of anything Greenberg might reveal in person. The job of listening to Greenberg fell to Joe alone.

"What've you got, Gabe?" he asked after the door had closed.

Greenberg didn't mince words or waste time. "I did Shriver and the guy in Gloucester on orders from Tom Bander."

Joe kept his voice flat. "How and when did this happen?"

But Greenberg demurred. "That's it. You want more— which I have—I want assurances from the three kings out there."

Joe frowned. A lifetime of dealing with such people had still not immunized him from the outrage he felt at their behavior. That sense of double entitlement—allowing them to kill and then manipulate the system—still infuriated him. "What about Katie Clark?" he asked, exacting a surprised look from Nichols, who clearly hadn't heard the name before.

Greenberg stared at him long enough for Joe to see the

cold-bloodedness behind the man's bland exterior. "Never heard of her."

Reluctantly, Joe pushed his chair back. He didn't believe that for a moment, but he could clearly do nothing about it. His irritation, however, did prompt him to ask, "I don't suppose Bander told you why he wanted them dead?"

It was a long shot, not one he thought would stimulate a response, so he was halfway to his feet when Greenberg answered, "He said they had the goods on him for a job he'd pulled when he was starting out—a store robbery where some old guy died."

Joe stared at him, the shadowy figure of Tom Bander finally secured to a reality that made some sense. All this time the man had floated by in conversations with the substance of smoke. Now, at last, he had a pedigree Joe could grab hold of, straight from the proverbial horse's mouth.

"Did that come as a surprise?" he asked on impulse. "That your boss had that kind of background?"

Nichols looked confused while Greenberg merely seemed amused. "He's a businessman," he said. "Of course he's a crook."

That was too pat—and explained nothing. Joe straightened, moved toward the door, and tried again. "Did he say he was the one who killed the store owner?

"Not in so many words."

Joe nodded. Naturally. He grabbed the doorknob and said, "Okay. Be right back."

In the outer room, the three attorneys faced him as he entered.

"He deal?" Kathy asked.

Joe nodded, still torn by his conflicting emotions. Greenberg's parting words had fulfilled all of Gunther's needs. To

secure a nontestimonial court order for a DNA sample, all
that was needed was something called "an articulable suspicion" that a crime had been committed. What Joe had
now was in the suburbs of probable cause—far sturdier
ground and a reason for true celebration. Except that now
that he was closing in at last on his own personal Holy
Grail, he had to wonder what might happen next.

"Yup," he told her. "He's giving up Bander, complete with
motive."

Thomas Bander lived outside Brattleboro in an upscale
neighborhood called Hillwinds. For the most part, the
houses here hovered between upper middle class and the
slumming wealthy, depending on whether the section was
freshly developed or dated back twenty years, since Hillwinds continued to spread slowly like a living ink blot. Not
surprisingly, Bander's house was off the beaten path, up a
long driveway, and secure behind a stone wall and an iron
fence—unusual affectations for an area that prided itself on
being neighborly, if slightly a cut above.

In a roundabout fashion, the trip here had taken several
days, even though, as the crow flies, the VBI office was
barely ten miles distant. That was testimony to the lawyer's
art, since the delay was due entirely to that.

Getting the nontestimonial court order had been as simple as expected. Getting Bander to comply had involved a
series of grandstanding maneuvers by his attorney, including a press conference in which the police were accused of
hounding a poor innocent man to distraction. As a com-
promise to Bander's delicate disposition, the order was
going to be met, but only discreetly, at his residence, and
would involve only a bare minimum of police officers.

In fact, there had also been a bit of back-and-forth on the

prosecutorial side of the equation. What Greenberg had given Kathy Bartlett was actually enough to generate an arrest warrant for Bander, rather than a mere nontestimonial order. But just barely. As a result, Bartlett was in no mood to let a fish this size strategize after being prematurely slapped with a double murder charge. She far preferred to let him swim while she accumulated as much damning evidence as possible.

By the same token, and to stretch the metaphor, she wasn't beyond giving the line a yank or two to remind Bander of his position. Joe's desire for a DNA sample fit in nicely there. Her earlier proposal, that he not secure the sample surreptitiously, but hit Bander straight on, had now grown to a tactical gambit.

"Jeez," Sammie Martens said as Joe turned the last curve in the long driveway and came within view of the house. "I didn't know places like this even existed in Vermont."

"They exist," Joe told her. "You just can't see them from the road."

"Too bad," she murmured, craning to take it all in.

It was enormous: multistoried, shingle-clad, wrapped in a porch, and crested with beautiful eyebrow windows and complicated woodwork along a vast roofline. It was less than twenty years old—Joe remembered hearing about its construction at the time—but it had been built as an Adirondack throwback, albeit with modern trimmings.

They rolled to a stop by an expanse of porch steps leading up to a huge front door and got out of the car, their shoes crunching on the pea-size stones of the drive.

Joe gestured to Sam to precede him, bowing slightly.

She smiled. "Thank you, sir. It does sort of set a mood, don't it?"

"It do." He smiled back.

The levity died as they reached the top. Across the broad width of the porch the door opened, and Walter Masius III, Tom Bander's lawyer, stood before them in a three-piece suit with his telegenic mane of white hair. An unknown entity to Joe until Bander's appearance in this case, Masius had become its media darling in a scant few days—eloquent, dramatic, charismatic, and eminently quotable. The press had taken him to their hearts.

Sam couldn't stand the man.

"Hey, Counselor," she greeted him. "They let you in, too?"

Masius smiled broadly. "Indeed they did, Agent Martens." He nodded graciously at Joe. "Agent Gunther, how are you today?"

"Impatient. Where is he?"

Masius stepped aside and ushered them in. "Mr. Bander's in the library."

"You sound like the butler," Sam commented.

But Masius was beyond such taunts. He merely gestured down a ballroom-size hallway. The man could afford a thick skin, Gunther thought, his footsteps lost in the softness of thick carpeting. Boston-based, with a who's-who list of shifty, well-heeled clients, Walter Masius hadn't achieved his stardom by being easily riled.

He passed ahead of them about halfway down the hall and opened a tall, carved wooden door to their left. "In here," he said, and again stood aside to let them in.

The room they entered was two stories high, with one wall of leaded-glass windows and the other three lined with solid rows of expensive books. A railed balcony ran above them like a suspended horseshoe. Persian rugs were scattered across the floor, fat leather furniture was gathered in clusters around old-looking lamps and low, claw-footed tables, and by the windows sat a desk, huge as a dry-docked aircraft carrier.

The whole room was as sumptuous as a movie set and looked just as fake. Gunther had no doubt that the entire collection of books had been purchased by an interior decorator and remained untouched by the home's owner.

"Mr. Bander will be right in," Masius purred. "Make yourselves comfortable." He backed out, drawing the door closed as he went.

"Christ," Sam said in a whisper, looking around.

"It's a *My Fair Lady* knockoff," Joe told her. "I've seen it before, only better." He sighed in frustration. "I knew he'd pull this kind of crap—soon as I heard we had to come here to collect. Goddamned theatrics."

Sam watched her boss walk over to the windows and stare out at the vast lawn, its surface flecked with dead leaves, pale and battered by the first frosts of the season. She'd seen him get increasingly tense as the days had crawled by, sitting far from the command post in his upstairs office, poring over files he'd studied a dozen times already. The contrast between that and their own progress downstairs had been palpable, since they'd been successfully strengthening their case against Greenberg with ever-growing piles of evidence, including having located his three colleagues from the Tunbridge Fair. Knowing that they were all involved in a major case was intoxicating, which only made Sam's awareness of Joe's isolation that much more poignant. Several times she'd found excuses to drop by to find out how he was doing, and each time, although he'd pretended to be working, she'd known he'd simply been waiting for today—for the evidence, true, but even more, she sensed, for the opportunity to bring a little peace to his spirit.

A different door, off to one side and designed to blend into the bookcases, opened to reveal the man they'd both seen only in news photos, on TV, and as a scruffy youngster in yellowed mug shots.

Walter Masius was on his heels, still acting like a windup majordomo.

"Mr. Bander, Agents Gunther and Martens."

Seeing his nemesis for the first time in person—a short, pale, unprepossessing man dressed in nondescript clothes— caught Joe unexpectedly. In a way, he'd anticipated something weightier, at least marginally dramatic—someone looking the role ascribed to him.

This was a nobody, a delivery man lost in a mansion, glancing around as if expecting to be thrown out.

Joe knew what Thomas Bander had done, both as T. J. Ralpher and under the guise of legitimate business. He knew that underneath the insipid exterior hid a man capable of ruthless cruelty.

But therein lay the distinction between what Joe had imagined and what faced him now—previously, Bander's evil had been shrouded with a convenient, though fictionalized, personality. Call it the spider of lore at the web's center, calculating, seductive, lethally larger than life—a monster deserving of the damage that Joe had carried around inside him for well over half his years.

But now, in this forgettable, unmemorable, utterly ordinary man, Joe suddenly saw the larger insult of simple amorality. Tom Bander was no dark creature. He was simply an opportunistic parasite.

"You can cut the crap, Masius," Gunther said shortly from across the large room, feeling the heat of pure rage wash over him. "This isn't *Masterpiece Theatre,* and you're not Alistair Cooke. Let's get this done." He waved at his colleague impatiently. "Sam."

Sam looked at him, startled, as she reached into her pocket to extract the small buccal swab kit needed for the sampling. She could count on one hand the times she'd seen Joe angry, always in response to an immediate crisis—never a real burn like this one.

She approached the slight man with Masius. "Mr. Bander? Sorry, but I need to confirm your identity before taking the swab."

Masius spoke for his client. "We attest that this is Thomas Bander, for the record."

"Driver's license," Joe said, still keeping his distance.

"I don't believe that's necessary," Masius stated dismissively. "My client is a well-known member of the community."

Gunther's voice remained hard. "It's a court order, goddamn it. Show her the license."

Masius opened his mouth to respond, but Bander merely extracted his wallet and displayed the ID. Sam peered at the photograph and nodded, handing Masius a copy of the judge's order.

"You want to sit down for this?" she asked Bander.

He smiled slightly. "Will it hurt?"

Joe suddenly broke from his position, crossed the carpeting quickly, and seized Bander by the upper arm as everyone, Sam included, tensed for a violent outburst. Instead, Gunther roughly drew him to a chair and sat him down like a child.

"Open your mouth," he ordered.

"Now, just a minute," Masius objected.

Joe turned on him. "You shut up."

Bander was looking up, from one to the other.

Gunther refocused on him. "Was there something you didn't understand?"

His mouth snapped open.

Sam moved around her boss, quickly slipped on a pair of latex gloves, and extracted the swab from its sealed envelope. The sooner they left, she hoped, the sooner she'd be able to prevent Joe from shooting someone.

"I'm sorry, Agent Gunther," Masius intoned, "But I'm going to have to take this up with your superiors. This is simply not acceptable behavior."

Joe took three fast steps toward him, forcing him to retreat until he bumped into the wall.

"You call anybody you like, Counselor. I don't happen to give a good goddamn. But while I'm here, doing what the law allows, I am not going to put up with your shit. Is that understood?"

"I will not . . . ," the other man began.

"Is that understood?" Gunther shouted, his face two inches from the lawyer's.

Masius paused, swallowed, and finally murmured, "Yes."

Gunther returned to Bander, who was licking his lips following Sam's careful swiping of both his inner cheeks with the buccal swab, which she was now repackaging at high speed.

"And you, *T. J.*," he said, leaning forward and emphasizing Bander's former name, "you better enjoy your last days in this place, 'cause your ass is mine. After all these years getting rich off other people's misery, you're in for some serious payback."

"Okay, boss," Sam said very quietly. "I'm all set."

Gunther nodded and was heading for the door when Masius spoke up again.

Sam didn't hear what he said. Joe whirled around so fast

and shouted, "*Don't*" so loudly, his finger pointed like a sword at the man, that only that one word reverberated around them.

Once again, Masius shut his mouth, his eyes narrow with anger.

Sam and Joe left the room—and the house—in total silence.

Used to weathering a lifetime of male outbursts, Sam made directly for the car, trusting time to settle Joe back down.

But he stayed standing at the bottom of the porch's broad steps for a moment, his head back, seemingly taking in the cold, overcast sky.

She hesitated by the car door, wondering whether to get in and wait, or stay where she was. When Willy acted out, it was so routine and she was so used to it, she rarely gave it a second's thought. It was one of the tricks of their unusual relationship that she had this knack, and thus the ability to keep them going as a couple.

But she was off balance here and unsure of how to behave. She finally decided to do nothing and merely stood stock-still, her hand resting on the car's fender.

As if suddenly losing air from within, Joe dropped his head, slumped his shoulders, and let out a long sigh. He then walked over to the car and brought his fist down on its hood with a crash, leaving a rock-size divot. All without uttering a word.

Sam glanced at the dent along with him for a slow count of five.

"Feel better?" she risked asking.

Almost reluctantly, he brought his eyes up to meet hers. "My hand hurts."

"Bad?"

He flexed his fingers. "No."

She tilted her head inquiringly to one side. "You want to get out of here before they hassle us for trespassing?"

He looked at the huge building with a contemptuous frown. "Right."

She waited until they'd regained the Upper Dummerston Road, off Hillwinds, before commenting, "This case must be taking its toll."

He laughed, to her relief, and admitted, "You noticed that, huh? Good investigator."

"You pick up on the little things," she said. "It's like an art."

He didn't answer for quite a while, his eyes on the road ahead, before adding, "Or a migraine."

"You're not happy about nailing this guy?" she asked.

He mulled that over. "Not really. I mean, I recognize the value of it, but it's too late. It won't repair the damage."

He glanced at her, allowing her a glimpse of unmitigated sadness and loss.

"It's been too long," he added. "And it's cut too deep."

Chapter 23

I finally met Tom Bander," Joe told Gail.

They were sitting opposite each other at the tiny counter that separated Joe's kitchen from the living room, the remains of a meal between them. Acquiescing to the rigors of the campaign and her own lack of time, Gail had let Joe cook dinner. He'd catered to her strict vegetarian habits by making an iceberg salad and glow-in-the-dark macaroni and cheese out of a box, and, much as she hated to admit it, it had been one of the best meals she'd enjoyed in months.

"I went to his house a few days ago," Joe continued, getting up to put the water on for some coffee. "First time I'd ever set eyes on him."

Gail thought she knew what was going on, or hoped she did.

"How was he?"

"Small, quiet. Not a guy to fill a room by just entering it. Not like his lawyer. With all that power and money, the ability to order people killed, he was a nobody."

"Why were you there?"

"To get a DNA sample," he said lightly, lining up the mugs and rooting through the fridge for milk.

She turned that over in her mind, trying to imagine the scene. "Must've been tough, finally meeting him after all this time."

Joe returned to his seat and took her hand in his. "I lost it. I pushed him into a chair, yelled at the lawyer, dented the hood of my car afterward with my fist. I may have put Sammie into therapy."

Gail rubbed his knuckles with her fingertips, in fact happy to hear he'd blown up. "She sleeps with Willy, for God's sake. She's got the hide of a rhino."

He smiled weakly. "Still, I remember seeing my father explode like that when his tractor broke down once, when I was a kid. Scared the hell out of me. I didn't want to talk to him for weeks afterward."

Gail raised her eyebrows. "And Sam's been running away every time she sees you?"

He granted her point. "No. I think I knew at the time it wasn't the tractor he was mad at—maybe that's what scared me. I didn't know what the real reasons were. I just suspected they were there."

"You ever find out?"

"Good Lord, no. My old man was like a sealed chest on those kinds of things. You didn't share your *feelings* with your kids—or anyone else, for that matter. Jesus, that would've really put me into shock."

"But you know what set you off at Bander's," she suggested.

He took his hand back and propped his chin up with it. "Maybe. I'm not so sure. I was there getting the evidence I'm hoping will put him in jail. Should've been a time to rejoice. Instead, I just felt incredibly pissed off at everything he's caused."

Gail pushed for more. "What has he caused, exactly? You've dealt with murderers before. Some of them have put you through the wringer a lot worse than this guy, it seems."

He looked at her, surprise on his face. "Partly, I think that's what got to me—no bluster, no acting out, no nothing. But now I think the bigger part was remembering Katie Clark, sitting in her chair, about as alone and defenseless as you can get. Why kill her? Or Shea or Hannah Shriver, for that matter. It was all so gratuitous. So totally self-serving."

"But not unique," she pushed.

To his credit, he didn't reject this outright. He took it in, turned it around, and finally said, "Maybe, for me, this once it was."

"Because of how it started?"

He nodded. "Maria Oberfeldt. We got to calling her the bat from hell, the way she went after us, day after day, week after week. At first it was a pain—we were doing what we could. We didn't have the resources to do much beyond catch people who were still standing over their victims. When we got the evidence implicating Pete Shea, I thought we'd gotten lucky. But then we never found him. As time went on, I kept dreaming about how I'd be able to put her mind at ease someday, so that she could just sit by her husband's side and pay attention to his dying."

"Like you were doing with Ellen?" Gail asked.

He stopped halfway to the stove, where the kettle was beginning to whistle. His face averted, he ran his hand through his hair before turning off the flame. He stood, staring at the steam pumping out of the spout like a miniature chimney fire. A man lost in a dream.

In the silence, Gail heard a truck rumble by the front of the house.

Finally, he picked up the kettle and poured hot water into both mugs. Instant coffee, naturally.

"I didn't do much for Ellen," he said at last, addressing the mugs. "I wasn't able to do much for anyone, as it turned out."

He spooned in the coffee, added milk and sugar to his, and brought them over to the counter.

"Did I ever tell you what happened to Maria Oberfeldt?" he asked.

"You've never told me much about any of this."

"She left town right after her husband died, which he did when she was at the police station, bugging us yet again. She returned to the hospital, was told that he'd passed, and she left, almost the next day."

He sat down and cradled the mug between his hands. "Two weeks later, she committed suicide. Seventy-four. They'd been married fifty-five years."

He let out a sigh, and she noticed that his eyes were glistening. "We'd both been widowed, almost on the same day. When I heard she'd died so soon after, it felt like being hit all over again."

He paused and took a deep breath. "That day, I told myself I'd never get that close to anyone ever again."

"You're talking about Ellen."

"Yeah."

He pressed his fingertips against his eyes. "The T. J. Ralphers of the world—or whatever they're called—have no clue how far out the ripples go. Maybe it was his total lack of character that made me blow up. Damned if I know."

Gail waited for him to take his time. She thought of how

little she'd understood of all this—not just recently, while she'd been distracted by her political ambitions, but during their whole time together, stretching back years. She'd heard some of it, certainly the broad outline, but without the attention it clearly deserved. Now she felt oddly unbalanced, torn between yielding to her own sentimentality, and the knowledge that what he'd revealed was a statement of fact. He would never get as close to anyone as he'd been to Ellen ever again—and despite the love that he and Gail had nurtured and nursed through the years, that included her.

She had fussed around identifying her own reasons for not committing conventionally to this union, through marriage or at least cohabitation. She'd looked at her upbringing, her own parents' struggles, the rape that had changed her life. But she'd rarely paused to look at him. To some degree, Joe Gunther had just been that lucky catch, the guy who would put up with her eccentricities.

Now, feeling a bit naive, she saw him in more depth—and while she was grateful for his devotion to her, this conversation had left her shaken.

She reached out, took his hand, and kissed it.

Kathy Bartlett's plan not to arrest Tom Bander prematurely was working well. While Walter Masius kept holding press conferences to decry the abuses being heaped on his client—little unconfirmed snippets of which, Joe was pretty certain, Bartlett was making sure got leaked—Bander himself had all but made a prison out of his sumptuous home. In the meantime, Greenberg was still talking, his three colleagues from the Tunbridge Fair had been rounded up and were adding their songs to his, and the Massachusetts State

Police were updating their case daily with new and damning evidence linking Greenberg to the death of Pete Shea.

The only problem with all this momentum was that nothing, aside from Greenberg's word, linked Bander with what Greenberg claimed he'd done on Bander's orders. Greenberg's henchmen had been hired by him, not Bander, and no notes, e-mails, letters, outside witnesses, or phone records could be found tying Bander to Shriver or Shea or to the events leading up to their deaths.

Bartlett's case so far was entirely circumstantial.

Even the DNA Sammie Martens had collected hadn't proved as damning as everyone had hoped it would. Upon hearing that the swab was a perfect match for the drops found in the Oberfeldt store, Masius immediately announced that his client had cut himself upon entering the place earlier that day. According to the lawyer, Oberfeldt himself had even helped T. J. Ralpher to bandage his wound, since he'd felt guilty that a nail protruding from the counter had been to blame for the injury. Masius had almost made it sound as if the two men were friends.

Bartlett brushed the denial aside, but Joe could read between the lines. If this case went to trial, who was to say the jury would be any less swayed by that argument than some people he'd overheard discussing it in the street? Tellingly, one of them had even mentioned the phrase, "the benefit of the doubt."

Which is what made finally getting a phone call from Penny Anderson of the Court Reporters Association such a relief.

"You have any luck?" Joe asked her after a perfunctory exchange of greetings.

"It was harder than I thought," she conceded. "It's a little like deciphering someone else's really bad handwriting."

"But you did get it?"

"Oh, I got it," she said cheerfully. "And I also understand why she wasn't on the job for long, too. She was pretty bad."

Gunther glanced out the window, repressing the urge to yell at the woman to tell him what he wanted to know.

"Anyhow," Penny continued, "you were absolutely right about there being a missing piece, and it was exactly where you said it would be. Guess that's why you're the detective, right?"

"Right."

Penny finally picked up that he wasn't in a chatty mood. "So, I'll fax you a copy of what I transcribed, but would you like a sneak preview now?"

"That would be great."

She laughed. "Thought I'd never ask, right?"

Joe made no response, but he reached out and extracted a copy of the transcribed deposition Hannah had given the lawyer, Mr. Jennings.

"Okay. Here goes. Ready?"

Joe sighed silently. "Yup."

> MR. JENNINGS: We need to know if anyone saw you doing that. Getting your mail.
>
> MR. CONANT: T. J. was there. Came in just as I opened the box.
>
> MR. JENNINGS: Does T. J. have a last name?
>
> MR. CONANT: Sure. Everybody does.
>
> MR. JENNINGS: And what is T. J.'s last name?
>
> MR. CONANT: Ralpher. T. J. Ralpher. I have no clue what the T. J.'s for, so don't bother askin'. But he was a mess that night, so he'd sure as

hell remember seein' me. He had a nosebleed to
beat all. There was blood all over his shirt.

Joe interrupted her. "You're absolutely sure that's what it
says?

"Oh, yes," was the response. "I know you wanted this
done right, so I had one of my colleagues check it as well,
to make double sure." She hesitated a moment and then
asked, "Was that all right? I didn't think to ask."

Joe smiled. "That was perfect. Keep going." In the document before him, all mention of a bloody nose was missing,
which is what made Conant's comment about not talking
less odd than it had first appeared. Clearly, what he'd meant
was that there had been no detailed discussion.

> MR. JENNINGS: Did you and T. J. talk?
> MR. CONANT: Nope. We're not like friends. He
> said hi, I said hi. We live in the same building.
> That's about it. All he said was that I should see
> the other guy. But he could vouch for me. I
> don't know shit about Mitch and that cow he
> calls a wife . . .

"That's good," Joe interrupted. "I got the rest in front of
me. He doesn't mention Ralpher again, does he?"

"No. That's it."

"Penny, you're a peach. Next time I'm in Burlington, dinner's on me—your choice of restaurants."

"I don't know what my husband would say about that."

"He's invited, too. Fax me the whole thing, would you?
And thanks again."

Lester Spinney was writing at his desk across from Joe,

and looked up as Gunther replaced the phone's receiver. "Good news?"

"Not bad," Joe answered, dialing the phone. "David, it's Joe Gunther," he said. "You got a minute?"

David Hawke was the head of the state's crime lab, a man well used to cops calling him out of the blue and disrupting his day.

"Sure," he responded affably. "What's up?"

"Is there any way you can tell if a blood sample originated from a nosebleed?"

"Not from the makeup of the blood itself. Blood is blood, Joe. What're you talking about, specifically?"

"That three-decade-old stuff I've been bugging you about."

"Let me put you on hold so I can retrieve that file."

Joe stared into middle space as he waited. Spinney correctly interpreted the body language. "On hold?"

Gunther nodded.

"What're you after?"

"Remember that doctored deposition? I was just told that the missing section identifies Ralpher as having a nosebleed right after the Oberfeldt beating—and admitting that he got it in a fight."

"I thought Masius said the blood came from a cut hand."

"Exactly. If I can prove otherwise, it not only makes his client a liar but, if Hawke comes through, it'll strengthen my case."

"You still there?" David Hawke asked, back on again.

"Yeah. Go ahead."

"Well, I looked it over again. I don't have anything probative, but there are a couple of details supporting a nosebleed. The first is the blood pattern on the floor. It's consistent with having fallen from a height of about five feet. How tall is your suspect?"

"About five eight. You saying it couldn't have come from a cut hand?"

"A lawyer could argue that your guy left the place with his hand held high, but that would cause the blood to run down his arm. No one I know would walk around that way—they'd stick the hand down and to one side."

"Plus," Joe mentioned, "the lawyer in question is claiming the wound was bandaged before his client left."

"Oh, I doubt that," David said, his voice surprised. "The blood drops are very consistent with a free-flowing cut. And you have the trail he took, out the back door after loitering around the hiding place in the floor."

"They're claiming now he went out the back on the victim's insistence—the old man didn't want anyone scared by a bloody man coming out the front door."

Joe could almost hear Hawke shrugging at the other end of the phone line. "Well, I'll leave that to you. If asked, I'd have to say that whoever was dropping that blood clearly stopped at the hiding place, even if I couldn't swear he actually opened it up."

"Okay," Joe allowed. "What about the second detail you mentioned?"

"Again, nothing to really hang your hat on, but among the samples gathered, there were a couple of tiny hairs as well, consistent with having come from the nose."

"Meaning what?"

"Meaning they're also consistent with being hair from any part of the body, more or less. Obviously, nose hairs are very small and short, and these two fit that bill perfectly, but I could never claim on the stand that that's where they came from—only that they could have."

Gunther nodded to no one in particular. "Okay. I got you. Still, that's good. I owe you one, David. Thanks."

He hung up, his expression thoughtful.

"Home run?" Lester asked.

Joe looked rueful. "Call it a solid single—another one." He sat back in his chair and put his feet up on his desk. "I just wish," he added, "that I could find some rock-solid piece of evidence that Bander couldn't dance away from." He reached out his hand and closed his fingers around thin air. "I am so close, I can almost grab it. I just can't see it yet."

Gail's run for the senate was hanging in limbo. More important to her personally, *she* was feeling in limbo. Sitting in her command center living room, surrounded by her front-rank lieutenants, she was having a hard time concentrating on what they were saying.

She had a headache and was still feeling woozy. In the last few days of the campaign, it was traditional, if a little dopey, for candidates to stand on the edge of Brattleboro's rush-hour traffic every night, waving and holding a banner with their name on it and, in her case, fighting the rising nausea from all the exhaust fumes. Supposedly, this ritual was so voters could catch a glimpse of the person behind the hype, but Gail was also suspicious that if she didn't do it, she'd be accused of being aloof and arrogant.

And she'd had enough of that. So far, she'd had her wealth, her birthplace, her lover, several of her past professions, and the fact that she'd been raped all used against her in one way or another, mostly to prove that she was a rich, uppity, moneygrubbing flatlander with no morals or scruples.

Not surprisingly, most of this had come from the near-anonymous "other side"—backers of the man she'd been told to refer to only as "my opponent" so as not to give him extra visibility. But she'd also been reading of her short-comings in letters to the editor, hearing them on the street, and listening to them discussed on the radio and TV.

Gail had begun to wonder, as anyone might against such a barrage, whether there might not be some truth to all the rumors. After all, hadn't she been brought up on the principle that all politicians were only after power and money? What made that so different now that she was one herself? Hadn't she been doing the same things as her opponents throughout both the primary and the general election?

Her present nausea from all that carbon monoxide gave her the answer to that one.

And the fact that she'd left Joe to fend for himself in the midst of what was clearly a crisis. She was still ruing having asked him to lobby on her behalf with his law enforcement contacts, even though she'd just as quickly told him not to. Too little, too late.

And, at their very last conversation over dinner at his place, even while overtaken by appreciation for the man and what he stood for, she'd felt guilty and somehow inadequate. He'd revealed himself to be as unrecovered from his emotional wound as she would be forever from her rape. But instead of helping him, she had left him in the lurch, much as Ellen had so many years ago, for different reasons, obviously, but, coincidentally, while he was investigating the exact same crime.

She knew this was all essentially the raving of an exhausted, stressed-out, almost irrational punch-drunk fighter, but Gail was nevertheless beginning to wonder, just days away from the election, whether any of it was worth the cost.

"You want another aspirin, Gail? Or a soda?" Susan Raffner asked her, intruding on her daydream. "You're still not looking too good."

Gail shook her head. "I'm fine. It's passing. So, what's the consensus?"

"Honestly?" Susan answered for them all. "Not great. You've been doing the right things. You haven't been acting or looking too much like a candidate and nothing else, and your pedigree as a selectperson and a prosecutor has stood you in good stead. It's just—the stats still aren't there."

Janet Grasso, the team's number cruncher went further. "We're doing fine among the people who saw you through the primary, and what endorsements we've got so far have been great, but that's the bedrock we expected all along: the *Reformer* backing, Women for Women, Planned Parenthood, the unions. The tough parts have been the western towns and places like Vernon—which we didn't expect to carry—but Townshend, too, and Westminster and Dummerston. Those are where we should be doing a whole lot better. Part of it may be that you lost a little credibility when you shifted slightly to the right after the primary win, but that was a gamble we all agreed to—trying to steal a little of Parker's thunder."

"It may be the economy, too, at least partly," Susan added. "People are feeling hopeful enough, they don't want to listen to bad news."

"I haven't been telling them bad news," Gail protested.

Susan rubbed her forehead. "I keep telling you this. Democrats by their very nature are about bad news. We need to help the poor, the hungry, the disadvantaged, to use our wealth to help those in need. The Republicans just say, 'Fuck 'em; the economy will see 'em through.' Sad but true, that's what people like to hear when they finally feel they have some money in their pockets. They don't want to share. They want to buy stuff. Parker is cleaning up just singing his 'Happy Days Are Here Again' message."

"Not to mention all the national security hoopla," Nancy Amidon, Gail's treasurer, chimed in. "That adds to the fortress mentality."

Gail held up both her hands. "All right, all right. Basically, you're saying I'm out of luck. We did it by the numbers, and we're about to lose. Is that it?"

"Yeah," Susan said.

"No," came from both Janet and Nancy.

The three others in the room, silent so far, remained so, damning with no praise.

"Is it money?" Gail asked. "Can we flush in another few thousand in a last-second blitz?"

Nancy shrugged. "We know we've reached well over twenty-five thousand households. We've already spent eighteen thousand doing it. That's a lot. Probably more than Parker has, not that we ever want that to get out."

"Let's hear it for having the *Reformer* in our pocket," muttered Susan.

Nancy continued. "We do have more cash available. If you want to go ahead with that."

"Do it," Susan ordered, and then rose to her feet to pace around the room. "What I don't get," she burst out, "is why the hell this thing with Tom Bander hasn't even touched Parker. If they were any closer, they'd have to exchange vows, for Christ's sake. It pisses me off how every Republican can hang out with thieves and murderers, while Democrats get slammed for getting blow jobs."

Despite her fury, a quick ripple of smiles passed through the room. Susan on a rant was always good spectator sport, assuming you were out of range.

"Parker and Bander go back years," she continued. "Everyone knows that. They golf together; they've done deals together. How the hell can anyone think Parker didn't know his playmate was a crook?"

"Probably because he didn't," Gail explained gently. "How much do you know about *your* friends' backgrounds?"

Susan stopped in her tracks. "Shit. Have you been holding something back?"

Gail felt her headache bounding back, realizing her friend wasn't joking. "No," she said tiredly.

Susan resumed walking, totally focused once more. "Damn, this is frustrating. If I could take a bullet, I would, but, so far, it looks like we've been the only ones shooting—right at our feet."

Chapter 24

Joe, come down to the basement," Sammie's voice told him on the phone. "You're going to want to see this. Better make it quick."

He was about to ask her why when the phone went dead in his hand—her subtle way of forcing the issue.

He sighed and rose from his desk, half expecting to hear roots tearing away from the chair seat. He'd been spending so much time here, endlessly going over the same documents and photographs, that he was starting to believe the rumors that he was going around the bend.

He didn't think he was obsessing, though. He'd been in regular touch with Kathy Bartlett, checking her progress on what they were now both calling her "modern" case, versus his "ancient" one. And despite her many inroads and a file the size of a small clothes closet, she still didn't have the highly vaunted and much desired smoking gun of legal lore. Hers remained a circumstantial case, if, admittedly, a strengthening one.

And he remained convinced that the key to it all lay in his dusty collection of old memories and artifacts.

He reached the basement two minutes later to find most of the people present clustered around the TV mounted in one corner of the room.

To his surprise, on the screen he saw Gail working her way through a throng in what looked like a town hall.

"What's going on?" he asked Sammie, feeling awkwardly out of touch.

"Apparently, earlier today, Susan Raffner held a press conference on her own. She said she was breaking with the campaign and had handed in her resignation as manager to ask the question no one was willing to ask: What does Ed Parker know about Tom Bander's criminal activities and when did he know it? Quite the bombshell for a Podunk, Vermont, election."

"I didn't hear anything about this," he said, immediately regretting how inane that sounded.

But Sam didn't notice. Her eyes still on the TV, she said, "None of us did. We only turned this thing on because someone walked in and said he'd heard something was about to happen."

On-screen, Gail reached a small podium equipped with a couple of microphones. "It is with regret," she began, "that I have had to accept the resignation of my campaign manager and friend, Susan Raffner, for some unfounded and unsubstantiated comments she made earlier today. My regret comes, it should be noted, not because I am losing a trusted advisor, but because she let the goal of winning override both her judgment and the whole point of the political process, which is to allow voters to choose between two candidates in a fair, impartial, and unsensationalistic setting. What she implied about my political opponent, Ed

Parker, has, to the best of my knowledge, no basis in fact,' and had she not resigned, I would have asked her to do so. Such comments represent to me all that politics should not be about in this country, and although her departure from my staff will no doubt dishearten my supporters at exactly the point when I would prefer them to be carrying my message all the way to election day, I would like to stress here that what has happened today is precisely why I should be sent to the state senate.

"Too often in this country, we have seen our political leaders tout loyalty to their friends and backers over the interests of the people. They have, time and again, retreated to their support base like cowards unsure of the hearts and minds of the very people who elected them. Democrats and Republicans alike have ducked responsibility, orchestrated cover-ups, and flat-out lied on national television, all in the wrongheaded and insulting belief that we who elected them would somehow swallow their baloney solely because they told us to.

"Well," she added, grabbing the edge of the podium with both hands and leaning forward for emphasis, "I won't have any of it. I will fire people who aren't honest. I will fire people who play politics. And I will do so regardless of the supposed fallout that comes from having integrity. I will never believe that good people finish last, and I will never believe that the voters of this county, of this state, and of this country will allow themselves to be hoodwinked and misled by a political status quo that's been doing the same thing for so long, they've come to see it as the truth. Politics for the sake of politics is a sham and a lie, and I won't have anything to do with it. Thank you."

They watched as she pulled away from the podium amid a chorus of ignored questions, and retreated the way she'd come. As someone turned down the sound on the TV set, Joe heard Sammie murmur, "You go, girl."

As a growing number of faces turned his way inquiringly, imitating Gail, he quickly made his escape.

"Some speech."

Joe looked up. Standing in the office doorway was Tony Brandt, looking, as usual, slightly bemused. Of all the people who might have crossed Joe's threshold right now, he was happy Brandt was the first. It was going to take some getting used to, being the shadowy companion of the latest political fireworks display, and he didn't relish the predictable attention. Sure as hell, he wasn't going home tonight. Nor would he be going to Gail's, although he'd already left a message for her to call him when she could.

"What did you think?" he asked noncommittally, indicating a chair for Tony to sit in.

"I think," his old boss said, settling in, "that we all just witnessed the Hail Mary pass to end all. If it works the way I think it will, it'll put her at the top of the very political game she was claiming to debunk."

Joe felt his spirits almost palpably sag. "That cynical?"

Tony raised one shoulder. "Maybe that idealistic and practical. It depends on whose side you're on, as usual. Me? I think it was a master stroke, but then, I've always admired the lady."

Joe went to what he felt was the most telling point of the question. "Do you think she and Susan cooked it up together?"

Tony smiled. "Joe, you know her better than anyone. You've loved her, lived with her, nursed her back to health. Hell, you almost died for her, indirectly. With that degree of familiarity, you're asking me?"

Joe didn't smile back. "Yes. I am."

Tony became serious. "No, I don't. Because Gail Zigman's not the only one we're talking about here. Susan Raffner is about as tough-minded as any man or woman I've ever met. I don't know what Gail might say if she were asked the same question because, despite her statement on TV, she's as loyal a friend as anyone could want. But I would bet my bottom dollar that Susan launched this boat all on her own, trusting Gail would have the intelligence—and the *heart*," he added emphatically, "to know what to do next. That's why I said earlier that this smacks more of idealism than cynicism."

He paused, looked at Joe quietly for a moment, and finally added, "But that's me."

"No," Joe conceded. "That's you *and* me. Nice to hear, though."

Tony chuckled half to himself and got to his feet, dispelling the tension. "You have to admit, though, if she was in a horse race before, Christ only knows what it's turned into now."

He walked to the door, paused, and repeated, "Hell of a speech. See ya, Joe."

Joe sat there for a while, thinking, retracing the conversation. There'd been something in its midst, totally unrelated, that had struck him, as occasional stray thoughts do, out of the blue, encouraged by the merest turn of phrase.

He swiveled in his seat and stared out the window, letting his mind drift. When it finally came to him, he could only admire the simplicity of it.

Shaking his head, he reached for the phone and dialed the crime lab again.

"David?" he said, once the lab director had picked up. "Can you do me another favor?"

With nothing more to go on than pure instinct, he knew he'd found the proverbial smoking gun.

Kathy Bartlett looked up as Gunther knocked on her open door.

"Joe," she said. "What're you doing in town? Have a seat."

"I was in Waterbury, picking up something from David Hawke," he said, sitting opposite her and placing a manila envelope on her desk.

She reached for it but didn't open it immediately. "My God, Gail sure has been making the news."

He smiled ruefully, knowing Kathy's politics were at odds with Gail's on most matters. "Yeah. It's a crapshoot now."

"I give her high marks for guts, though. The woman knows how to fight. If I lived down that way, I might reconsider my vote." She hefted the thin envelope. "What's this?"

"I think it may be what you've been looking for," he told her, happy to move off a subject that had been filling the air ever since Gail's announcement. He and Gail had spoken just once thereafter, mostly for him to wish her luck and for both of them to agree to stay out of each other's way, for everyone's sake. It had been a practical, forlorn conversation. "I was having a chat with Tony Brandt a few days ago, in part about knowing people and things so well and so intimately, that a sudden surprise no longer seems possible. Made me rethink how I'd been looking at the Oberfeldt case."

"Oh?" she prompted, still holding the envelope. Like the prosecutor she was, she knew the value of occasional patience.

"The switchblade at the scene bugged me from the start,"

he explained. "It wasn't used, although it was open, and the thumbprint on it pointed directly to Pete Shea—which, as it turned out, was the intention."

"The surrogate thief," Kathy said with a smile.

"Right—and eventually the surrogate killer. The gun planted under Shea's mattress was clearly supposed to be the deal closer—no prints, but still covered with Oberfeldt's blood. Of course, Shea found it before we got a lead on him, had his girlfriend hide it, and beat feet, in short order. But the plan worked anyway—we believed Pete was Oberfeldt's killer."

"Okay," Kathy said neutrally.

"If you're going to set someone up like that, you do the deed and then plant the evidence. Makes sense. But as Ralpher or Bander or whatever you want to call him was putting the old man into a coma, Oberfeldt got one good shot at him, maybe with his elbow, and hit him square in the nose—produced a real gusher.

"Following my conversation with Tony, I replayed that scene in my head, based on no more than what I would've done in Bander's place. I visualized tossing aside the gun I'd used to beat Oberfeldt, feeling my nose to assess the damage—and thus covering my hand with my own blood—and *then* extracting the switchblade to place it by the body."

Kathy's eyes narrowed as she now tore open the envelope. "You're kidding me," she said. "Bander's blood is on the switchblade along with Oberfeldt's?"

Joe smiled. "Exactly. I had the crime lab test the knife from end to end. Before, reasonably enough—especially for back then—they'd taken but one small sample, which turned out to be only the victim's. Pure dumb luck."

Kathy scanned the printed results before her. "There's no

such thing, Joe—it's all part of the cosmic plan." She looked up at him. "Especially when it works in your favor."

She rose and shook his hand, a rare gesture for her. "I'll have an arrest warrant for Thomas Bander in a few hours. You want to be the one to serve it?"

Chapter 25

J oe didn't get to serve the arrest warrant on Tom Bander. When he and Lester pulled up to the mansion's familiar broad porch steps, they were met by a woman in a maid's uniform, looking dazed and shivering in the cold without a coat.

Joe swung out of the car and quickly looked around. "Ma'am?" he asked. "You all right?"

"It's Mr. Bander," she said vaguely, pointing inside the house.

On edge, both officers bypassed her and quickly checked the open doorway. There was nothing to see beyond the cavernous hall Gunther remembered from his earlier visit.

With Lester still watchful, Joe pulled the woman in from outside and shut the door quietly.

"What's your name?" he asked her.

"Louise."

"You work here, is that right?"

"Yes, sir. I didn't know what to do."

"You did fine, Louise, and now I want you to stay put. Where's Mr. Bander?"

"In the library. It's down . . ."

"I know where it is. Is there anyone else in the house?"

"The cook's in the kitchen. There's a man outside covering the plants for winter."

"All right. You stay here."

Gesturing to Lester, Joe led the way down the hall to the towering double doors leading into the library. One of them was slightly ajar.

Gunther pounded on it with his fist, his other hand resting on the butt of his holstered gun. "Thomas Bander? It's the police."

Total silence greeted them.

Joe pushed the door back to reveal the room in whole. At first, distracted by the windows and the light pouring through them, he couldn't see anyone.

Spinney then touched his arm. "Joe. Over there."

He shifted his gaze to a corner of the room, where a metal spiral staircase twisted up to meet the narrow balcony running alongside the rows of untouched books. Next to the stairs, a body was hanging from a rope tied to the railing above. Its feet were dangling almost within reach of the floor.

Joe quickly crossed the room and touched Tom Bander's hand. It was cold and stiff. Rigor mortis had already set in.

"He's dead," he told his partner. "Call for backup, the ME, the state's attorney. Might as well call the crime lab, too, just so they're alerted, but don't tell them to roll yet. Better use your cell phone."

Lester left the room. Joe stood still for a moment, peering at Bander's discolored face, its eyes and mouth half open, looking like a poorly executed wax model.

He shifted his gaze to the railing, the nearby staircase, following in his mind the man's last actions, studying for inconsistencies and finding none.

Finally, he stepped away, watching the floor carefully so as not to disrupt any possible evidence, and approached the enormous desk, where a single sheet of paper seemed to be glowing in the reflected light.

The handwriting was plain, as was the message: "My name is Tom Bander. It used to be Travis Ralpher. I've done some things that will send me to jail and I don't want to go there. I mailed a letter to my lawyer, Mr. Masius, with all the details. Thanks."

Joe sat on the edge of the desk, his legs weak. He could hear his own breathing, feel the beating of his heart. The sunlight gently warmed one side of his face.

Thirty-two years ago, fresh from having buried Klaus Oberfeldt and then Ellen, feeling empty and grieving and instinctively knowing that the case would remain unresolved, Joe had sat at his desk in the detective bureau's bullpen, thinking about Maria Oberfeldt. The phone had rung at that precise moment—a call from the state police— to inform him that Maria had just been found dead by her own hand. A hanging.

It was over. A full and finished circle, completed on a note of thanks.

Joe walked down the gleaming white-walled hallway, his footsteps sounding loud against the linoleum. There weren't as many people milling about as there'd been last time, but then again, it was late, as attested to by the faint odor of dinner and the muffled sounds of TV sets.

He turned one final corner and knocked on a door no

different in appearance from the dozens he'd already passed—so many lives cloaked in ubiquitous anonymity.

"Come in."

He opened the door and stepped inside. Natalie Shriver was seated as usual by the window, but the lights were out, allowing her to gaze onto the moon-washed lawn without any competing reflection.

"Who is it?" she asked.

He realized the hall light behind him had made him into a featureless shadow. He quickly closed the door. "Joe Gunther. I visited you the other day?"

"I remember. Would you like to rest for a while? I apologize for the darkness. You may turn a light on if you wish."

"No. That's fine," he said, taking his chair across from her. "It's actually very restful this way."

"Yes, I agree. That's why I do it. I read a little later, generally. But after supper, it's nice to simply sit and think for a while. I don't believe people do enough of that in this busy world."

"I'm sure you're right."

He couldn't really see her face. It was mostly in darkness, one cheek only being touched by the moonlight.

"What's on your mind? I can't imagine you came by to simply stare out the window with me."

"I did say I'd be back to visit."

He saw her nod, if just barely. "That's true. I remember that. A nice gesture. Do you have many friends?"

"Enough."

"I would imagine they're happy to have you in their lives."

He was startled by the remark. It so closely echoed something Gail had told him just hours earlier. Flush from her near-miraculous victory over Ed Parker, and now a newly anointed state senator, she'd dropped by his house on Green Street with flowers, a box of mac and cheese as a joke, and an admission that despite the important place he held in her heart, she was fearful that she too often took him for granted.

He'd been deeply touched by that. He'd never laid claim to her, and although he'd felt cast away sometimes as she wrestled with her inner conflicts, he'd always known he might lose her to a course not yet charted. It was a defense mechanism, no doubt, a hedge against disappointment, and perhaps not the soundest emotional raft to cling to. But in the end, it worked for him.

"I'm certainly happy to have them in mine," he told Natalie.

She was silent for a moment, and he feared he might have reminded her of her losses.

"But you are here for a reason, nevertheless," she suddenly said, her voice still strong.

"That's up to you—whether you'd like to know about Hannah or not."

"Why she was killed?"

"Yes."

Again, there was a prolonged pause, during which Gunther became aware, for the first time, of the distant ticking of a clock somewhere.

"I think I would. I have my own theories, but it would be a comfort of sorts to actually be told. How do you know, by the way?"

"A man she knew, a long time ago, died recently and left a note—a long confession, in fact. With his lawyer."

"A suicide, you mean." She said it matter-of-factly.

"Yes." He paused. "Hannah had taken a deposition when she was a court reporter. This man discovered he was mentioned in it, by pure chance—had that gotten out, it might've ruined him. So he approached her, first with money, and then with his own dreams and ambitions."

"They were lovers, then?"

"For a while. That's why she dropped out. He'd heard from an ex-employee about a large cache of money hidden under the floor of a small store in Brattleboro. He stole it to start a new life, and I guess Hannah hoped she could make his dream her own. But it didn't last between them."

"Poor girl," her mother murmured. "It never did."

"Anyway, the man did well. He made a few lucky choices, hired people who knew what to do, became very wealthy. I only met him once, but I sensed he may have been as surprised by his own success as anyone, as if maybe he were just along on somebody's else's ride."

"That's happened to more than a few people."

"He wasn't really, though," Joe corrected himself. "I guess I meant that he seemed ill suited to the trappings of wealth. But he had the necessary ruthlessness. Money hadn't changed him from what he'd been."

"A bad man, then?"

"Maybe worse—an amoral one. Bland and brutal, both. When Hannah heard a few months ago that his past might be threatening to catch up with him, she contacted him and told him her continued silence could be bought."

Natalie Shriver reacted with a small but sharp intake of breath. "Oh—foolish girl."

"I'm afraid so. I am sorry."

The old woman sighed. "We make choices, Mr. Gunther, usually based on what we think is right, even when all around us see our folly for what it is. Hannah led a sort of wishful life, really—an approximation of the one that actually stretched out before her. She was never in a position to choose wisely."

Joe thought back to the lives he'd encountered lately, of people now both living and dead, and at the watershed events that had helped shape his own.

"I wonder how many of us are."